Breakout

Breakout

ALSO BY THE *BREAKOUT* TEAM

Blackout

Whiteout

DHONIELLE CLAYTON

TIFFANY D. JACKSON

NIC STONE

Break out

ANGIE THOMAS

ASHLEY WOODFOLK

NICOLA YOON

Quill Tree Books
An Imprint of HarperCollins*Publishers*

HarperCollins Children's Books, a division of HarperCollins Publishers,
195 Broadway, New York, NY 10007

HarperCollins Publishers, Macken House,
39/40 Mayor Street Upper, Dublin 1, D01 C9W8, Ireland

Quill Tree Books is an imprint of HarperCollins Publishers.

Breakout

This book was cowritten by Dhonielle Clayton, Tiffany D. Jackson, Nic Stone, Angela Thomas, Ashley Woodfolk, and Nicola Yoon.

harpercollins.com

ISBN 978-0-06-321750-8

Typography by David DeWitt
26 27 28 29 30 LBC 5 4 3 2 1
FIRST EDITION

To the ones who have learned to maneuver.

We see you. Keep it up.

PRESENT DAY

NOELLE CLARKE

April 6
2:16 p.m.

A LIE TASTED delicious. A cherry ice pop on a hot day or a pumpkin-spiced latte as the weather cooled. There were as many flavors of lies as there were of the petit macarons in the glass windows of Noelle Clarke's favorite patisserie in Georgetown. Some lies were savory, with bits of pistachios and matcha, the truth folded into the fabrication to make them more sincere. Some were even gory, like her father's signature dish at Red Bone, his world-renowned restaurant: a luxurious beef bone, sliced open to reveal the decadent marrow inside, pomegranate reduction drizzled on top, like blood.

But the lie leaving Noelle's mouth was thick and salty, like burnt caramel crystallized along the edges of an expensive saucepan.

"I didn't do anything, you know?" she told the nurse who was slipping a blood pressure cuff around her bicep. "It wasn't me."

The red-faced woman didn't glance up from her chart. "I'm just here to get your vitals, honey."

"Then I can go home?" Noelle searched the woman's face for the truth. Every person she'd encountered since leaving the boat was lying. The sweet kind of lies. And she knew it.

"Of course. You've all been through a trauma. We have to run tests to make sure you're both physically and mentally okay. It's just terrible what happened."

Noelle didn't need a reminder that the last few days had been awful—monstrous, in fact. She'd barely made it out. "But how long will it take?" Her front teeth nibbled her bottom lip until she got what she was after: blood. She felt bad about breaking the skin, but only a little bit. The *nasty habit*, as her mother called it, should've been "fixed" by now with all the expensive therapy appointments, stimming objects, and menthol-laced lip gloss her parents had invested in to deter the compulsion. But as the first metallic pearl oozed through the cut, throbbing with heat, Noelle was reminded that she was still alive. That she'd survived what had happened on that godforsaken island.

The nurse shook her head. "What did I tell you about doing that?" She handed Noelle a piece of gauze to apply pressure before wiping it with stinging antiseptic.

Noelle flinched as her skin sizzled. "I want to go home." This was probably the hundredth time she'd said it.

"The officers will be back soon, and we need the results of your bloodwork and tests. Some of you were in such bad shape . . ." The nurse's statement had a question underneath: *How did you get hurt like this?*

The machine beeped. They watched together as Noelle's heart

rate spiked. She didn't know how to respond. She didn't know where to begin. She didn't know if she even wanted to.

So she avoided eye contact, instead surveying the small hospital room again, counting each item like she did when she'd prepare to bake one of her award-winning creations. (She'd won the Washington, DC, Capital City Junior Bake-Off Championship two years in a row.) She'd assess each ingredient, making a mental inventory of what she was working with. In this current reality: a tiny bathroom with a leaky faucet she could hear when the room got too quiet; one wobbly chair; a hospital bed that she reluctantly occupied; a single window overlooking the Atlantic Ocean (a body of water she never wanted to see again if she could help it); and one door leading to a hall clogged with police officers, detectives, and security. Aka her only exit led right to the people who wanted to keep her here.

The machine beeped again, and the blood pressure cuff pulled her focus back to the nurse. The woman's blue gaze was fixed on Noelle's injuries with curiosity. Noelle wondered if she could see deeper, beyond the cuts and bruises, down to her heart, where the real damage lay. Noelle knew if she caught a glimpse of herself in the small wall mirror, she'd see just how terrible she looked. Her brown skin boasted a constellation of bruises. The whites of her eyes were streaked with red. Dried blood crusted in the stitches holding the gash in her chin shut. And her twists had unraveled, releasing her thick curls: a lion's mane dirtied with sand, salt, and seaweed.

"Your blood pressure is higher than it should be," the nurse reported. "You need to rest and try to stay calm." She rubbed Noelle's shoulder. "I may need to add something to your IV to help."

Noelle bit her bottom lip again, the weak, half-formed scab easily giving in to her anxieties. "They're going to lie about me," she said as fresh blood hit her tongue. "They always do."

The nurse's eyebrows lifted. "Who?"

Noelle glared out the window. "My friends."

"Well, if they're *good* friends, they won't."

Noelle gritted her teeth. "You don't know them. They're—"

The door swung open. A man entered, a gun at his hip, and a streak of sunburn on his white nose noticeable against his all-black clothes. "Are you ready to talk now?"

"I'll be back to check on you later." The nurse patted Noelle's leg, then nodded at the detective and left the room.

Noelle stared forward, eyes fixed on bursts of lightning illuminating dark storm clouds rolling in over the ocean. A week ago, she would've been in awe of the view.

The detective dragged the chair closer to the bed, and the screech of the legs set her nerves on edge. "I'm Detective Franco. We can start at the beginning."

Noelle crossed her arms and refused to look at him. "I don't have anything to say."

"Oh, that can't be true. Not when each of your friends called you the ringleader." He tapped his notepad.

Noelle squirmed, fixating on the storm outside. It grew closer and closer by the minute. "Yeah, okay . . ."

He flipped the pages and read. "They said you control everything. That you run the crew . . . the Six, is it?" He gazed up, and Noelle felt his eyes burning into her. "Oh, and Keisha White was your best friend?"

"Keisha White is dead," Noelle replied matter-of-factly, willing her mind not to summon images of Key's dead face. The bulge of her pretty heterochromic eyes, one blue and one green. The blue tinge in her full lips. The graying of her light brown skin.

"She died last year around this time, right? Very sad. Heartbreaking for everyone involved, I'm sure. Very sorry for your loss."

Noelle gulped down the lump in her throat. "I don't want to talk about her."

"Maybe you'll want to talk about Anthony Brooks, then?"

A shiver raced across Noelle's skin. She shoved her hands beneath her thighs to keep them from trembling and forced herself to meet his eyes this time. "Like I told you before, I didn't do anything. I don't know anything." She looked away. "I want to talk to my parents."

"They're on their way now that those twin hurricanes have passed. Boarded a plane from Washington, DC, thirty minutes ago. In the meantime, we need some answers." The man clicked his pen. "Anthony was your boyfriend, yes?"

Tears welled in her eyes despite her attempts to fight them. "Yes," she muttered.

"Mm-hmm . . ." Noelle didn't know what he was scribbling, but it made her neck itch. "So, what happened on the island, Noelle?" he pressed.

She clenched her jaw.

"The Six—your crew—all of them said you were to blame. That *you* did this."

Noelle's head snapped up, her breaking point reached. "They're fucking lying!" she screamed. "They're terrible people, all of them! They'll never tell you what *really* happened!"

She pulled her knees to her chest and rocked back and forth, willing her pulse to slow, but it galloped. As the man asked more questions, her ears filled with the beeping of machines and the slamming of doors and the crashing of thunder outside.

The storm inside Noelle raged, mirroring the one through the window. People always said they wanted to know the truth. They told lies about how revealing your secrets would set you free. But what happened when the truth was ugly? No one actually wanted to know how a person's neck snapped like a twig or how their lungs filled with water or how they choked to death. No one wanted the details of what it was like to watch the light leave a person's eyes.

At seventeen, Noelle understood that humans preferred their truth sweetened and softened with lies like brown sugar melted into butter. So she would bake the most beautiful lies.

She had no choice.

THE WEEK BEFORE:

SUNDAY

CHAPTER ONE

ANTHONY

8:48 a.m.

AS THE GROUP piled out of the Sprinter van into the late-afternoon sun, Anthony Brooks exhaled and let his shoulders drop.

"Bruh, I'm not a road trip guy *at all*, but I could go some places in that joint," Dwayne said, looking back at the glistening black vehicle. "The hours flew by. Is everything in your life that smooth?"

Ant smiled but didn't respond. Just inhaled deep. The sun was high and bright in a cloudless sky, and the ocean-salted air was cool and fresh. Everything was going according to plan.

"Ant, that's *you*, dawg?" asked Quintin. Or Quatro, as everyone called him. "Damn, son!"

Ant grinned. His dad's yacht was impressive for sure: The *Nocturna* was all black with clean lines, chrome accents, and a wraparound ebony deck that never got too hot to lie on. There was a plunge pool in the front and a hot tub in the back, and Ant had no doubt everyone would lose their minds when they went down into the belly of the boat and discovered the movie theater and game room: billiards, air hockey, pinball, *Pac-Man*, and six different gaming consoles all hooked up to an eighty-five-inch TV. With surround sound.

He loved that they'd just gotten off a private jet from DC to Key West, but everyone still had room to be impressed. And all with him.

"Mmmmm . . . that sure is a lot of water," Noelle said, materializing on Ant's right side. She grabbed his hand, but he wasn't really in the mood for the PDA. He needed to keep a little distance for his own sake.

"I'm the varsity swim captain, babe," he said, pulling away and giving her a pat on the back. "You know I'm not gonna let you drown."

Ant fixed his gaze on the yacht and let the rest of the tension melt from his broad shoulders. Though not the favorite—that honor went to a McLaren convertible his dad had won off a bet with an oil magnate in the UAE—the yacht was, by far, Kelvin Brooks's most expensive toy. And he'd stuffed it to the gills with his preferred sources of entertainment from his late-twentieth-century childhood. In truth, Ant hadn't been entirely sure the yacht was going to be docked: dear ol' Pops could be a little wishy-washy when it came to his only son, especially when said son's requests involved the use of Pops's precious things.

But it seemed like sending his father the list of names, which included the offspring of politicians—two of whom were trying to land the Democratic nomination for president—as well as the son of an NFL Hall of Famer and the daughter of their illustrious private school's founder, had done the trick. Did Ant have a backup plan in case the yacht hadn't been waiting for them? Of course he did. And a backup to the backup. Obviously. He knew how to flex and impress. And he had big plans that needed to go perfectly.

He was relieved everything seemed to be working out. Ant knew how difficult it was for Pops to resist anything that smelled like a networking opportunity, especially for his "progeny," as he referred to Ant, and Ant couldn't have been more thrilled that the name-dropping tactic had worked.

It felt like a good omen, and Ant was thankful. He needed all the luck he could get to pull off "the week of a lifetime" he'd promised his new friends.

He let the rest of the group pull a little bit ahead of him as they made their way down the port. When Ant had initially pitched the idea for this little spring break getaway at Kuzimu, an all-inclusive resort on a private island in the Florida Keys—both of which were owned by his "Hospitality King" father—he wasn't sure any of his classmates would bite. Yeah, he'd been at Thurgood Marshall Academy since the beginning of the school year, and he'd had at least one class with all but two members of the final spring break crew, but he was still the new kid. One who hadn't even been able to come up with a dope enough backstory to wow them. He'd realized too late that the lie he told people was actually really boring: he'd moved to DC from Atlanta because his mom wanted a change of scenery, and they already owned a home in the nation's capital.

And though Ant had managed to form a couple of decent acquaintanceships, he—and everyone else on that campus—was well aware that one group of kids held sway over just about everything Thurgood-related: which classes were offered, which other schools were invited to their annual gala, what kind of food was served in the cafeteria, and which events would make it onto the school social calendar.

The Six.

Noelle Clarke. Sydney Davis. Quintin McCallum IV. Dwayne Harris. River Reynolds. Keisha White.

And most of them were right there in front of him. All but Keisha—or *Key,* as he'd heard them refer to her. She'd passed away the previous year, but despite having been the proverbial queen bee of their group (or so was the word around school), no one ever wanted to talk about her. At any rate, what once had been the Six was now the Five. And even without Key, they were still the most powerful kids at Thurgood Marshall Academy.

Ant let his eyes roam over their heads and smiled. It was *his* family's yacht they were about to board. He'd actually pulled it off. Which both blew him away and scared the shit out of him. He'd spent seven months learning as much as he could about them: The Six had met in kindergarten. They'd gone to some super-exclusive private elementary school full of diplomat offspring and had been the only Black kids in the building. So their parents bonded. Noelle's mom, a PhD-level, National Hall of Fame educator who'd been on *Oprah* back in the early 2000s, decided enough was enough and started Thurgood Marshall Academy with Keisha's mom, a tech titan who'd left San Francisco to work for the government.

The story was so well known, it might as well have been on a plaque near the school's entrance.

For as long as Ant could remember, Pops had drilled one thing into him: *People couldn't care less about* what *you know until they know* who *you know.*

Ant had *plans,* and the Five had all sorts of access. And knowledge. It was a no-brainer. He had to impress them. He had to know them. He'd already made himself invaluable to each of them in different ways. Now he just had to continue to deliver on all his promises.

There was a burst of static before a female voice crackled through a two-way radio: "Johnson, I'm gonna head onto the vessel and do a sweep. Hold the group back until you get the all clear."

"Roger that," said a giant of a man clad in all black hovering just behind Ant's left shoulder. He'd almost forgotten ol' dude was there. The reminder dampened Ant's mood. As thrilled as he was that they'd all come, accomplishing that came with some unfortunate stipulations. Like the inclusion of a literal security detail for two of the members. ("This is what happens when your mom is a damn senator," Sydney told Ant when she let him know there would be two "executive protection security guards" with them on the trip. One for her and one for Dwayne, the kid of a governor.)

In the long run, though, Ant guessed it didn't really matter: once the yacht left the port, there'd be no turning back. It was go time, and follow-through was paramount.

This *would* be the trip of a lifetime. And no one would ever forget it. He'd bet the boat in front of them on that. He was *that* good.

Ant absentmindedly adjusted his gold rope chain so the clasp was centered at the back of his neck. He let his gaze lock on Noelle, whose waist-length twists were already swollen from the Florida humidity. She was up near the front of the group now and had just thrown her head back in laughter, likely telling an unfunny joke in an attempt to try to get one of them to talk to her again. The sound hit Ant's ears as powerfully as the drop of his favorite hip-hop beat—neurotic as she sometimes could be, Noelle could light up a room with her smile—so he took his laptop from his backpack. He had to stay focused. Having the playlist queued up so he could turn it on in the rec room as they entered (to show off the surround sound) was nonnegotiable. Yes, he'd gotten in with the Five as intended, but there was far more he wanted—no, *needed*—to learn.

"Man, that chain don't make your neck itch in all this heat?" Quintin—Quatro—asked as he looked at Ant over his shoulder. "No doubt it's *real* considering the water castle we're getting on, but don't sweat plus metal—even if it's precious—cause some sort of reaction?"

Ant shrugged and started his ultimate playlist. "Never been a problem for me before. I even swim in it when I'm allowed to. Brings me luck."

Quatro and Dwayne smirked in tandem. "Of course it does," Dwayne said.

Ant debated sniping back, but the moment he opened his mouth, the two-way radio beeped on Johnson's shoulder.

"We're all clear," came the voice of the female bodyguard. "All aboard, I guess."

"Ten four," Johnson said.

Ant grinned and let Dwayne's little dig drop. It wasn't important. Not anymore. The sound from beneath his feet changed as they shifted from walking on concrete to the wood of the dock. They were almost there.

"Oh my God, this yacht is *sick*," called out one of the girls as she entered the boat.

Ant smiled so hard, he looked at the ground so no one would see. That approval was the last vote of confidence he needed.

Go time, baby.

CHAPTER TWO

RIVER

10:42 a.m.

RIVER REYNOLDS HAD never seen water so black.

From the sun deck of the yacht, the Atlantic Ocean looked like Onyx Ink, the newest color from her favorite nail polish line, Mineral Manicure: it was shiny and sleek as a raven's feather, so smooth it looked fake.

She squinted into the distance, lifting her hand to shield her eyes from the sun, but there were only the tiniest ripples in the ocean's glassy surface, and all caused by their boat, like the bow was a knife, the ocean a cake. She'd been at sea before (her uncle had been a naval officer since she was three), so she was used to both rough and calm waters. But in the fourteen years since she'd first stepped foot on a ship, she'd never seen water look like this.

River felt a warm presence at her elbow and tensed. Before she could turn around, the scent of hazelwood and honey flooded her nostrils.

Quintin McCallum IV. Her endlessly adorable—and wildly

infuriating—crush. Who she'd always refused to call Quatro like everyone else did.

"Whatchu up here thinking about?" he asked as he joined her at the railing. She felt the tension leave her muscles. And hated it. Quintin had precisely no right to make her so comfortable. With a mom like Dana Reynolds, DC's most sought-after crisis manager, River had been trained to prepare for the worst while hoping for the best. It was survival, but it'd also split her, she realized, into both an optimist and a realist.

A Gemini through and through.

There was the River who did everything right and chased what she knew she could catch (as Mama demanded). But there was also the River who knew that certain things were impossible.

Like actually being with Quintin.

River noticed that she'd been morphing more into Dana's Daughter around her friends since last year—the "perfect" River that she worked hard to be, instead of Real River, which is what she called her hidden self.

But she felt more like her real self around Quintin. Softer. Less guarded.

Safe.

She didn't feel the familiar instinct to put up her wall with him. And though it should've been a relief not to be *on*, it just frustrated her. Made her want things she knew she couldn't have. She sighed and forced herself to turn and take in his warm smile.

And instantly regretted it.

One of the problems with Quintin was that he was beautiful. Gorgeous, even. Gleaming copper skin, a fresh cut edged up sharp as broken glass, heavy brows over soulful eyes, a dimpled grin that always looked like trouble. And then there was the rest of him: broad shoulders, long legs, and an ass that made her wonder why his position on the football team wasn't tight end.

His expression morphed into one of concern. "Yo, you good, love?"

She wanted to scream. Even his beauty couldn't lure her into telling him the truth—that the darkness of the ocean was frightening in a way she didn't know how to explain. That it was making her feel weird and jumpy, on edge about this trip and the future. She couldn't say what she wanted to say: that ever since last year, being close to water had felt inherently unsafe.

And that him standing this close and gazing at her that way was both helping and hurting. That she wanted him to leave her the hell alone. Stop acting like he cared. But she also wanted him to come closer.

See? Infuriating.

So, she pointed to their friends, who were gathered on the main deck. "I'm thinking about how much it sucks that we're stuck rooming with Noelle. Sydney didn't even want her to come, so you know she's only here because of Ant."

Quintin leaned over the railing beside her, so close their pinkies nearly touched, and looked down at everyone else. The girls were beside the small pool at the front of the boat—Sydney's locs hanging almost to the deck as she threw her head back laughing and

Noelle anxiously twirling her twists around her finger. And there were the boys: Ant, tall and slim, and Dwayne, whose arms and legs were thick with muscle like Quintin's, were at a table tossing playing cards and money around in what looked like a rigged poker game. River could see Dwayne peeling cards off the bottom of the deck when Ant wasn't looking.

"I know, Riv," Quintin replied. The nickname hit River's ear like Styrofoam, but she couldn't tell him it grated on her because she'd have to explain why. That would bring up the topic they most wanted to avoid: Keisha White. Their dead best friend.

His dead former girlfriend.

"But it'll all be fine," he continued. "We've known Noelle practically our whole lives. And even though she's been kinda . . . difficult these last few months, I'm sure she's coming around."

River nodded, but she *wasn't* so sure. Yes, they'd all been friends for years, but with one member of their group gone, the balance had been off for a while.

Honestly, River had never fully trusted Noelle. Call it intuition, a sixth sense, but it had been too strong for River to ignore over the years. So she'd always kept Noelle at arm's length. She was a person who would never meet Real River. And now River would be trapped with her for a week.

Everything had been off-kilter since spring break last year. And River didn't know how to stomach any of it: that Quintin was beautiful and kind despite the loss of his girlfriend. That they were all trying hard not to talk or think about said girlfriend—the girl Noelle had blabbed to a reporter about despite the pact they'd made when Key died. That beautiful, kind Quintin wasn't with Key anymore solely because she was dead.

That she, River, wanted Quintin for herself, now *and* when Key had still been alive.

Even though she'd been gone for a year, Key still lorded over them all.

River felt her wall creeping back up, Dana's Daughter slipping in. "You think Sydney and Dwayne will finally hook up this week?" she asked, trying to bury the dark thoughts that were attempting to rise to the surface.

As though she'd heard River, Sydney called out to Dwayne, and despite the ache in her own heart, River couldn't help but smile at the way Dwayne leaped up from the card table at the sound of her voice. A shy but hopeful grin settled at the corner of his full lips, like he'd been waiting for her summons, and he hovered next to her: a hungry hummingbird hoping to taste a flower's nectar without ever touching down. He was so loud and confident except when it came to Sydney. With her he seemed like he was afraid to get too close.

"God, I hope so," Quintin said, laughing.

But River knew Sydney and Dwayne's situation was just as complicated as her own with Quintin. Despite the fact that they had all grown up together, Sydney's mom—a senator—and Dwayne's dad—the governor of Maryland—had become political rivals. So Sydney and Dwayne were star-crossed, too. It ate Sydney alive.

River glanced at her best friend and wondered how things might change between them if Sydney did start officially dating Dwayne. Then she looked at Noelle and felt something awful deep in her gut. At least she still *had* Sydney. Yeah, the Six had always rolled pretty tight, but they each still had their singular person: River + Sydney; Quintin + Dwayne . . . Noelle's person—Key—was . . . gone.

River turned to face Quintin then. His lashes looked almost fake in the sun.

She lifted her hand to point to the captain, about to make a joke that he looked like somebody's uncle at a cookout in his sandals and socks. But Quintin caught her wrist and brought her hand closer to his face.

"I like these," he said, admiring her nails. She'd started giving herself elaborate manicures the year she turned twelve to kill a nasty nail-biting habit she'd formed after her grandmother passed. Her mother had started batting her hand away from her mouth if they were in public, and it was getting embarrassing. The habit had flared up again last year after everything happened with Key. But River squashed it as soon as her mother told her it made her look like she was guilty of something. Looking guilty is as good as being guilty in Dana's book.

For this trip River had chosen a shimmering shade of blue that glimmered like gems in the sun. She wiggled her fingers, and her nails looked like they were covered in sapphires.

"Thank you," she said, and she wanted to flirt back, but she could feel their friends' eyes on her. She could only imagine what they must be thinking: *Really, River? Flirting with the dead girl's boyfriend?*

She pulled out of his grip and stepped away from him.

"I guess I'm just glad you're here," he said, and River couldn't help but smile then even though she was still thinking about how different last year had been and about the person who should be standing next to him instead of her.

"I'm glad you're here too," she said. And dammit, there was Quintin's troublemaker grin. He was like her, she realized—a coin with two sides. She wondered what secrets he might be keeping. That curiosity drew her even closer to him.

River looked out at the dark water again. She'd chosen this color for her nails thinking they'd match the sea, but she'd been so wrong. She swallowed hard, pulled a pair of sunglasses out of her purse, and slipped them on like they could hide her real feelings as easily as they hid her eyes. "I just hope this trip goes as well as we want it to."

"You worry too much," Quintin told her. "Of course it will." But River could tell by the small crease in his brow that he wasn't as confident about their long-awaited spring break as he was making himself out to be.

Over Quintin's shoulder, River saw Ant pull out his laptop, walk over to the cabin, and duck inside, his infamous gold chain glinting in the sunlight.

They were headed to an island resort called Kuzimu, which was owned by Ant's father, and she watched as Noelle followed Ant into the cabin, panic evident in her wide eyes and the hot spots of red against the light brown of her cheeks. River knew that panic. She'd felt it whenever her mother told her that mistakes could follow a person for life if they weren't careful.

"How do you think everyone's feeling about the anniversary?" she asked Quintin.

She *had* to ask. The question had been haunting her for weeks.

He didn't immediately respond, and River wished she could take it back. But whether she brought it up or not, it was a shadow hanging over everything: a year ago this week Keisha White had died.

Quintin sighed and shifted away from her. "I think it's good we're going away. That news story Noelle did is probably gonna break soon, but I think we all want to put the whole thing behind us. Pretend none of that shit ever happened."

"But what if she told that reporter things we promised to keep secret?" River whispered.

He met her eyes. "Maybe we should just focus on senior year coming and college and shit, Riv."

That nickname again. It was what Key used to call her.

River wished she could pretend none of it had ever happened. That the events of that night would die too. There were things no one knew about Key and River, the gala, the after-party, and the weeks leading up to it . . . and she wanted to keep it that way.

The yacht picked up speed. River swallowed hard and smoothed her hands over her braids and the fabric of her summer dress. The ocean's breeze made both ripple in waves behind her, so she turned to face Quintin and squinted up at him, trying to read his expression.

Before she could say more, River felt the baseline of a song drop as the whole yacht began to vibrate with music. She looked back down at her friends as Sydney grabbed Dwayne's hand and started dancing, and Ant emerged from the cabin, laptop still open, headphones on and arm in the air like the DJ he was pretending to be with Noelle trailing him like a tail.

Quintin pumped a fist in the air. "Yo, this my song!" He put out his arm like a gentleman inviting a lady to dance in an old movie and River laughed. She took it despite her head being full of Key and the anniversary. The movement felt like it was made for forgetting. And she desperately needed to forget.

When the song changed, she and Quintin descended the stairs and joined their friends on the lower deck. Soon the whole boat felt like one of the parties they would've thrown back in DC. Which should've been a *good* thing: the Six's parties were legendary. But it just made River think of last spring break, after the gala. The last party where they'd seen Key alive.

She could see the island in the distance. It looked lush and green, like Emerald Envy, the color she'd brought to paint Sydney's nails because it matched her friend's new swimsuit. But as they got closer, the water became choppier, eventually rocking them in a way that felt like a warning. Still, the island looked like paradise. And River was excited.

There was only one problem. In paradise it was easy to forget that sometimes you couldn't do anything to stop bad things from happening.

CRUZ RAMIREZ

Bellhop
11:31 a.m.

CRUZ CHECKED HIS money clip as he stood at the mouth of the temporary arrival dock waiting for the final boatful of VIP guests to arrive.

He should've been happy. He barely had fifty dollars to his name. The official grand reopening of Kuzimu Horizons Resort and Beach was still six weeks away, but when his boss had called with the promise of overtime pay for staffing a "sneak preview" of the remodeled resort for friends and family of the owner, it had taken him less than thirty seconds to agree to come back to the island.

He shoved the almost-empty clip into his uniform pocket. Only one VIP had arrived so far—a grumpy writer—and she was a tightwad with a nasty attitude. He could only guess her books weren't bestsellers. If they were all like her, this was going to be a rough week.

But maybe rich assholes would part with their money easier—and they had to be rich if they were tight with the owner, right? He needed the tips. He straightened himself, dabbed at the beads of sweat on his upper lip, and adjusted his uniform, making sure everything was on the up and up. Part of his job was to look like he gave a shit. Not that the weather was making it easy. The humidity was off the charts. And the water—usually clear and calm this close to shore—churned a dark, muddy green. It almost looked black.

Below him, the makeshift dock shifted with a strong gust of wind, and Cruz widened his stance, then glanced back at the bags of concrete for the new "disembarking pier" to be built to keep precious VIP guests from having to suffer arriving on the leeward side of the island, then fussing about their luxurious air-conditioned shuttle ride through the mangroves to the resort.

Thundering hip-hop beats snatched his attention. He looked out over the water, spotting the guests on the yacht deck.

These "VIPs" were teenagers.

The only people Cruz hated more than the old rich people he was forced to cater to were the young rich people he was forced to cater to. The old ones you could imagine had earned their money, though he was sure most of them had probably just been born lucky and inherited that shit.

The young rich ones, though? Cruz hated them most. He hated the way they glided through life, the path greased, and every door held wide open. He hated the way he was beholden to their generosity to feed his family. Were they in a good mood? Maybe he'd get a generous tip. If he ever got a significant amount, he had better act extremely grateful. He had to pretend that this job of hauling expensive designer bags from luxury yachts and hoisting them onto carts, careful not to scuff or dirty them, was the job he'd dreamed of all his life. Had to pretend that all he wanted was to be a servant to rich dumbshit assholes and their rich dumbshit asshole children.

The other thing he hated? The way most of them couldn't be bothered to look him in the eye. Like he was some kind of soulless robot only there to meet their needs. Then there were the chatty ones who liked to act as if they were on the same level as him. They'd dap him up and pretend that the mountain of money they had didn't make a lick of difference. But that was bullshit. The money mattered. Sometimes, Cruz was *sure* it was the only thing that mattered.

Cruz sighed. Now that he could see them approaching, the voice of his boss, the general manager, filled his head: "We follow the plan I laid out, and all should go smoothly. The son of Kuzimu's owner and his friends are to get anything and everything they want, no questions asked."

Must be nice.

There were six of them. Even from this distance, Cruz saw a glint of gold around one of their necks that he knew cost more than a month of tips. For a few seconds he indulged a fantasy that maybe a wave would swell and crash over them, that the ocean would swallow them up, and they'd spend eternity at the bottom of the sea. But then, he realized, he wouldn't get paid.

A small wind kicked up and sent a spray of salt water into his eyes. Cruz wiped at his face and checked the weather on his phone. Earlier in the day the forecast had called for scattered showers. Now it looked like a tropical storm was developing. Spring break wasn't going to be as sunny and beautiful and perfect as these kids were expecting.

Cruz put his phone away and exhaled, preparing to go and greet his new guests. Sometimes people got exactly what they deserved.

CHAPTER THREE

NOELLE

4:07 p.m.

THE THING ABOUT this trip was that Noelle would do whatever it took to get her life back.

As she stood on the dock and watched her ex-friends head down the path to the Kuzimu Horizons Resort and Beach entrance, she thought about how her therapist might say that this obsession with reclaiming her old life by any means necessary was a bad idea. But it made her feel more like *herself* again. The Noelle who hadn't lost control and lost her friends too.

Her gaze locked on Ant, who was watching the bellhop unload their group's luggage with an eagle eye. The sun glowed behind him, and she noticed how beautiful his skin looked: the perfect molasses batter before it was poured into a cake mold. Sometimes she wondered why he was into her. Key used to say, "You'd choose baking over boys like a weirdo every time." And she was right. But Noelle wondered what Key would think now. She had the most popular junior at school—the mysterious, hot new guy. Every girl wanted him, but he'd chosen her.

If she was *sticking to the facts* like her therapist urged her to, he was the only reason she was here. If Sydney and River had had their way, Noelle would be at home, her only glimpses of the vacation stolen from photos and videos the others posted online. Well, the ones who hadn't blocked her.

Noelle felt grateful to be there but hated that she had to depend on Ant. Especially since he currently ignored her almost as much as everyone else.

"Is the glass-bottom boat scheduled for tonight?" she asked, desperate for his attention. "The bioluminescence peaks around midnight."

"Yeah."

But he didn't look at her. Panic bloomed like a blood-colored rose at the base of her breastbone. "Will they have the key lime tarts for dessert based on my recipe? They didn't confirm via email. Oh! And I requested a tour of the mangrove forest in the morning and a visit to Vista Village on the other side of the island—"

"I really need you to chill," he said, cutting her off. "The staff will do their best. Don't forget: the resort isn't actually reopened yet. There are renovations and shit still in progress. My pops is doing me a big favor by letting us stay here."

"I just want it all to be perfect."

"Yeah, I hear you." He headed down the arrival dock, and she scampered behind him. "It'll be as good as it'll be, all right?"

She bit her tongue to keep the bark inside: she hated when he did the "It's gone be what it's gone be" thing.

She'd laid out the entire trip before she'd messed everything up. That's who she was in this group: the planner. The one who organized the parties, picked the movies they were going to watch, coordinated the snacks, orchestrated the itinerary. She could whip up new recipes in an instant, and a group trip was nothing more than an experience made from a set of ingredients. Being the daughter of a high-performing school principal and an award-winning hospitality mogul meant she'd learned how to organize and execute.

But now she was the one nobody wanted around.

She missed Key. Her best friend, who would rather yell at her than give her the silent treatment. Key knew silence was the hardest thing for Noelle to take. She nibbled her bottom lip, telling herself not to bite too hard and pierce the skin.

Noelle paused at the bottom of the dock. The sticky heat coated her skin and sweat poured down her back. She didn't know if it was from the weather, her nerves, or both.

Ant turned back to her. "You coming?"

Part of her wanted to say no. To turn around and return home. That was probably what she should've done. Everyone hated her, and maybe if they knew just how much she hated herself right now they'd let up.

Noelle squeezed her eyes shut, pushing flashes of Key's face away. The freckles on her nose. The way she tucked a sneaky smile into the corner of her mouth. The baby hairs she could never control around her hairline. The intensity of her haunting eyes and how they made her face always look like it was beckoning.

"Hey, can you not kill the vibe, please?" Ant whispered, suddenly right in front of her.

Noelle talking to that reporter had already done that. And now the story would be published. Her version of the story, at least. Sydney, River, Quatro, and Dwayne had shut her out because they claimed she'd broken their little pact or whatever, but Noelle had never actually agreed to it that night. They all seemed to have forgotten that part.

Ant reached out his hand.

"Sorry," she said.

Noelle glanced over her shoulder and caught one last glimpse of the yacht. She was really stuck here and there was nothing she could do about it. She took a deep breath, steeled herself, and continued forward. "Refire. Replate. Don't stop. Keep moving." Red Bone's executive chef David Donaldson's barking refrain droned in her head. She hated the way even the *thought* of it spiked her heart rate but also hoped it would make her brave.

"Wait," she said as they stepped off the pier and onto the path. "You forgot your laptop."

Ant winked down at her, then patted his backpack. "I'll grab it later; don't worry. I left a few other valuables on board with Captain Ade, too, in a little travel case. He'll be chilling and waiting to take us back to Key West at the end of the week. I'll go check in and get whatever I need from him or he'll bring it to me."

Noelle nodded, trying to let Ant's confidence tuck itself into her broken parts. He had everything covered. She wasn't needed.

The Kuzimu Horizons Resort and Beach spread out before her like the most beautiful bakery window display: coral-pink buildings with icing-white shutters arranged in a loose octagonal shape, perfectly landscaped lawns and gardens freckled by gazebos and walking paths, and pretty wicker furniture. "Great bones and smart details," her mother would've said. She'd overseen all the interior design of their boutique hotel, Vermilion Park, and its restaurant, Red Bone.

Even though Ant said renovations weren't complete, the central building hub sparkled. A spiderweb of cobblestone walkways led to the other areas, all named for the path the sun takes across the horizon each day. Through the open-air lobby she spotted a trio of glittering pools and four additional buildings covered in construction scaffolding.

The entry foyer brought a welcome breeze from the overhead fans and trickle of air-conditioning. But the heat of everyone's eyes prevented Noelle from cooling off.

An older white man greeted Ant; his overly tanned skin reminded Noelle of leather. They whispered for a moment, then turned to the group.

"Yo, yo, yo!" Ant yelled. "So, there's a bunch of construction—"

"Is there, now?" Quatro teased.

Everyone laughed.

Noelle watched Ant play off his annoyance.

"Our grand reopening isn't for another month, but my pops made sure we could stay in the part where the upgrades are done."

"Welcome, welcome to Kuzimu," the white man said. "I'm Glenn Chandler, the general manager. Your group will have the run of the place aside from one other VIP guest. As Mr. Brooks pointed out, please be mindful of the ongoing construction zones. We apologize in advance but know that this should be an amazing week."

"It's going to be the best one of our lives," Ant replied.

Everyone cheered like they were in the stands of one of Quatro's football games.

Mr. Chandler continued, "The only amenities available will be here in the Dawn wing, where you are now." He motioned in various directions. "You'll find all that you need—our front desk, concierge, and award-winning restaurant, First Light. There's also the sundry shop, activities center, and our trio of swimming pools." He turned toward a set of sliding doors. "You'll be staying in our Sunset wing, where all of our VIP suites are located. It has its own stretch of private beach. However, the Meridian, Sunrise, Twilight, and Dusk wings are off-limits. Additional apologies that the spa, steam room, and sauna aren't ready yet. We shall make up for it with our signature Kuzimu hospitality." He grinned and gestured at the staff. "I've assembled a small and mighty crew to cater to your every need."

The hodgepodge group flanked his sides like soldiers ready to do his bidding. He introduced them one by one: the front desk lady, the concierge, the bellhop, the bartender, the chef, Starlie, who Noelle knew from Red Bone, the lifeguard (who happened to be Starlie's son), the head of housekeeping, and the groundskeeper.

Noelle would never remember all their names, except Starlie's of course, but she tried to flash them her best and brightest smile. She knew they were the ones who kept the place running like the line cooks in a kitchen.

Ant nodded. "Time for room keys!"

The bellhop ordered them all to line up their suitcases and get checked in.

Ant rattled off the plans for that night: dinner, then a midnight trip out on the resort's glass-bottom boat.

Noelle's plans. But he didn't mention her at all.

She slipped her hand in her pocket, where her copy of the itinerary sat tucked away. She'd agreed that Ant could pass off the agenda as his own—no one would be interested if they knew she'd done all the planning—but it still stung standing on the sidelines.

Everyone held up their cell phones, trying to get service. Noelle checked hers and the letters *SOS* screamed from the upper right corner of her screen. She felt like it was the theme for her life right now.

"Restaurant at seven for dinner," Ant announced, then turned, slipping her one of his extra keys to the presidential suite and winking.

The front desk lady handed out everyone else's keys. Noelle stepped forward but River cut her off, flashing Noelle a nasty look. It'd been three weeks of this, so Noelle should've been used to it, but the unnecessary gesture still made her heart plummet.

Anthony stepped off to the side with Mr. Chandler. She watched the pair have what looked like a serious conversation. But she didn't get to be fully nosy because something slapped her arm. She whipped around. Sydney glared at the floor, and Noelle followed her gaze. To a key card. Sydney had thrown it at her. "First floor," she said, and it sounded like a curse. "139."

Noelle tried to offer a weak smile. *Kill them with kindness*, her mother would say, but her upset was morphing into an angry knot by the minute.

Everyone headed for their rooms. She ignored the bellhop's insistence that he'd deliver her luggage promptly and took her own bag. She needed something to do with her hands.

She lugged her suitcase, letting the melody of the wheels' soft clicks grow louder than the worries. She walked as slowly as possible to avoid catching up with River and Sydney—and Prescott, the glorified bodyguard who followed Sydney around. She'd had her fill of dirty looks and judgment for the day.

As she entered the Sunset building, beautiful wall sconces left stripes across the open-air limestone hallway. A floral mural snaked along the walls, each detail reminiscent of a gorgeous tropical cake brimming with mangos, passion fruit, guavas, and pineapples. She tried to let the beauty of it fill her up. She was in paradise. She should be happy. Key would be singing at the top of her lungs, guzzling her second margarita, and hustling Noelle into the pool by now if she were here.

Suite 139 loomed ahead. Prescott stood beside the door. Noelle hesitated, and in that moment, a nearby door swung open. Noelle smacked right into a beautiful middle-aged Black woman and her ice bucket, sending it flying.

"Oh, I'm so, so, so sorry." Noelle crouched to rescue the fallen ice.

"Stop." The woman sucked her teeth. "You think I want that filthy bucket now? It would pollute my bottle of wine!"

Noelle's eyebrow arched as she thought about how a dirty bucket could contaminate a glass bottle. This had to be the other "VIP" the general manager had mentioned.

"You kids better stay out of my way while I'm here. This isn't a playground." The woman shooed Noelle away while mumbling about Ant's dad and how she hated all these resort renovations.

Prescott smiled at Noelle, giving her courage to approach the room. She decided to drop her bags before going to see Ant. More beauty awaited her inside the suite: a large living room held two cozy couches, a wet bar and fridge, a pretty powder room, a large spa-like bathroom, and three bedrooms. Chocolate-covered strawberries and freshly sliced pineapple sat on a coffee table.

Noelle heard the girls in their rooms. "Hello," she called out.

River peeked her head out. "Oh, I thought you were the bellhop with the suitcases." She pointed to the door in the back corner. "You get that room."

Noelle glanced out the sliding glass doors, admiring how they led onto a small patio and then the white sand beach. "It's gorgeous out there," she said, trying to get River to talk to her.

River turned away without a word and slammed her bedroom door.

Noelle retreated to her room. The bedspread looked like whipped cream topped with guava-colored pillows. A cupboard held a stack of board games and kiddie toys; a folded crib sat in the corner alongside a changing table. She realized the other girls had given her the suite's kid room. She sighed and set her suitcase down.

A soft knock echoed through the suite. Noelle left her room

and opened the door. The sweaty bellhop lugged in suitcases. River darted into the living room, thanking him.

"Do you need cash for a tip?" Noelle asked, but River didn't respond. Sydney exited her room and grabbed her suitcase without a word.

A text message pinged on Noelle's phone. One bar of cell phone service, finally. Her therapist's response blinked. An answer to the panicked text Noelle had shot off earlier about this trip.

Noelle, consider telling your friends the truth. They aren't obligated to forgive you, but maybe if you tell them what really happened, you can begin to forgive yourself.

Noelle tasted the blood from her bottom lip before she realized she'd bitten it. Maybe her therapist was right. Maybe if she just told River. It was one person.

She peeked her head into River's room. "River, can I talk to you?"

River looked up from her suitcase, her pretty eyes narrowing to angry slits. "Gonna tell me what you told that reporter?"

A pit burned in Noelle's stomach.

"Didn't think so," River said when Noelle didn't respond.

She felt her pocket for Ant's extra key card and rushed out of the room.

Noelle sprawled across Ant's bed, staring up at the skylight. Her short legs tangled with his long, athletic ones, and she buried her nose in his neck, trying to disappear into the scent of his skin and their closeness. It helped her forget that she felt adrift.

Ant left a trail of kisses along Noelle's neck. "Your heart's racing . . ." he whispered into her skin, his voice sending a shiver through her.

Noelle kissed him instead of answering his implied question about why her heart was galloping. His tongue tasted like the sliced pineapple left for them by the hotel staff. She tried to enjoy his touch, but each time she tried to forget what had happened, she'd see a flash of Key's face, her clever grin and startling eyes, or hear her shrill laugh. And worse, she'd see the permanent scowls on Sydney's and River's faces and Dwayne's and Quatro's dismissive grimaces.

Ant sat up. "You're not kissing me back. What's up?"

She couldn't find new words to describe a situation he already understood. *Pathetic*, Key would've said had she been able to hear her obsessive inner monologue about being on the outs with everyone.

He took her chin between his fingers. Her eyes burned into his. "Do you trust me?"

"I do," she replied.

"Then stop worrying." He went back to kissing her neck, a little more fervently this time.

It felt good. He was surprisingly gentle for such a strong-looking guy—with his swimmer's shoulders and toned arms—and the way he'd breathe against her skin before allowing his lips to make contact always made her flesh erupt with goose bumps. He ran one hand over her hip before slipping the other one up her shirt and turning her to butterscotch pudding.

The suite phone rang, and Ant groaned, rolling off her. He said a bunch of things she didn't understand to someone on the other end before hanging up and pulling on his T-shirt. "Gotta go talk to Chandler. Meet me at dinner." He kissed her forehead and was out of the room before she could react or respond.

Noelle left to grab a few things from her room, then doubled back to Ant's suite to get ready for dinner away from River's and Sydney's nasty glares. She caught a glimpse of herself in the mirror. Her mouth was a puffy, frayed rose from abusing her lips with her front teeth. Her long twists were in need of more mousse and gel to fight the humidity.

"Pull yourself together." She heard Key's voice inside her head. "You're supposed to be my beautiful best friend." A bubble of sadness grew in her chest, and she swallowed hard. She couldn't afford to cry right now. She had to gear up for dinner and the hot anger of her ex-friends. As distant thunder boomed and lightning streaks cut through darkening clouds, she felt those skies mirrored her life right now: a tangle of sad rain, angry booms, and jagged bolts of random electricity.

"Fix it," she grumbled to herself, then darted out of the suite.

The noise from First Light, the resort's restaurant, found her in the hall. Sydney's and Dwayne's security were posted at the entrance like sweaty sentries. They nodded at Noelle as she walked by.

Noelle held her breath as she faced all of her ex-friends in the midst of an argument. Their table stretched across the patio, which was decorated to exact specifications: floating candles in tiny bowls nestled between local flower arrangements on a blush-pink tablecloth.

The pool glowed as the underwater lights changed every few seconds. It was better than she'd imagined, and she'd have to leave a handwritten note thanking the general manager for nailing all her requests. She was filled with a momentary surge of happiness.

Noelle watched her friends, wondering if they knew how much she'd done. Would they even care if they did?

Of course they wouldn't care, a tiny voice whispered. *Well, not anymore. You ruined everything.*

"But why do *you* care so much?" The memory of Key's voice settled over her. The thing Key would always say to her.

Noelle cared about *everything* while Key hadn't cared at all, and Noelle had secretly envied Key's ability to ignore what anyone had to say about her. Tonight she'd need to be a little more like Key and less like herself. She steeled herself and strode up to the table.

Her table.

"No welcome committee for me?" Noelle said, then started to giggle at her own joke. She used to be the welcome committee head for Thurgood Marshall Academy.

Everyone looked up, sucked their teeth, and immediately looked away.

Noelle felt the rest of her temporary bravado crumble.

Ant pulled out the empty seat beside him. Everyone else acted as if she didn't exist.

"Bruh, you didn't tell us the cell service was gonna be shit out here." Quatro held his phone in the air.

"Settle into island life," Ant teased. "Unplug a little. Time to relax. Plus, everybody you text is right here. Ain't nobody checking for you."

"Uh, hello, my mom," Quatro spat back.

"Okay, big mama's boy," Ant said before guzzling his drink.

"But c'mon, what about Wi-Fi, though?" Sydney added.

Ant laughed. "General manager said it'll be back up in the morning, hopefully."

As the others piled on the complaints, a server and a woman in a chef jacket approached the table.

Ant stood, beaming. "Yo, everybody, this is Chef Starlie and she's a Michelin-star—"

"Enough with the flattery," she mumbled with a shy smile, mopping sweat from her brow.

"She makes the dopest dishes for me and my dad when we're here, and she's going to let us know what she's cooking up tonight."

Chef Starlie smiled. "Now, unfortunately we haven't gotten our shipment in from Key West due to this evening's rough waters, so I'm doing my best. We're going to make do."

"What we eating, then?" Quatro yelled out, joking.

River swatted at him. "RUDE!"

"Something delicious. I've been in contact with the wonderful Noelle Clarke to design this week's menu, so if you have any questions, talk to her. Good to see you, Noelle."

Noelle smiled, happy to see a familiar and friendly face from back home, and Chef Starlie winked at her. It sent a wave of warmth across her skin, reigniting some of her courage.

Sydney sighed and Quatro shook his head. But Noelle smiled a real smile for what felt like the first time since they'd left DC. They *had* to talk to her if they wanted to know what they were eating. She wondered if Ant had taken care of this, too, and made sure Chef said this tonight.

The chef bowed and returned to the kitchen. The courses arrived one after the other just as she'd designed: hamachi crudo for Sydney, seared scallops and shrimp for Quatro, wagyu beef for River, pineapple fried rice for Dwayne, and spicy calamari for herself. Plus, a key lime cake and pie for dessert as a reminder of Keisha in memoriam.

But none of them acknowledged her thoughtfulness as they feasted, nor did they include her in dinner conversations.

Sydney and River took their thousandth selfie.

"Everyone wishes they could be here," Sydney said.

"Well, no one's gonna be jealous if we can't post." River waved her phone around. "And I don't want my mother coming to find me if she doesn't hear from me soon. You know how she is."

Dwayne pointed out at the pool and surroundings. "Ant, this really all your dad's?"

"Yeah," Ant replied. "He's about to expand it too. Adding two more restaurants on the property next year in the Dusk wing."

"Five stars so far," River chimed in. "Everything's perfect. It's like they know everything we like."

"Well"—Ant put a hand on Noelle's shoulder—"couldn't have planned it without her help."

An uneasy silence left only the scraping sounds of forks scooping up last bites of dessert. Noelle tried to push away her anxiety and intrusive thoughts. *Don't bite your lip harder. Don't bite harder.*

"Want to raid the bar like old times? Get some tequila or rum and hit the pool while we wait for the midnight glass-bottom boat ride?" Her words hung in the air, betraying the unspoken rule that she wasn't supposed to be talking at all. She'd already broken everyone's trust. But she wanted to conjure memories of good times back when the Six had been stuck at stupid DC fundraisers or political galas with their well-connected parents and found ways to sneak off, pilfer the bar, and start their own party away from snobby adults who asked questions about where they planned to go to college or if they were going to follow in their parents' footsteps into politics or business.

No response.

If Key had been there, Noelle wouldn't have been dismissed even if the crew was upset with her. Key wouldn't have allowed it. Key's energy was like a bolt of lightning: electric, volatile, undeniable. No one would dare ignore her.

The memory of the night Key died rushed into her bubble of loneliness.

The Thoroughgood Gala. Their school's yearly fundraiser. (The parents "had to find a way to use Justice Marshall's given first name," and a gala was apparently as good a use as any.)

It'd been black-tie and hosted in the ballroom at her family's hotel. They'd been on top of the world, sneaking out before the dessert course and headed to get in the pool and hot tub.

Noelle blinked away images of Key's mouth, how her smile had slackened, and the glassy look in her eyes as life left them. She balled her dress in her fists, willing the memory away.

The restaurant's lights flickered overhead.

"Ant, no boat tonight, okay?" River said, a nervous edge to her voice.

"It's probably wack, anyways," Dwayne added.

"Yeah. Cancel it." Sydney's eyes landed straight on Noelle. "The air doesn't feel right, and none of us actually care about glowing fish."

Another knot twisted in Noelle's stomach. Distant thunder boomed and she felt like the universe had sent it to give her a voice. "I'm sorry, okay? You guys can't ice me out forever, you know!" she shouted.

"We can try," River replied.

The table burst out laughing.

Ant touched Noelle's hand. "Chill, okay? You're good. Relax."

There it was again: *relax*. A firework exploded behind her ribs, and she slapped his hand away.

"Yo, she's losing it . . ." Sydney mumbled.

"Again, you mean?" Quatro added.

River crossed her arms over her chest. "Don't sit here and act like you don't know what you did, Noelle."

"Right." Dwayne grimaced. "You're buggin', popping off like that."

Ant's eyebrows lifted, but he didn't step in to defend her like he typically would've. He wouldn't even look at her.

She knew every good and bad thing that had ever happened to Sydney Davis, Quintin McCallum IV, River Reynolds, and Dwayne Harris. But she'd kept every secret, every embarrassing moment, every worry, every mistake. Did all those years of friendship really get erased by one crap decision?

She jumped to her feet. "You know what? Fuck all of you. None of you have a clue what *I'm* going through. I wish y'all had died instead of Key . . . At least she gave a shit about me. And that's exactly why I told that reporter *everything* she wanted to know."

Noelle stomped away from the table. This was exactly what her therapist had told her *not* to do: continue to blow up her life. But when her feelings bubbled up inside her, she became a shaken bottle of champagne.

The minute she was out of sight, she ran. And she didn't stop until the noise of the restaurant and the approaching storm had turned to whispers.

CHAPTER FOUR

QUATRO

9:52 p.m.

THE ENTRANCE TO the pool loomed up ahead, and the din of voices let Quatro know he and Dwayne weren't the first to arrive. Which made Quatro that much more unsettled. His low-flying hope that everyone would recognize they should *reject* Noelle's pick-me-ass suggestion that they do the same stupid shit they'd done the last time they were gathered near a pool? Shot right outta the sky.

You know . . . despite the fact that someone had died then.

Adding to the anxiety: as he and Dwayne headed for the resort's largest pool, a brown-skinned guy in red trunks—carrying a matching red tube with the word GUARD on it all big and bold—appeared to be . . . leaving?

"Enjoy, guys," he said in passing. "I'm off-duty. Swim at your own risk."

"Umm . . ."

"Come on in, fellas! The water's fiiiiiine," Ant called out the moment he saw Quatro and Dwayne. He sat on the little ledge that ran along the pool's waterfall edge. Noelle was tucked up under his arm looking just as sour as she'd been when she'd made her dramatic restaurant exit.

Ant reached for his phone, which was perched on a floating tray.

"Friend, you got your phone *in* the pool?" Dwayne said, baffled.

Noelle laughed (it sounded almost as fake to Quatro as her apology for breaking their pact and talking to that reporter). "He keeps that thing closer to him than me."

Irritation flashed across Ant's face, but he forced a smile. "My life in the palm of my hand. Plus, I figured I'd look more into this whole A.S.S. investigation."

"The *what* investigation, now?" Quatro asked.

"Oh, you haven't heard about this?"

It was one of a handful of things Quatro *really* didn't like about Anthony Brooks: his tendency to condescend by making himself seem more in the know than everyone else. "Nah. I haven't."

"There's an areawide investigation of anonymous slander sites, and there's one on the list that's reportedly connected to our school. MANIfest the Mess?"

"Wait, for real?" from Dwayne.

"Yep," Ant replied. "I'm determined to figure out who's behind it, but for now . . ." He did some tapping, and hip-hop filled the air from speakers Quatro couldn't see.

"Well, hot damn," Dwayne said under his breath.

"Huh?" Quatro looked at him and then followed his gaze.

Sydney and River had just entered the pool area and were removing the cover-ups they had over their bathing suits.

River stared at Ant's phone—apparently also shocked to see it on the water. Which gave Quatro just enough time to take in the fullness of her . . . *her*ness. And River looked . . . *well, hot damn* indeed.

Quatro quickly turned away and walked over to a lounger under one of the nearest cabanas to drop his towel and slides. Then he dove into the pool. Even submerged, he could hear a clap of thunder that shook the sky.

This whole trip was going to be a disaster. He just *knew* it.

The moment he surfaced and wiped the water off his face, he and River caught eyes. She cut hers to Noelle and then to the sky before meeting Quatro's again.

So she was feeling it too. It shocked Quatro how desperately he suddenly wanted to grab her, pull her out of the pool, and whisk her to the yacht—which he would hijack so he could get her safely back to Key West.

"Yo, Ant, where them drinks at?" Quatro yelled, tearing his gaze away from her.

"Should be here any second." Ant flashed him his signature smug I-can-get-anything-for-anyone smile. "Then the *real* fun can begin, am I right?"

Sydney waved him off. "So Quatro, you dating anyone?" She turned to face him. He saw her eyes cut to River and back again. "Things are way easier now regardless of who you're interested in, correct?"

The second question—which really wasn't a question at all—landed with the force of an elephant falling from the sky. Quatro didn't have to look around to know that every member of the OG crew heard Sydney . . . and knew exactly what she meant. No one was willing to say it outright, but *most* things had become "way easier" for *everyone* with Key no longer around. She was notorious for collecting secrets and using them as leverage to get people to do what she wanted them to. Himself included. There was nothing Quatro hated more than being reminded of Keisha White. He'd only stayed with her as long as he had because she knew things he didn't want anyone else to know.

It took everything in him not to look at River right then. The only thing worse for him than having a crush on one of his dead girlfriend's closest friends was knowing that (1) he'd had the crush long before he had the girlfriend, but (2) because the girlfriend had *died*, he couldn't bring himself to make a *real* move on the crush.

Even in death, Key held sway.

The friendly bartender—Lamar, he thought that was the dude's name—rolled a cart with bottles of liquor and mixers, plastic cups, and two buckets of ice to the edge of the pool. "That's what I'm talkin' about." Ant swam away from his perch to check the delivery. Noelle hugged her knees and looked away from the group.

Another big boom of thunder rumbled in the distance.

As Anthony played bartender, Quatro did his best not to make eye contact with anyone. It was impossible not to notice how quiet it had gotten since Sydney said what she said.

Thankfully, it didn't take long for another floating tray laden with drinks to appear on the surface of the pool. "This round is on me," Ant said as he waded back over to Noelle, a cup in each hand. "Feel free to make your own refills. Just use the same cup. Pops is real fussy about maintaining this place's sustainability rating."

Quatro couldn't grab a drink quick enough.

No clue what Ant had mixed up, but cup one dulled the edges of Quatro's overactive mind just enough for him to exhale.

Halfway through cup two—which Dwayne had mixed—Ant suggested they play truth or dare, but it didn't take long to recognize no one was choosing *truth*. And the dares were pretty mild as the group consisted of one official couple, one pair of "friends" who clearly had the hots for each other despite a parental political rivalry (he truly hoped Dwayne and Sydney would get it together soon), and himself and River. By the time Sydney was handing Quatro his third refill, they'd abandoned the whole thing.

Speaking of River, after guzzling cup three, she looked too good to resist. Didn't help that she was eyeballing him too.

"My God, can you two just hook up already?" Sydney said, snapping Quatro out of his trance. "Why you insist on acting like you don't like each other is *baffling* to me."

"Oh, you're *certainly* one to talk." River looked Sydney dead in the eye. "Hey, Dwayne, you like Sydney's bathing suit?"

Dwayne choked and spat out his drink.

Quatro waved them off as he finished his cup and made his way over to the cart for a refill.

When he turned around, Ant was watching him. "Careful not to put a damper on your, uhh . . . *performance*. Yeah, Quatro?"

"Pause," Dwayne said. "Say *what*, now?"

"Well, if *that* wasn't the most ridiculous thing I've ever heard," Noelle chimed in.

Everyone turned to her and stared.

"I mean—"

"What are y'all, twelve?" River said.

Their eyes met again, and Quatro was so overcome by an urge to kiss her, it made him dizzy. (Or perhaps that was the booze?) Her eyes always got him. Since second grade, she'd sworn they were too far apart, but he thought they were perfect.

"Hey, I'm not the one talking about Quatro's *performance*," Dwayne began. "I mean . . . not that there would be anything *wrong* with you—"

"Think your mind can survive outside the gutter for five minutes, Dwayne?" Quatro slurred. "He's not talking about *that* kinda performance."

"So, what sort of performance could he mean?" Sydney asked.

Which was when Quatro picked up what Ant was laying down. It was something he'd told Quatro before, and the stark reminder of why he was even here—how he and Ant had gotten to know each other.

It had all been so random: on his way to his car after the worst football practice of his life, Quatro ran into a teammate who looked to be in the midst of a shady exchange with the new kid, Anthony

Brooks. Said teammate decided that was the perfect time to return the set of resistance bands he'd borrowed from Quatro, so when he rushed off to *his* car, Quatro was left standing with Ant. Who instantly asked, "You good, man? You look a little down."

And Quatro didn't know what it was about Ant, but he told him the truth: the closer they got to senior year, the more pressure Quatro felt to perform well on the football field, especially since his super-macho dad was a Hall of Famer. Quintin "Quatro" McCallum IV had to *prove* his mettle. He needed to be exceptional, as borne out by his stats. He had to line up athletic scholarship offers he didn't need and earn a spot on a D-I team. Be the *best* of the best.

Largely so people wouldn't be able to say he'd received an unfair advantage because of his dad.

He told Ant all of it for some reason that day.

When Quatro was done, Ant had looked at him as though studying a photograph (which was a little awkward, but Quatro refused to flinch). Then Ant said, "You know, I think I got something for you. It'll give you a little boost. Take some of the pressure off."

Thus began Quatro's foray into the forbidden realm of performance-enhancing drugs—the effectiveness of which were hampered by excessive alcohol consumption.

Quatro looked down at his half-empty cup. Had Ant brought Quatro's "vitamin" re-up as Quatro had requested? He'd have to wait until they were alone to ask. Quatro obviously didn't want anyone to know what he'd been doing. And he low-key hated Ant for putting his business out there like this.

"Welp, that was a raindrop," Sydney said, making her way to the pool steps.

Quatro thanked Mother Nature under his breath.

Dwayne's expression wilted like a day-old salad. "Really? You're gonna leave?"

She snapped her towel and began to dry off. "You could come with me," she said with a quiet smile.

"I'm also gonna head in." The voice came from below Quatro, so he looked down. To where River, whose head didn't quite reach his chin, was staring up at him. There was so much longing in her pretty eyes, Quatro couldn't look away. Or form any other words. Or see or hear or feel anything else. His heart beat faster, and he got the sinking feeling that his soul was about to be sucked into the black centers of the light brown irises he'd been daydreaming about since before he could tie his shoes.

This was bad.

"You should come to my and Syd's room," she said to him then. Zero malice, snark, bite, anger . . . anything of the like. It made his toes tingle. So he wiggled them. You know, to try and ground himself.

He waited to get out of the pool until she'd walked under the overhang, heading along the path back to Sunset. And as soon as he grabbed his towel, the rain began to fall in fatter drops.

Noelle tugged on Ant's arm. "Guess that's *our* cue, too."

"You go ahead." He gave her a kiss. "Go to my suite and wait for me. I'll be up in a few."

She looked annoyed, but it didn't last long: the harder it rained, the faster she moved. She disappeared, hustling as Quatro (tipsily) worked his feet into his slides, then made his way back to his suite with Dwayne, not wanting to be alone with Ant despite needing to figure out whether he'd brought the package. With the memory of Keisha in the air, there were too many other secrets churning inside Quatro, and Ant had a way of drawing them out.

He really did need that re-up, though. He peeped around to make sure the coast was clear and then turned to ask Ant flat out if he'd brought it.

But Ant was swimming. Hard. Broad shoulders and toned arms broke the waterline and then disappeared beneath it again. Just when he was almost at the far wall, he flipped and came back in the opposite direction.

Of course, the captain of the swim team would be swimming laps at every opportunity. Even during a lightning storm.

If only Quatro was that dedicated to football.

He shook his head and went inside as the loudest clap of thunder of all shook the world around him.

ORION PARSONS

Lifeguard
11:44 p.m.

ORION HAD ALWAYS loved water. And because the public pool down the street from his apartment had been an unpredictable place—with badass kids who would splash you to the point where you felt waterboarded, push you in fully clothed, or even hold you under—Orion had known he'd need to get really good at swimming if his anxious mother was ever going to let him go to the pool alone.

Ever since he was ten—the year he could finally swim well enough to be allowed to walk to the pool without her—he'd spend hours challenging his friends to see who could hold their breath the longest, making bets that kept his pockets fat and his ego fatter.

He always won.

He never swam on a team, but he'd been a lifeguard since turning sixteen. So when his Aunt Nova suggested he come to the Kuzimu resort with his mom, the chef, to earn a little extra cash before heading back to his university in the fall, it seemed like a no-brainer. "Easy money," she'd told him. "I got the hook-up."

But something had been off since they'd arrived. He'd thought his mom was just being extra when she said she had a bad feeling shortly before they left home. That she was overreacting the way she did about everything.

Orion knew the world record for holding breath underwater was twenty-four minutes—a feat that felt impossible. He knew from timing himself that he could hold his breath for almost four and a half minutes.

But that was when he was in control—when he knew he could come up for air at any moment.

When he was calm.

Not thrashing, terrified, and panicking, his blood turning to ice in his veins.

Not feeling the pound of a torrential downpour on his back.

Now, as the large hand pressed down and continued holding his head underwater, he thought of how many breath-holding bets he'd made and won. He thought of how many times he'd escaped situations like this at the public pool down the street from his house. He thought of his mother.

How she'd been right this time.

He hoped she could feel how much he loved her.

PRESENT DAY

DETECTIVE LUCA FRANCO

April 6

3:37 p.m.

"I'M SORRY, SIR. I just don't think we can safely wake this patient. There's no way for you to continue with your line of questioning right now," the doctor said.

Detective Franco rubbed a hand down his face. This investigation was proving more difficult than he'd anticipated. What had all these kids—and that's what they were: *kids*—been doing on that island without supervision?

"We need information only this individual can provide. Do you think we could do this in a few hours?"

The doctor looked at the clipboard in her hands. It seemed like she was doing it for show, not to actually check or read anything. Detective Franco shoved his hands in his pockets, frustrated.

"Sir, we had to induce a coma due to the extent of these injuries. The patient would still be in too much pain to answer anything if we stopped the medication in a few *days*, let alone a few hours."

"Goddamn it," Detective Franco breathed. "Fine. Is there anyone *else* from the group who's healthy enough to speak? I really need to get to the bottom of this mess—"

There was a knock on the door, and both the detective and the doctor turned. "Nurse Delgado is finishing up with one of the other kids now. Maybe the detective can speak with him instead?"

Detective Franco frowned. He was so tired of talking to children.

The doctor nodded. "Thank you," she said.

"He's the next room over." And the nurse left.

The doctor turned to Detective Franco, relief evident in her slight smile. "Let's let this one rest," she said, gently touching the patient's hand. The patient was the only other adult he had access to, and she couldn't speak.

"Maybe the boy next door will be more helpful than you think."

THE WEEK BEFORE:

MONDAY

ADE DIALLO

Captain of the Nocturna
12:36 a.m.

ADE CRACKED OPEN his fifth beer. He knew he'd had too many, but it was raining, and this yacht was better than his whole damn house in Key West. He was about to enjoy himself. He flipped up Anthony's laptop and started streaming another movie to Mr. Brooks's sick flat-screen. The boy had a better catalog than all them streaming apps combined.

As he burped and rubbed his stomach, he sniffed the air. Was that gas? He chuckled to himself and farted so loud it made the whole bench under him vibrate. "Must be me." He was thrilled his complaining-ass wife, Faridah, wasn't around to nag him.

He sure liked this job. These next six days were gonna go by way too fast. It honestly didn't get any better than this: being paid to vacation. That was why he always said yes to anything Mr. Brooks asked. Best boss he'd ever had. He ain't even mind that Ade's captain license had expired and he didn't have the money to retake those exams. Mr. Brooks had hired him anyway. He was that kinda brother. Always looking out.

Ade guzzled the last of the can and got one more. What was the harm? He'd watch a movie and then mosey on out into the rain to head for his room at the resort. Another perk of this gig. He'd continue to be in the lap of luxury.

"Don't forget to bring Ant's stuff," he told himself, remembering little boss man's instructions. He glanced at the laptop again, a small monogrammed bag, and the travel case.

He sighed, more content than he'd been in a while.

Ade Diallo. In Kuzimu paradise . . . who would've thought it?

He'd won the lottery. Another jagged blast of lightning ripped through the sky, followed almost instantly by a thunderclap so loud, it rattled Ade's bones. The smell of gasoline tickled his nose again. Whole thing made the beer swim in his gut this time, but he shook it off. Not like Ade hadn't weathered worse storms—his marriage included. He took another swig, hoping to dull the irritating edge that was creeping into his bliss. He tilted his head back. "Every ting a gonna be all RIGHT!" he sang into the sky.

If only he knew.

CHAPTER FIVE

DWAYNE

7:16 a.m.

DWAYNE DIDN'T HAVE a clue how he'd slept through the rager of a storm last night. At home, he couldn't sleep at all without his seventy-five-inch TV on, set to C-SPAN twenty-four/seven. But here, he'd slept hard, only stirring as dull sunlight streamed through the thin gold curtains in their hotel suite.

He stared up at the unmoving ceiling fan, sweat dripping down his neck. He and Quatro must've forgotten to switch the AC on last night—though it felt odd knowing they'd gotten turndown service, but the housekeeping staff hadn't made sure the room would be at a comfortable temperature. Ant had boasted for weeks about how fancy these suites were, how exclusive the island was, how famous rappers and models vacationed here, how it was an industry secret, blah, blah, blah. And yeah, the rooms were nice, but why was it so hot inside this one?

Dwayne climbed out of bed and peeked his head out into the suite's common area. Quatro sat on the couch staring at his cell phone.

"The power's out," Quatro said, not looking up.

"Ah, so that's why it's so hot." Dwayne wiped his brow.

"That storm was really nuts last night. How'd you not wake up *at all*, bro? And there's even *less* cell service this morning than there was yesterday. Been trying to text my mom for over an hour."

"Wonderful," Dwayne grumbled. So much for a relaxing vacation. He could've stayed home with his trio of little sisters if he wanted to sit in the middle of a tropical storm or hurricane or whatever was still lashing the building with wind and rain.

Seven days in paradise with his oldest and closest friends. That was what he'd been after. Let the sun and water and ocean air set them free from the nightmare that was last spring break. But what he'd gotten so far was the opposite: confinement to their rooms as a storm raged, and now without power, air-conditioning, Wi-Fi, or cell service.

It almost felt like retribution.

As he glanced around the dim, window-lit room at the supposed "luxury amenities"—like the (useless) eighty-five-inch TV—Dwayne was reminded of how expensive the trip had been.

Not that money was an issue. Business with Ant kept his pockets fat and happy. And even if it hadn't, he could've siphoned money from his aunts, uncles, and grandparents. All he had to do was place high at Model UN conference, win at a debate tournament, or have a word with state legislators about some of his family members' grievances.

They were the rare kind of Black family that was old money—second and third homes in Oak Bluffs and Sag Harbor; scholarship funds and buildings in the Harris name at a number of HBCUs; a yearly invitation to the White House, and that was *before* his father had been elected governor of Maryland. Dwayne's family—and especially his father—knew people in high places.

But Dwayne took great satisfaction in the fact that he didn't have to ask anyone—Governor Harris especially—for money at all.

He looked around the suite's common area again. At the high ceilings and big, cushy furniture. If his father found out just how fancy the place was, he'd start asking questions about how Dwayne afforded the trip without parental assistance. He'd been able to dodge the third degree by asking if he could go—and making it clear that he'd pay his own way from all the allowance he'd been saving—as his father was rushing out for some meeting.

So yeah: even though he too was feeling nervous about . . . well, every damn thing, Dwayne would not be calling his dad like Quatro was calling his mom.

A whistling wind catcalled the boys from outside. Quatro leaned over and peeled back a slice of curtain, revealing a cloudy slate-gray sky with trees swaying on the distant mountains.

"Is it over?" Dwayne asked.

Quatro shrugged. "Maybe. Seems like the rain is easing up right now, but before the power went out, I saw a weather report about how this hurricane randomly changed course. Didn't even know they could do that. It was supposed to miss the Keys completely, but here we are. Hoping the worst of it passed last night. I've never seen anything like it."

Dwayne rubbed his groggy eyes. "Sydney had me doing the most. I think we might've had one too many drinks."

"Well, that would explain a lot . . ." Quatro said, not looking up from his phone.

"Mmmm . . . what's that supposed to mean?"

Quatro glanced up, *concerned best friend* etched into his furrowed eyebrows. "What do you remember from last night?"

"Uhhh." Dwayne took a quick scan of his body. He wasn't that hungover, just a little groggy, like he hadn't gotten much sleep. Which he knew wasn't true: one thing he *did* remember was being pissed that he was in bed before midnight. He hadn't wanted to stop partying—the vibe was right, the music was good, and Sydney was doing something with her hips that had his mind in a blissful blender. But then the storm really picked up. And as all the passageways between rooms were outdoors, everyone had to get to their assigned one, stat.

He just couldn't remember the journey back to the suite. Or where he'd been before he made it. Or who all had been there with him.

The black hole where his memories should have been made his blood run cold. One of his father's favorite sayings was "Self-control is the ultimate power move, son."

What the hell had he done?

Dwayne gulped, bracing himself. "So, what *did* happen last night?"

Quatro opened his mouth, but before he could elaborate, three hard knocks startled them both.

Dwayne was closer to the door, so he answered it.

And almost shut it again instantly. There was Sydney. Standing like a ray of bright sunshine with her locs wrapped up in a bun and her gorgeous brown skin on display in an emerald bikini with a long sheer skirt over her bottom half. Raindrops freckled her bare shoulders. She wiggled her glittery toenails in her sandals, and Dwayne shifted his gaze to her face and kept it there.

Behind her, both Johnson *and* Prescott lurked like overly serious babysitters. His bliss bubble popped like it'd been poked with a toothpick. Dwayne hated having a security guard, and he knew Sydney did too.

But alas.

"Good morning." She handed him a cool glass bottle with a smile. "Fresh mint water. It's not super cold, and there's sadly no ice. But it'll keep you hydrated after last night."

Dwayne stared at the bottle. Surely looking like an idiot.

"Are you good?" she asked. "I know today is likely to be tricky, but I figured we could try and make the best of it."

"Huh?" Now Dwayne was confused.

Which seemed to confuse Sydney. "You do know what day it is, right?"

It clicked then: today was the anniversary of . . . last spring break's night from hell.

Now he really wanted to close the door.

He felt Sydney's eyes rove over his face. "Let's go grab some breakfast, yeah? Come on." She grabbed his hand and pulled him out of the room, and they headed down the stairs to the first floor.

"So, about last night . . ." she said once there was a bit of distance between them and the security guards.

Definitely caught Dwayne off guard. "Uhhh, yeah. About that . . ."

She burst out laughing and looked at him. "You don't remember a thing, huh?"

Dwayne sighed and hung his head. "Can't say that I do."

"Figures." Sydney gently elbowed him in the side. "Something I've been daydreaming about for over a year finally happens, and you were too faded to even catalog it." She shook her head.

"Umm . . . I'm sorry?"

"It's fine. We did have a *lot* of fun, though." She slipped her hand into his and interlocked their fingers. "It's too bad you don't remember."

Dwayne forced a smile. Under different circumstances, this whole holding-hands-and-bantering-with-Sydney-Davis thing would've been a trip highlight. But between the weight of the anniversary and the fact that they had their babysitters in tow, Dwayne couldn't enjoy a single thing about his ideal girl's soft palm against his own. All he could think about as they walked was how screwed he would be if one of the security guards snitched to either of their political parents about their romantic stroll.

It'd taken Dwayne a while to realize he was even *into* Sydney. Yeah, Quatro and Key had become an item freshman year, but the thought of dating a girl he used to play freeze tag with had been a bit of a hurdle for Dwayne despite their budding mutual attraction as they all got into the groove of high school.

Dwayne had been shocked the morning his parents announced over family breakfast that his father had decided to seek out the Democratic nomination for president. And not only because Dad was barely over a year into his governorship and politics in general. Sydney's mom had announced her bid just two weeks earlier. And she'd been instrumental in helping Dwayne's father get elected governor.

It was a whole scandal. Made the gossip blogs and everything.

And now the offspring were holding hands?

Also not helping: as they made their way across the resort, Dwayne could see just how bad the storm had actually been.

"Oh my God," Sydney said as they looked around; the rain was letting up briefly.

It was worse than he could've imagined. Palm trees littered the resort property like toothpicks. Lounge chairs were tipped on their sides. Inches-deep puddles overtook pathways at varying intervals. Wooden scaffolding was splintered into pieces. Loose tarps flapped in the wind. Tipped paint buckets spilled all over the lawns.

An eerie silence blanketed the property, too, like they were in the middle of a ghost town. Only them, the one other guest, and the small team of staff in a place that could accommodate a few hundred.

"This is wild," Sydney said, pulling Dwayne back to the present.

"Truly." He gulped. A storm this destructive just happening to sweep in on the eve of Key's death date? It made Dwayne's chest feel tight. Every inch of Kuzimu now looked—and felt—like a bad omen.

Just before they reached the main pool deck, Sydney stopped. So Dwayne turned back.

"I don't think I'm okay, Dwayne." She looked like she might be about to cry.

And now Dwayne was ready to fight whoever was responsible for Sydney being near tears. "What's wrong?"

Sydney waved a hand around. "I mean, all of it? The storm. No power. No cell service. This mess. The anniversary . . ." She put her hands over her face. "I don't want to ruin your vacation—our vacation—but I kinda want to leave. Don't you?"

"I mean, I hadn't thought about it." Dwayne looked off into the distance. "But I can't really disagree with you."

"Resorts usually have plans for disasters like this, don't they?" Sydney asked. "Like, why the hell don't they have generators or something?"

And that's when Dwayne looked a little more closely at her. Her nails, which were normally flawless (she once told him that was a prerequisite for being best friends with River) were chipped and bitten. Her eyes were vaguely puffy.

He couldn't help it: he pulled her closer. Hovering guards be damned. "I'm sorry, Sydney. I didn't realize you were this freaked out."

"I've tried to put on a brave face, put the anniversary out of my mind—which is why I came over so early. I was looking for a distraction. Sorry about that, by the way."

Dwayne smiled. "I've had worse wake-up calls."

She grinned and looked at her feet.

"Everything is gonna be fine, okay? Tomorrow will be better."

"I just . . ." She peeked up at him through her crazy long eyelashes—something he'd noticed about her when they were eight. "I'm not upset that she's gone, you know? And a part of me feels guilty about that."

Now Dwayne was the one to drop his eyes. He did his best to never let the G-word—*guilty*—enter his consciousness. But here was the girl of his literal dreams serving it up to him on a storm-dented platter.

It'd never been a secret that Dwayne Harris wasn't fond of Keisha White.

Actually, that was a euphemism. He'd hated Key with every molecule in his body. Had since the first time he watched her bully a new kid out of her pepperoni pizza in second grade.

The night she died . . .

No. He'd done too good of a job shoving the whole thing into the deepest recesses of his mind, and he wouldn't let it overtake him now.

"Yeah, I hear you," he said, setting his hands on her shoulders and looking into her (frickin' gorgeous) eyes. "But that was then, and this is now, okay? Let's try and focus on what's in front of us—"

A loud bang near the pool made them both jump. One of the cabanas had collapsed. Dwayne looked and gasped. There was all sorts of debris in the water.

His hands fell from Sydney's shoulders, and he moved closer, drawn by something he couldn't explain. The bad feeling spread from his chest to his extremities like there were centipedes inside his veins. Flipped pool loungers, resort towels, strips of a shredded umbrella . . . and something else.

A break in the clouds flooded the deck with sunshine, and something gold glinted in the light. It was wrapped around . . .

"Oh my God!" Dwayne shouted, making a break for the water. A part of him knew it was too late. That Ant was . . .

He jumped in anyway.

The last thing he heard before going under was Sydney's scream.

CHAPTER SIX

RIVER

8:08 a.m.

RIVER WOKE TO screaming. She shot up in bed and looked through her window. All she saw was the storm-strewn beach, but the high-pitched screaming continued. River stood, ran to her bedroom door, and threw it open. Noelle was already standing in her own doorway.

"What is that?" she asked, eyes wild.

Noelle was the last person River wanted to see this morning, or ever. "How would I know?" River said.

They both rushed out of their suite and down to the main walkway that led to the heart of the resort. Someone was still screaming. They ran toward the sound, toward the pool. River hopped over palm leaves and bounded through warm, gritty puddles barefoot with Noelle at her heels.

When they reached the source of the sound, River stopped dead.

The pools in front of her looked all wrong. The water was murky from the storm and seemed almost as dark as the ocean had felt that first day on the yacht—dark as the thick clouds clustering overhead right now when both the sky and the pool had been crystal clear the day before. It reminded River of the way her mother could codeswitch in a second when she was talking to clients; the way River knew she herself could shed her true personality and shift into Dana's Daughter as easily as she changed her nail color. She blinked, hoping this, too, was somebody pretending.

Maybe none of this was real.

Dwayne couldn't be dripping wet, pacing, as the bellhop was doing compressions the same way physicians in her mother's favorite medical dramas did.

The general manager couldn't be yelling at them all to "Get back!" and "Give Cruz some room!"

The body couldn't really be Ant's, unmoving as it was; his gold chain twisted around his bloated neck.

She wanted to be imagining Noelle's eerily warm hand squeezing hers.

And Sydney couldn't possibly still be screaming. But she was.

And none of it was River's imagination.

The groundskeeper and concierge blocked them from getting closer, keeping them on the grass.

Dwayne's sobbing crescendoed as he pleaded with Ant to "Please wake up, man," and Quintin turning his back on all of them as if he couldn't stand to see anything else was what made her finally return to her body. Her feet and legs were wet and dirty. She was still in her sleep shorts and tank top. She was sweating.

The bellhop looked up, shaking his head. "He's gone."

And the general manager's mouth fell open.

"Gone?" Noelle said. "What do you mean, gone?"

River looked down at where Noelle's hand still held hers and yanked her own hand away.

Then she just stood there, watching it all unfold. Unable to fully accept what was happening.

"He's dead?" Dwayne asked.

Noelle crumbled, wailing like her soul was being sucked from her body, and River's stomach twisted.

She turned away from the pool and puked. All that came out was water, like she was drowning too.

"Noooo," Noelle cried over and over, her voice echoing through the empty resort. Her screams replaced Sydney's, who stood, limbs slack, behind a soaked Dwayne, still being held back, almost pushed, by the general manager.

An eerie sense of déjà vu passed over River like a shadow. Goose bumps covered her arms, as if she was being haunted.

Moments later, shouts filled the air. Dwayne's and Sydney's security appeared, going off on the rest of the staff slowly spilling out of the surrounding buildings. The suited guards bustled around, holding their phones up as if they could command a cell signal to appear by pure will.

Quintin walked over and wrapped his arm around River's shoulders, like he could stop her from trembling. But she wasn't cold. River shook with dread, with fear, with grief, even as she tried her hardest not to.

River wished her mom was here. Dana Reynolds would know exactly what to do.

But Real River? She didn't have a clue.

The general manager disappeared, muttering about going for help, but the bellhop and the groundskeeper still loomed by Ant's body, keeping everyone else away. "This is now a crime scene," the bellhop announced as the groundskeeper covered Ant with a nearby towel. "No one passes this line." He'd laid a palm frond across the ground like caution tape, and River wanted to laugh at the absurdity of it all. Instead she did her best to look steadily away.

The whole nightmare scenario was made so much worse because of the actual date. Because of the anniversary they were all trying not to think about.

Keisha had died. And now, exactly a year later, so had Ant.

"I can't believe this is happening," Sydney said. The *again* was implied.

"Yo, where the hell are the police?" Quintin asked as he rubbed circles on River's back.

"It's private security like us, not quite police. But that's what we're trying to find out," Johnson replied. "They're on the other side of the island."

"Man, you can't be serious."

"Certainly wish I wasn't," the security guard went on. "The guard—Callum, I think his name is—didn't make it here last night at all."

"Trees are down and the roads through the mangrove forests are badly flooded," Prescott added. "We're completely cut off from the other side of the island. But we're going to try to contact the other nearest island in the Keys."

River felt Quintin's grip tighten around her. "So, what you're saying is nobody will be here anytime soon."

She didn't know how long they'd all been standing there when the general manager finally showed up again. He strode past her and her remaining friends and made a beeline for the guards.

Even though River still felt like she was floating outside her body—in shock, her mother would have told her—she still heard bits and pieces of their tense conversation. A small medical clinic had been destroyed. The village shops had taken a beating along with the staff's seasonal housing unit. Flash flooding had wiped out the island's major roads, leaving only one small one.

He sounded more pissed about the damage to the resort than upset that someone had died.

Sydney stood. "This is terrible. Worse than terrible."

"We gotta be cursed," Quintin whispered.

Noelle flailed. Her eyes were bloodshot and wet. "Does he have to just lie here like this? Can't they move him somewhere?" She pointed at Ant, clearly in shock too. "It's starting to rain again."

"We'll figure it out," Prescott said. She turned to Sydney. "I'm so sorry, Miss Davis. You have my word that we're trying to find help."

"You should all head to your rooms," Johnson said. "There's nothing we can do right now."

The guards walked off with the general manager.

"Who's going to tell his parents?" Dwayne choked out. He looked like a plug had been pulled and all the life had drained out of him.

No one answered.

"Maybe he fell in last night?" Sydney said. "He was drinking, right?"

"He was definitely drinking," River heard herself reply. "We all were."

Quintin shook his head. "The hell was he doing out in the storm?"

This felt all wrong.

River shook her head, forcing herself to pull it together. "Let's focus," she said. Clearly someone needed to take charge. Everyone fell silent. River grabbed Quintin's arm. "We have to keep cool heads if we want to figure this out."

It was silent for a moment and then . . .

"Riv's right." It was the worst possible time for Quintin to call her that, but she clenched her teeth, thankful he was backing her up.

"Do you have something specific in mind?" Sydney asked.

And River didn't. But she could feel her wall going up, the one that meant she needed to channel her mother. "Well, since the adults aren't telling us anything, maybe we need to figure this out ourselves. What are the facts? What do we know?"

Quintin looked at Dwayne. "How did you find him, bro?"

Dwayne shook his head. "You were there when Sydney showed up at our door this morning. We were just trying to find some breakfast—" His voice broke.

Sydney returned to his side and put a hand on his shoulder. "We were standing over there, talking and taking in the damage from the storm. Then Dwayne actually *looked* at the water and . . ." She hung her head. "He was floating face down."

Noelle stood and whipped around. "So, you're telling me you walked right past here on your way to *their* room, and didn't see a thing?"

Sydney's eyes widened . . . and then narrowed. "I didn't look up. I was on my phone, trying to find a signal so I could text Dwayne. I wasn't looking over there." Her chin dropped. "Didn't know I needed to."

"It's just weird, is all," Noelle said, crossing her arms.

"Doesn't seem weird to me," Dwayne said. "Even if Sydney *had* seen him the moment she stepped out of her room this morning. There was nothing she could've done. He was already gone."

"How could you possibly know that?" Noelle barked.

"Y'all saw the blood!"

River had tried to ignore the blood. Told herself the water's reddish tint was a trick of the light. Or some paint from the renovation had somehow wound up in the pool.

"Something had to have hit him," Dwayne went on. "Hard."

"Or someone," River muttered.

In the silence that followed, she realized she'd said it aloud.

"Why would you say that?" Noelle whispered, but you could tell she was trying hard not to scream.

River needed to get a grip, and fast. Keep her speculations to herself.

"It's not like she doesn't have a point," Sydney chimed in. "He was a nationally ranked swimmer. They typically don't just *drown.*"

Quintin spoke up next. "Maybe he went for an early swim. Y'all know Ant. He's usually up at four thirty, training. Maybe he did that this morning."

Thunder shook the sky, and everyone flinched.

"I thought I told you guys to get back inside," Johnson called as both security guards and the general manager returned to the pool area. "Can you not hear another storm is rolling in? It's not safe for you to be outdoors."

Noelle's face pinched as she wrapped her arms tight around her chest. "And we're just supposed to *leave* Ant here?"

The general manager cleared his throat. "There's nothing you can do about Mr. Brooks. What happened to him was unfortunate—"

"Unfortunate?" Noelle practically yelled. "We don't even know what actually happened! Was this an accident? Did some random piece of metal come flying in his direction mid-breaststroke? Or was it something else? Some*one* else, as River put it?" She dissolved into another fit of tears.

Quintin took a deep breath and touched River's shoulder.

"Let's get out of here," he whispered into her ear.

River nodded and followed, even as their friends continued

arguing and crying behind them. They walked in silence for a bit, but it felt louder than Sydney's scream had.

"Real talk, do you really think someone hurt Ant?" Quintin asked as they stepped onto the covered pathway to the Sunset wing.

She wished he had kept quiet.

River looked up at him. His skin lacked its usual vibrance, and his pupils were wide.

There was only one other time she'd ever seen him this afraid: when he'd checked Key's neck for a pulse and hadn't found one.

She could feel the other version of herself—Dana's Daughter—descending completely like the storm overhead.

"I don't know," she said, locking in. "But I'm going to get to the bottom of it."

There were very few moments when River didn't hear her mother's voice in her head.

Dana Reynolds's standards had shaped River's life from the moment Dana had chosen to be a single mother, selecting River's biological father from a donor database according to her preferred criteria. Most people were alive because of a twist of fate, but fate had little to do with River's existence. A strong-willed Black woman had done the heavy lifting.

And that strong-willed Black woman always made sure River knew that working twice as hard to be considered half as good wouldn't cut it.

Perfection was the standard. River had to be the sharpest mind in the room. And when River was Dana's Daughter, there wasn't a room on earth that contained anyone sharper.

Today, that room happened to be inside the scaffolded Twilight wing, just east of Sunset, the wing that held their suites. She'd asked the boys to meet in the girls' room, but when the security guards disappeared again with the general manager, Sydney suggested they chat somewhere they wouldn't be overheard. River immediately knew where they should plot their next move.

It probably seemed heartless to be thinking of "moves" so soon after Ant had lost his life, but River could hear her mother's voice, clear and sharp, as if she were standing next to her.

Control the narrative, or the narrative will control you.

It's what Dana told so-called "family-first" politicians who built their brands on the backs of their wholesome images, only to come crawling to Dana for help after being caught with one sex worker too many.

The narrative was always the priority. Not the truth. Not emotions. The narrative. And after what had happened last spring break, River knew how to deal with situations like this one.

She had to be four steps ahead of everyone else. She had to know their stories, their motives, their secrets . . . It was a game of chess in every sense, and by having everyone together, River was positioning her pieces.

River pushed at the front door of the unfinished building, and it was open. She looked back at her friends, who were all standing just behind her, getting wet in the softly falling rain, and waved them forward into the Twilight wing. They crept through the entryway and turned down a hallway in silence.

"Why is no one talking?" Sydney whispered. "Wasn't the whole point of meeting here so we could speak freely?"

River heard Noelle's voice next. "Why are you whispering? Probably for the same reason no one else is talking at all. We're freaked the hell out!"

"Can both of you just shut up?" River scanned the expansive lobby. There was no furniture yet, but she could imagine where the front desk would sit, where the concierge and bellhop would be stationed, waiting to be at guests' beck and call. The high ceilings made their shuffling voices sound like they were at the bottom of a well. "The guest rooms must be upstairs."

"You good?" Quintin asked, appearing at her side. He gripped one of her hands gently and squeezed.

"Not really," she answered honestly. "But I'll be better once we're in a safe spot."

River pushed aside a heavy canvas tarp hanging in front of an archway that led to a set of stairs. "Let's go this way," she said.

As soon as they reached the second floor, River realized that the suites in the Twilight wing must be smaller than the ones in Sunset. There were more doors off this hall than on theirs in the other building.

She pushed the first door open and they all filed inside. The room was still dusty from its recent construction.

"Sooo . . ." Noelle began, crossing her arms. She stood by the door as though ready to make a run for it at any minute. Her eyes were still puffy from crying, and her hair was a mess. "Why are we here again?"

River shot her a sharp look but quickly schooled her expression. During a crisis, emotions had to be kept in check.

"We need to figure out what to do next," River replied. "I would think that's pretty important, wouldn't you?"

"Whatever you say, Miss Mini-Fixer." Noelle looked away from the group, and River bit her tongue so she wouldn't say what she wanted to.

"I know this situation is difficult," River continued, "but we need to get on the same page so things don't get worse—"

"Oh, you mean worse than my boyfriend *dying*?" Noelle retorted. "Do you actually care about that part, or are you all about the optics? Just like last time . . ."

River straightened her shoulders, her perfect posture a function of years with Dana resting her hand on River's spine to correct her stance at even the hint of a slouch. Honestly, she *was* more concerned about the optics.

When it came to River's relationship with Anthony Brooks, things had been complicated. He'd always seemed to know things, things River didn't understand exactly how he knew, and she had been planning to use this week to find out exactly how much he'd known about *her*. And after she'd heard him say the words "MANIfest the Mess" at the pool last night as she and Sydney had walked in, she'd been even more determined to get him alone and figure it all out.

But now that couldn't happen.

Unfortunately, River couldn't even be relieved at the thought that he might have taken her biggest secret to the grave with him. Because incriminating details about that secret might be somewhere on his phone. *He keeps that phone closer than me*, like Noelle had said.

She hadn't gotten to talk to him, so she had no idea what he knew or where the phone could be now. She had to believe it was with him while he was swimming—maybe, hopefully, ruined in the water? But . . . oh shit . . . then there was his laptop . . . Where was his laptop?

She cleared her throat. "I do care, Noelle. What happened to Ant is so, so awful," she said. "But let's not act like we don't have a huge problem: we're a bunch of Black kids with a *second* dead body on our hands in a year. The cops are gonna be all over us, all over this. Hell, they might even decide to reinvestigate what happened to Key. Especially after you talked to that reporter. Is that what you want?"

Noelle's face scrunched up, and a fresh set of tears slipped from her eyes.

River took a deep breath. She felt bad making Noelle cry, but the girl talked far too much—she always had. "Look, our imperative is controlling the narrative so it doesn't get out of hand, okay? That means we need to get our stories straight. Where did all of you go last night after you left the pool?"

Dwayne started to answer, but Noelle cut him off. "So, you think one of *us* did it, then?"

"Should we think you did it?" The look Sydney gave Noelle

could've sliced through a polar ice cap. "You were closer to Ant than any of us. Just like with Keisha. So where were *you* last night, Noelle?"

Noelle looked ready to combust. "I *know* you're not accusing me of—"

"Nobody is accusing anyone of anything," River cut in. "It's simply a question. And a valid one."

"Who died and made you chief detective?" Noelle snarked.

"I mean, technically your man did," Dwayne replied.

Noelle's eyes narrowed. "Did you really just say that?"

"Too soon, Dwayne," Quintin said. And River agreed.

"Noelle," River said. "Why is it always *something* with you? Can you just tell us where you were so we can move on—"

"You seem mighty worried about where *we* were, River," Noelle bit back. "Why don't you go first? Where exactly were you?"

"I was in our room, puking my guts out," River said. "I haven't had a drink since last year . . . last spring break. So I drank too much at the pool, and it caught up with me. Once Quintin and Dwayne were gone, I spent the entire night between my bathroom and bed. Which is how I know *you* weren't there, Noelle."

Noelle crossed her arms again. "Yeah, okay."

"The housekeeper came at some point and brought me extra towels," River continued. "She can vouch for me. What about you, Sydney? I know you walked Dwayne up to the guys' room, but I didn't see when you got back."

Her best friend shifted slightly . . . a tell. One River did her best to ignore.

"I walked to the Dawn wing to get a snack," Sydney said. "When I called down to the front desk, the concierge said the chef—Starlie, right?—had left a basket of treats for us in the hospitality suite across from the restaurant."

River didn't take her eyes off Sydney. Who she was *sure* was hiding something. It was evident in her clipped response. River's best friend was a lot of things, but short on words had never been one of them. "Is there someone who can back you up?"

Sydney shrugged. "Maybe some staff saw me."

River nodded. "Great. Dwayne? Where were you?"

"I crashed as soon as I got back to my room," he said.

"Do you have a solid alibi?" River asked. Which made Dwayne's eyebrows knit together. "If the cops question us, we'll need proof of our stories," River explained. "Is there anyone or anything that can verify what you're telling us?"

"Johnson," Dwayne said, but River shook her head. "Someone who doesn't work for you."

"I guess Quatro," he said, glancing over at his suitemate. "Did you hear me snoring? I admittedly don't remember you coming back to the room."

"Oh, I definitely came back!" Quintin said. "As evidenced by the fact that I woke up in my bed. I honestly can't remember what time it was. I'd also had a lot to drink."

Noelle shook her head. "Quatro was too wasted to even know his name—"

"I can vouch for him," River said immediately. "He was with

me. I walked with him up to his room and when I got back Sydney was leaving *our* room with Dwayne."

"You still haven't told us where *you* were, Noelle," Sydney repeated. "River left and came back with the pukes. I left and came back with a stack of French macarons. But you were still missing from our suite by the time I went to sleep."

"What are you trying to say?" Noelle snapped.

River titled her head. "Sydney's just telling the truth."

"Not that Noelle would know anything about *truth*," Dwayne added.

He might as well have set off a bomb. Suddenly, everyone *but* River was slinging insinuations.

She tiredly wiped her face. This hadn't been what she'd had in mind when she asked them all to meet up. But now she had questions.

She nibbled on her thumbnail, ignoring the fact that it would mess up her manicure. She could hear her mom's voice in her head: *That's not very becoming of you.* Dana also wouldn't think the mess River got herself into with Anthony was becoming. Nor would the cops. And all it would take was them snooping on Anthony's laptop for the entire narrative to switch and for River to wind up in even *more* trouble.

That laptop could literally ruin her life.

BOOOM!

River jumped as the noise shook the room.

"What the hell was that?" Quintin asked.

"Maybe thunder?" Sydney replied.

River wanted to agree, but then actual thunder rumbled much more softly.

Sydney walked over to a tarp that looked like it was covering a window. She pulled it back, sending dust motes flying as soft, stormy light spilled into the room, and gasped. "Uhh, guys?"

River, Quintin, and Dwayne crowded around her to look outside. Rain fell in sheets, but they could still see the plume of fire in the near distance, coating the sky in orange and red.

Anthony's dad's yacht was on fire.

"What the fuck?" Dwayne said.

River blinked, unable to believe what she was seeing. "Did . . . lightning do that?"

Quintin shook his head. "I don't think lightning could cause that sort of explosion."

"It could have been a gas leak . . . or something, right?" Sydney asked.

"A leak would still need fire to explode," Quintin replied.

Dwayne glanced at him. "Is that your way of suggesting that . . . someone blew it up . . . on purpose?"

Quintin didn't answer. Which was an answer itself.

Sydney had a hand over her mouth. "What if . . . what if . . . what if Mr. Ade was still on there?"

"H-he's got a room here at the resort," Noelle stammered as she watched the flames dance wildly across the water, heat and smoke billowing into the stormy sky. "Ant told me. It's not protocol for him to stay on the boat, but I haven't seen him around. Have any of you?"

No one answered. Before River could think about what to do next, Noelle was rushing from the room. They heard her footsteps echoing through the empty hall as she ran down the steps, and River called after her to stop.

"Noelle, wait! It could be dangerous! We still don't know what's going on!"

But Noelle didn't stop. She didn't even turn around.

River followed her, and Sydney followed River, and then the boys were running after them too.

Once outside, River could see Noelle running toward the burning boat. River saw Noelle freeze, and then drop to her knees again, just like she had that morning by the pool.

So River stopped running. She didn't want to see whatever Noelle had seen, and she held her arm out to stop Sydney from getting any closer either.

"Call for help!" Noelle screamed. Her voice came out strangled and wet. "It's Captain Ade. He's right here. And he's . . . not moving."

When the boys caught up to them, Dwayne said, "I'll go get Johnson." He approached Noelle, helped her up, and led her away, back toward the Sunset wing. And that was when River saw it, washed up beside the pier: a badly burned body, charred and bloody, still wearing socks and sandals.

River grabbed Sydney and they hugged each other, holding

on so tightly their grip felt more like claws than fingers. Quintin wrapped his big arms around them both as they shook and sobbed.

River didn't know if it was Real River's fear or her mother's training her to expect the worst, but all she could think about was how it seemed like someone didn't want them to leave.

CHAPTER SEVEN

SYDNEY

2:26 p.m.

GRAVE ROBBERS. THAT was what they used to call the thieves who crept into cemeteries late at night, dug down deep into freshly packed soil, pried open the coffins of the newly dead, and stole their precious valuables: a ring, a necklace, some other sentimental trinket left to them by the living. In some cases, the robbers stole entire bodies and sold them to medical schools for parts.

Had they, Sydney wondered, felt the way she did now, like she'd crossed over some cursed line that there was no coming back from?

It felt like a sin, though Sydney knew from years spent in Sunday school that it wasn't. She touched the cross at her throat and asked for forgiveness for what she was about to do anyway.

She sucked in a breath and felt the bitter cold air of the walk-in freezer in the resort kitchens invade her lungs. Felt it invade the marrow of her bones. Turned out the resort did in fact have a generator, but the only building it powered was the one that held the food. She imagined shards of ice ripping her apart from the inside, turning her into someone new. Someone who could do this next terrible thing: ransack a dead body—Ant's dead body—to get what she needed, so that everything she and her mother had worked so hard for wouldn't have drowned in that pool along with Ant.

It didn't take long to spot his body. It—he—was right there, a long, bumpy lump laid out on the cold floor and pushed up against the back wall. He was partially hidden behind two room-service delivery carts. Someone had even covered him completely with the plush monogrammed guest towels Sydney had admired just the day before.

She eased one of the carts aside. A piece of pink-and-green plastic—a shower curtain from one of the guest rooms—peeked out from beneath the towels. The resort staff had probably wrapped up his body. Sydney tried to picture it. One person gripped Ant's shoulders—had his lifeless head lolled to one side?—while another held his legs, and still another smoothed the curtain down flat. Then they'd had to tuck the curtain beneath his forearms and thighs before rolling him over and over until he was sealed.

Sydney doubled over and dry-heaved. What was that smell? Rot? She slapped a hand over her mouth and held it there until her revulsion subsided. Now was not the time for regrets or sentimentality. Later, she could retch. Later, she could allow herself to feel everything.

Another mincing step took her even closer to Ant. What were the chances his phone was in here with his body, of all places? Slim to none. But she had to look. Had to find it before the police arrived from the other side of the island to investigate what happened. Before Prescott notified her mother. Before the press got wind of it and blew up her mother's campaign.

It was hard to tell which end of the lump was Ant's head. More than anything, Sydney didn't want to see his face. She was already plagued by the memory of Key's lifeless one. She didn't need more lifeless features haunting her.

God, she'd forgotten so many details of the night Key died, but there were a few things she'd never forget, not ever. The absolute stillness of Key's face. The sound of Noelle's voice, broken and helpless, like a lost child's. The chemically sweet smell of chlorine. The silver-blue shimmer of the pool. For a brief moment, Sydney had wanted to dive in. *Come in*, it seemed to say. *Be baptized.*

Those memories weren't even the worst part of that awful night. The worst part was what she'd begged all her friends to do in the aftermath of Key's death. It was unforgivable, really. But it wasn't the first unforgivable thing she'd done in the service of her mother's ambition to be president. It wouldn't be the last.

Sydney went to her knees next to Ant's body and shook her head. Enough. She had to get what she'd come for. She reached for the towel closest to her. Before she could lift it, the walk-in door scraped open behind her.

Her heart beat so hard she felt the pulse of it in her throat. It took all her self-discipline not to scream. The trick with situations like these was to act like you had every right to be wherever it was that you were. That attitude, the one that said she belonged in whatever room she was in, didn't come naturally to her. It was something she'd had to cultivate. There was no way to exist in her mother's orbit without it. The higher in politics her mother climbed, the better an actress Sydney was forced to become. It was why she and River were so close: they both knew how to pretend.

She stood, squared her shoulders, and tilted her chin up.

Whoever was at the door took two steps closer. "Jesus, Sydney, what are you doing in here?"

She spun around. Dwayne. It was just Dwayne.

Relief flooded her and pressed her hands to her heart. "Holy shit. You scared me half to—" She cut herself off. No need to finish that sentence given the circumstances.

Dwayne moved closer and frowned over her shoulder to where Ant's body was. "What are you doing?"

"I could ask you the same thing," she said, using offense as defense, the way her mother did so effectively during her more combative interviews with the DC press corps.

But Dwayne wasn't buying it. He was too smart to fool so easily. He simply went still and waited for an actual answer to his question.

Sydney stepped closer to him, not just because she wanted to distract him and give herself time to come up with an excuse. Lately, being close to him was the only thing that made her feel safe—made her feel right—in her own skin.

"I just wanted to say a last goodbye to him," she whispered, surprised the lie had come so easily.

Silently, Dwayne opened his arms and Sydney stepped into them.

Tears she hadn't anticipated sprang to her eyes. It was, all of it, too much. Key's death and now Ant's. Her mother's demands. Lying to Dwayne, who she liked more than she'd expected to.

More than she was supposed to.

The guilt of it all.

She let herself be held for another few seconds and then pulled away. The only reason she'd known the kitchen and walk-in freezer would be empty of people was because she'd overheard someone at the front desk say that the general manager had called an all-hands meeting for the resort staff. Who knew how long that meeting would last? They could be back at any second. Not to mention Prescott, who was so busy trying to lock down the situation that Sydney had managed to give her the slip.

She had to get Ant's phone right now.

She widened her eyes and looked up at Dwayne. "You think you could give me a minute alone with him?"

Dwayne cupped her face in his hands, wiped her tears with his thumbs. "Whatever you need," he said. "I'll be outside the door."

She didn't deserve his . . . friendship, or whatever it was that was between them. She didn't deserve him, but maybe somehow, some way, after all this was over, she'd get to keep him.

As soon as the door sighed shut, Sydney went to Ant's body. She held her breath and lifted the towel. Luckily, she'd uncovered his feet and not his face. Even luckier still, there was a small black bag tucked between his leg and the wall. Carefully, she unzipped it and reached inside. Her fingers found his phone almost immediately. Relief sagged her shoulders, and she cradled it against her chest before dropping it into her purse. Later, when she had time, she'd figure out how to get what she needed from it despite the probable water damage. For now, it was time to go.

She zippered the bag and put the towel back into place. "I'm sorry . . . so very sorry," she whispered to Ant's body. "I didn't want any of this to happen, even though you—" She pressed a fist to her mouth and squeezed her eyes closed. "God," she whispered, looking up at the ceiling. "God, please." She didn't even know what she was asking Him for. She really had to get herself together.

She stood. "I'm sorry," she whispered again, and hurried to the door.

Like he said he would be, Dwayne was waiting just outside. "You good?" he asked.

She nodded and gave him a small smile.

He wiped his hand down his face. "With all that's going on, I got worried when I couldn't find you. Chef Starlie said you'd come to the kitchen to grab a soda. You stay sneaking off to get a snack, girl. First last night, now today . . ." His eyes narrowed in a way that made her nervous.

She grabbed his hand and squeezed it. "I promise you I'm fine."

His fingers curled around hers and, again, Sydney let herself be held. His hands were warm and strong. How simple it would be to fold herself into his easygoing, big-hearted warmth. How simple it would be to let herself fall for him.

And what a mistake it would be, too.

Despite the fact that they'd known each other since kindergarten and despite the fact that their families were close—Sydney's mother, the senior senator from the great state of Virginia, had helped Dwayne's father, the extremely popular sitting governor of Maryland, get elected—Sydney hadn't started noticing Dwayne in more than a friendly way until sophomore year. She wasn't sure when her feelings had gone from platonic to not-even-a-little-bit-platonic. Maybe it was because he'd grown a few inches over the summer and developed muscles along with a lopsided smile. That, plus he had taken to staring at her for a beat too long.

When it came out mid-sophomore year that Key and Quatro had been secretly dating each other, something none of the Six had ever done before, Sydney had begun to wonder if she and Dwayne could too. They'd started hanging out more. At first they'd mostly commiserated about the trials of being the children of high-powered politicians, but soon they moved past that. They'd talk late into the night about their hopes for the future. Dwayne could always get her to laugh no matter the mood she was in. She could always get him to tilt his head and consider some new angle on whatever they were talking about. They were opposites in every way, and Sydney couldn't help but love the way he rebelled against what was expected of him while she couldn't imagine doing anything other than exactly what was asked of her. Maybe it was the church girl in her loving the bad boy in him.

It seemed to Sydney that things between them were headed in the right direction when all hell broke loose.

As she'd planned for years, Sydney's mother announced her intention to seek the Democratic party nomination to become president. She'd seemed like a shoo-in. She had high approval ratings and years of national political experience under her belt. She was also a policy pro, an effective speaker, and beautifully photogenic. For a while, she had no serious competitors.

But then Dwayne's father threw his hat into the ring, and everything changed. Sydney's mother had been enraged. As far as she was concerned, Dwayne's father had betrayed her. She'd worked her ass off, called in political favors to help get him elected. And this—becoming her fiercest competition for a position that was meant to be hers—was how he repaid her? The vitriol between the campaigns grew toxic enough to deeply complicate whatever had been growing between Sydney and Dwayne.

As primary season grew closer, the rhetoric of the campaigns went from bad to reprehensible. Dwayne's father's campaign ratcheted up the smears by implying that her mother had slept her way to her position. Sydney's mother's campaign responded by insinuating he'd fathered a child out of wedlock.

Things got so bad, her mother hired a second firm to do opposition research on Dwayne's father. Within days, she'd approached Sydney with what she called a suggestion, but what was really an order: get some dirt on Dwayne or his father that they could use against him. At first, Sydney resisted. But her mother was a force. What if Dwayne's father's smears worked? What if Sydney's unwillingness to help cost her mother the nomination and by extension the presidency? Would she be able to live with that?

In the end, Sydney had given in to her mother.

She always did.

Sydney let go of Dwayne's hand and took a step back from him. What she was doing wasn't right, no matter what her mother said about Dwayne's father deserving what was coming to him. What she said about the ends always justifying the means.

She liked Dwayne. She liked the way he teased her and saw her so clearly. She liked how easygoing he was, how he took life in stride. She liked not having to be perfect around him and not having to know exactly what to say next. The only time she got to be her true self—Syd, not Sydney Katherine Davis, future First Daughter—was when she was with him.

"We should get going," Dwayne said. "Quatro found some working plugs in the restaurant. We can charge our phones and all that."

Sydney nodded. She had a sudden urge to confess everything to him. She opened her mouth. Closed it again. No. Now was not the time to come clean. First, she had to make things right for her mother, for Dwayne, and for herself.

"Thanks for being so understanding earlier," she said.

His eyes searched hers. "Anytime, Syd," he said. "I'm always here for you."

First Light had the somber air of an afternoon funeral. Rain hit the glass windows like tiny bullets, and strong gales slipped inside like wailing cries. Everyone except Quatro was already there and charging their phones. No one was talking. Sydney mouthed hello to River.

"There's an outlet free over there," Dwayne said, and gestured toward the left side of the room.

After they were seated on the floor and plugged in, Sydney surveyed their surroundings. It finally settled into her that they were the only guests at the resort besides the grumpy woman in the suite next door to theirs, but she wasn't here right now. Maybe she'd ignored the paper notice that the bellhop had slid beneath their doors a few hours ago about coming to First Light by three p.m.

Noelle was on the floor next to the main doorway. Her arms were wrapped tight around her waist, and she was rocking back and forth slightly. She looked so miserable, so alone, that Sydney couldn't help but feel bad for her. First Key and now Ant. That was too much loss. Still, Sydney's sympathy fizzled when she remembered how Noelle had gone blabbing to the press about Key. How Noelle had risked all their lives and reputations. Noelle always needed to be the center of attention. It didn't matter whether the attention was good or bad.

"Try not to look at her like that," Dwayne said. "You know she'll figure out a way to use it against you."

Sydney smiled over at him. "Always looking out," she said.

Dwayne looked her up and down. "You know me," he said.

Sydney's eyes softened. He had his secret half smile on.

"I do," she said.

Dwayne grinned and bumped his shoulder into hers. How did he manage to take her out of her head and make her feel as if the world and its worries didn't matter?

From across the room, River caught her eye and winked knowingly. She kept telling Sydney that she and Dwayne should be more than just friends. But not even River knew the real reason she'd gotten so close to Dwayne over the past few months.

Sydney tilted her head back against the wall and closed her eyes.

Was she really in another room with these same people in the aftermath of another death? They said tragedy bonded people, but she wasn't sure she believed that. After they got off this godforsaken island and after she got what she needed from Ant's phone, she was going to put some distance between herself and the group. Maybe it was time for the Six to disband or for her to exit for good. Maybe it'd been time since the moment the Six became five. She'd keep River, of course. And Dwayne, if he still wanted her. But she needed to focus on getting ready for senior year.

The main door banged open. Everyone was so on edge, they all jumped.

Quatro stumbled inside looking ragged and disheveled, like he'd been in a fight and lost. A half-empty bottle of whiskey dangled from his hand.

"Oh shit," Dwayne muttered.

Sydney looked over at River, who just stared in disbelief.

Quatro almost tripped over his own feet. Sydney couldn't remember seeing him be anything less than graceful.

He staggered over to the exit door at the back of the room and sank down to the floor.

Next to her, Dwayne sighed. "Let me go check on him," he said, and pushed to his feet.

Quatro took a swig and let out a loud, nasty hiccup. "You ever think maybe we're cursed?" he yelled, voice slurred.

Dwayne squatted down next to him and whispered something in his ear.

Whatever Dwayne said didn't work. Quatro shook his head and clutched the bottle tight against his chest. "I mean it," he continued. "Maybe we were all born with a curse. Or maybe we brought it down on ourselves." He took another swig. "Know what I think? It's punishment. For what we did to Key."

Noelle sprang to her feet. Her fists were balled at her sides. "We didn't do anything to Key! What happened to her was an accident! Just like Ant was an accident!" She sounded to Sydney like a child having a tantrum and looked the part, too, glaring around the room, daring anyone to disagree with her as she bit her lips and fussed with her long twists.

For a long time no one said anything, but River broke the silence. "Ant *just* placed at nationals in swimming," she said in her low, steady voice. "It doesn't make sense he would drown." She looked at her nails like she wanted to nibble on them (Sydney knew all her tells), but then she pulled one of her braids over her shoulder and twisted it around her finger instead.

Sydney nodded without meaning to. River was right. They'd all seen Ant swim before. He was a natural in the water, like he was born there.

Noelle shook her head, tears streaming down her face. "Accidents happen," she insisted, voice quieter this time. She fussed with her long twists, unraveling and retwisting one over and over again.

They sank into a silence that didn't last. From the doorway, the general manager cleared his throat. The way everyone straightened up and gave him their attention, you would think he was a general commanding his army. Right now, Sydney supposed he was. From the satisfied smirk on his face, she could tell he was enjoying his new power.

"Listen up, and listen good, because I'm not going to repeat myself. The arrival deck on this side of the island is messed up from the storm. We're also investigating the explosion on the yacht I'm sure you guys heard or saw this morning. And I haven't been able to contact the leeward side about damages yet. And unfortunately, another storm system seems to be rolling in. There's no getting on or off the island from this side for now. Those of you waiting on Mommy and Daddy to come save you are shit out of luck."

Sydney frowned. This man's whole attitude had done a 180 since the sweet-talking welcome he'd given the day they arrived. He suddenly seemed to really have it out for them.

"Who are you again?" Quatro slurred.

The man crinkled his sunburnt nose. "The general manager. The person responsible. Glenn Chandler, Mr. Chandler to you."

Mr. Chandler rocked back on his heels and continued. "As of right this second, there's a mandatory shelter-in-place order in effect. Each and every one of you needs to go back to your room right now and stay there. This hurricane will be on top of us for the next twenty-four to forty-eight hours."

Dwayne said what they were all thinking. "What? Why? That doesn't make any sense. Aren't we safer in here?"

Mr. Chandler gave him a look filled with so much poison, Sydney was surprised Dwayne didn't keel over.

"I know you all are not used to taking orders, but today is your lucky day. You will do what I tell you to do when I tell you to do it." He folded his arms and glared. "Don't test me. Trust that when the security team arrives, I'll be letting them know about anyone who gives me trouble." He wagged his fingers. "I'm taking notes for the Islamorada police too."

"What's your problem?" Quatro tried to push to his feet. Thankfully, Dwayne put a hand on his shoulder to hold him back. Sydney walked over to River and reached for her hand.

Prescott stepped forward. "How do you know the security team is en route? You said the satellite phone didn't work when I asked earlier."

Mr. Chandler pursed his lips. "The battery died after we sent out the distress call, but we are scouring the resort for replacements. Our supply rooms and storage facilities flooded last night. We're doing the best we can. All we've got are flashlights for now." He nodded at the front desk lady, Ms. Gloria, who began to hand them out.

"Well, do better," Quatro muttered.

The general manager glared at Quatro for a few seconds before turning to them. "I'm not the one with a problem. You're the ones with the problem," he said with a smile that was really a sneer. "As for your friend Anthony? We've stored his body for now. None of you are allowed near it." He rubbed his hands together like he was excited for what he was going to say next. "If I catch any one of you even close to there, well, then, I guess I'll have to make sure the police know who to investigate first for this murder."

Murder. The word was a bomb, and the room exploded into shocked curses and denials. Noelle cried even harder. River buried her face in Sydney's shoulder.

Quatro started to laugh. "Told y'all. We're cursed. Some things God don't forgive."

Sydney squeezed her eyes closed. What a nightmare. She clutched her purse close and felt for the outline of Ant's phone. The sooner she got what she needed from it, the sooner this would all be over. She forced herself to take three long, slow, calming breaths and fiddled with the cross at her throat. All she wanted right now was to be alone with Dwayne in the bubble they created between them. He always made her feel safe. But when she opened her eyes, Dwayne was no longer seated next to Quatro. He was no longer in the room at all.

SABINE RICHARDSON

Guest in Room 140

5:19 p.m.

SABINE RICHARDSON HADN'T come to Kuzimu Horizons Resort to deal with a bunch of spoiled kids and all their goddamn noise. She also hadn't come to the resort to deal with a power outage and a terrible storm, and she most definitely hadn't come to paradise to be in the middle of a murder mystery or accidental-death investigation.

She always came here to work on the latest book in her bestselling romance series, The Young, the Black, and the Powerful. There was a reason she was at the top of the *USA Today* bestseller list. She delivered on her tropes. And she left her teenage kids home with her husband where they belonged.

But she'd done this to herself by requesting special permission to come to the resort while it was still being remodeled. And when her deadline had moved, she'd decided to come a week earlier than she'd planned. She should've asked whether anyone, especially a bunch of rowdy spring breakers, would be on the island. She'd felt hysterical when she'd seen that gaudy yacht dock from her beach hut. Regrets hardened into a knot in her stomach.

Her fans demanded the best from her. Mr. Brooks knew this. She paid a premium for the peace and quiet and her usual two-floor Sunset suite decked out with all she needed to enter the writing zone: freshly sliced pineapple and mango at sunrise, three shots of espresso and her breakfast order of fried eggs, bacon, and avocado toast right at nine a.m., only a pot of coffee for lunch on her private patio overlooking the beach, a glass of pinot noir, and a steak dinner on her upstairs balcony with a view of the gorgeous infinity pools, and a midnight taco trio to get her through to three a.m. Rinse and repeat for two weeks and she'd have her book done. Mr. Brooks's renovations and lengthy closure had thrown her behind, and she was just so happy to be back. This place unlocked her words.

But last night around one a.m., as Sabine reached outside her door, searching for her prescheduled snack, she'd found nothing. She'd barely hit her word goal, and hearing those kids partying in the pool had pissed her off more than her missing snack. Then, when the rain started and the noise subsided, she'd gone up to the second-floor balcony to check and make sure she'd have peace for her last writing sprint. She spotted one of them—she couldn't tell which—doing laps in the downpour. Foolishness.

Now one of them had up and died, and Sabine's whole trip had been ruined. She'd have to tell her editor that the book would be late. Again. And she hated writing those kinds of emails. That woman didn't want to hear about her writing retreat taking a turn.

All she wanted from Sabine was words. She sighed. She could see the disgruntled comments now. Her fans hated to wait, and they were never nice about it.

Sabine stepped out onto her balcony again, this time to smoke, her nerves fried. She looked toward the resort's center, another downpour pounding those pretty pools. A little earlier there'd been all sorts of yelling and screaming. The commotion had found her, instead of her breakfast, and she'd foolishly gone to investigate. Too nosy for her own good. Now her thoughts spun on a loop. The deadly incident with those teens would surely ruin the whole week alongside that nasty storm.

See, she thought, *they shouldn't even be here and especially without supervision.* Even though she knew that those kids were related to the owner, she didn't believe in nepotism. Nepo babies always ended up in some shit.

But as Sabine took a long drag of her clove cigarette, she felt a little bad. She wasn't really into big feelings, but the Brookses had been through a lot. A dark cloud seemed to follow them, she thought. Just like the ones thickening overhead right now. Bad energy. What a shame.

Maybe she needed to find a new place to write. She couldn't afford any bad luck coming her way. And there seemed to be a lot of it here . . . with more, she could sense, on the horizon.

CHAPTER EIGHT

RIVER

11:59 p.m.

RIVER'S PHONE LIT up like an explosion in the dark, and for a moment she thought she was dreaming.

There had been a real explosion earlier, one that had taken them all by surprise, so River was relieved when she realized the light was coming from where her cell sat on the bedside table this time, and not the arrival dock. The whole trip was starting to feel like a waking nightmare, so as the notifications slid in and stacked along her screen—a Jenga tower of information, one right after the other—she couldn't fully believe it.

She sat up quietly and grabbed the device to make sure she wasn't imagining the buzzing and blinking. It was real. She had a single bar of service—a few pixels that felt like something sent from heaven instead of a flimsy, fleeting connection to some satellite or tower—so she tried to stay as still as possible, desperately hopeful that maybe if she didn't move, she'd be able to sustain the signal.

She typed in her passcode quickly—the room was too dark for

the phone's camera to recognize her face—and scanned the list of alerts. Dozens of texts from her mom, eight voice mails, and a bunch of new likes and follows on her various social accounts filled her screen. Just before she was about to attempt to resend an unsent text to her mother and beg her to use her fixing skills and get River out of here, she noticed something else: a few messages had come in on that long-abandoned video channel Ant had mentioned at the pool.

River squinted at the notification. **You have 3 new direct messages from Lo_KeyKeisha.**

"What the . . . ?" River whispered, frozen. Instead of using the single bar of service to try to contact her mom—or anyone—River couldn't keep her eager finger from tapping the notification. She watched as her screen flashed to open the app.

MANIfest the Mess was . . . messy.

It had all begun innocently enough: ever since she was a kid, River had kept journals—notebooks where she sketched, jotted down her observations about the world, and experimented with color, thoughts, and theories. She'd started the journals because of a book series she'd loved that featured a girl detective who solved crimes in her apartment building. The books kept her company when she had to tag along to fundraisers and galas with her mother and her clients. And emulating the main character became her favorite pastime. The notes she took about her surroundings ended up helping her too; she'd remember some random detail about one of her mother's clients that would save the day, or something she'd drawn in her notebook would earn her a compliment from a kid of some high-powered politician. Like Sydney. The next thing she knew, other kids of high-powered people were asking to meet with her at lunch or to come over after school, and their parents were hiring her mom.

As she got older, keeping her unfiltered thoughts and feelings in the notebooks seemed more dangerous than sharing them anonymously online. So she wrote less and less in her journals, and more on the internet. Eventually she started making videos. Notebooks could be lost or found, but videos that hid her face and disguised her voice gave River the kind of freedom of expression she'd been missing. A safe place she could be Real River more often without worrying what her mother might think.

Before long, she was not only talking about herself in the content she created, but also including her observations about other people. And after one of her videos went viral, things spiraled a little out of control. River had been trying for months to forget about all the gossip she'd spread and the messes she'd made.

Before opening the messages she knew were waiting for her, River scrolled past thumbnail after thumbnail of her own hands—freeze frames of the manicure tutorials that the channel was known for (the MANI part of MANIfest the Mess). Of course, when she was done recording, she'd have to remove her hard work and repolish so no one at school would recognize her hands (it was the price she had to pay for anonymous internet notoriety), but River had made over sixty videos where she expertly painted and designed her nails, accompanied by a sped-up voice-over that spilled the details about featured nail colors along with secrets that were never River's to share. Videos with the manis and messes were all River spent most of her free time making for a full year before Keisha died. Ironically, they helped distract her from the fact that Key was with Quatro.

And now it was coming back to bite her in the ass.

She'd just tapped on the tiny envelope to open her messages when the screen went black. The sudden dark she was plunged into felt like a sign, the blackness reminding her of the water surrounding the island, and the shadow of Ant's and Key's deaths hanging like a veil over everything.

As River slid open the patio door near her bed, she prayed Noelle and Sydney would remain asleep. She was thankful that all the rooms in the Sunset wing had direct access to the beach. She paused mid-step when she thought she heard movement in the suite, sheets rustling, or maybe someone getting up to use the bathroom, and she held her breath until she could make out the soft sound of gentle snores starting again.

She couldn't leave through the front door without possibly waking them both, and she didn't want anyone to catch her on the main paths.

The thickly humid island air outside made the darkness of the beach feel like something she had to wade through, but she'd always been good at swimming. The thought made her momentarily sick.

Ant.

She eased the door shut and crossed the short patio, weaving through the lounge chairs and onto the soggy sand, grateful that the soft ground would do the work of keeping her footsteps silent. She moved as quickly as possible, knowing the rain would be back any moment.

She tried to put Ant out of her mind. She needed a clear head because she could see only what was directly in front of her—whatever fell into the thin beam of the flashlight she carried—and there was debris everywhere. And because she had so much else she needed to focus on at the moment.

Her phone had died just before she had a chance to read the messages from Lo_KeyKeisha (DMs that seemed to have come—impossibly—from a dead girl), so River needed to get to the only place on the island where she could charge her phone: the restaurant. As she tramped quickly across the storm-strewn sand, her heart pounding as heavily as her footsteps, River kept close to the water so as not to lose her way. But when her foot touched something that felt like wet, ice-cold skin, she stopped dead in her tracks and screamed.

She aimed the flashlight down, and she could see that a thick tendril of seaweed was wrapped around her bare foot, its slimy surface clinging to her skin like the roots of a wet, waxy weed. No matter how hard she kicked to try to get it off, it didn't budge. She was carrying her sandals—lace-up espadrilles she loved—in the same hand that held the flashlight, and her phone and charger in the other. Though she didn't want to, she cringed, balanced on one foot, and tried to gently push the seaweed off the other with her big toe.

Once it slid off, she turned, convinced her scream must have woken the whole island. But she didn't hear any footsteps behind her and couldn't see anyone else on the beach when she swung the flashlight's beam side to side like a lighthouse.

Still, she had a sinking feeling in her stomach when she thought of the messages on her phone, and it reminded her of the way she'd felt when she was recording some of the last videos she'd done—like she was making a huge mistake. Like her body knew what she was doing was wrong. She'd felt that way the night Key died, too—achy in the pit of her belly, and faint, the dark closing in.

She put her head down and kept walking. Priority one was now reading those messages and finding out who they were from, since they couldn't really be from Key.

The Dawn wing glowed golden as a false sunlight in the dark, and she shut off her flashlight. The night immediately felt like a yawning void, and River hated it, but she didn't want to risk being seen. She thought she heard voices. Instead of entering through the big glass doors, she ducked behind one of the outdoor tables that had been blown onto its side in the storm and waited. Sweat skated down her back.

Before long, two figures approached. River could see their silhouettes, backlit by the brightness coming through the glass doors to the lobby. This was the only place on the island that was lit tonight, so people would probably swarm, like moths to a candle. River kicked herself for not thinking about that before now.

"I saw the bitchy one who says he was her boyfriend arguing with him by the pool," River heard a voice say. It was light and airy, despite the woman's nasty words. "What if she did it, you know? She's pissed off, he's drunk, she pushes him. Maybe he hits his head on the edge of the pool, and he passes out. And it's over, just like that."

"A crime of passion?" a second voice replied.

River didn't recognize that one. She peeked around the edge of the table and saw the shape of a short, curvy woman. It was the front desk lady, Ms. Gloria, and the housekeeper, Ms. Florence.

"I could see that," Ms. Florence said, "but it's still such a shame."

River dry heaved at the implication: that Noelle had killed Ant. But after taking a few slow deep breaths to pull herself together, she wished she'd brought one of her journals, or at least that her phone wasn't dead, so she could write this down. If the staff was theorizing that one of her classmates killed Ant, she needed to stay ahead of it. On top of it.

Control the narrative.

Because the truth was, River *had* come back to the pool last night. That's why she didn't have a real alibi.

The *other* truth was, Noelle had come back, too. And she and Ant were arguing about something—him still in the pool, her standing at the water's edge, and River had waited and watched.

And another truth was, after Noelle stormed off and Ant went back to swimming in the rain, River had approached to talk to him, too.

But the messiest part of it all was she'd been really drunk and didn't remember most of the conversation. All she knew for sure was it involved MANIfest the Mess.

And that she hadn't killed him.

They had unfinished business. But not the type that would lead to murder. Now River had to figure out who did it before anyone could point a finger at her.

Once the housekeeper and the front desk lady disappeared from view, River waited and slipped into the expansive lobby, just missing the next downpour. She waited long enough that if she bumped into them, it would be as though she'd just arrived and hadn't overheard anything. But as she ventured deeper inside toward the restaurant's main dining room, they were nowhere to be seen.

The noise of other voices drifted through the air. River craned to listen. They seemed to be coming from the kitchen. Part of it made her want to run, not knowing who she might bump into here, but she swallowed hard, steeling her nerves and reminding herself of the task at hand. *Priorities*, her mom would say.

She took a few steps forward, the light at least a comfort. Still, she wanted to stay out of sight.

Unfortunately, she still had to charge her phone. River crept along the back wall of the room and tucked herself in the corner farthest from the kitchen. She ducked behind a table, grateful the pristine linen tablecloths had already been replaced after dinner service (she assumed) in preparation for breakfast, so that she was completely hidden from most of the room. She plugged in her phone and watched it glow to life.

The voices grew louder, closer. River tried to make herself as small as possible. All she could see without revealing herself were shoes in the gap between the bottom of the tablecloth and the floor. A pair of dark leather loafers and a pair of brown boat shoes moved into view. Both pairs looked like they belonged to men.

"He wasn't even supposed to be here," said one voice. "So I'm glad he's been . . . taken care of."

River felt an ache at the back of her throat.

The loafers shifted in a way that suggested the statement had come from the man in those shoes. "I haven't gotten a raise three years in a row despite the fact that I've brought in a dozen families who visit annually, and overseen the renovation of the spa," he went on. "I didn't leave Hilton to babysit drunk teenagers, but this week is just more proof that the whole family uses this place like it's their personal backyard. This isn't some cheap motel or sleazy time-share. This is a *luxury resort*. And a place of business. Maybe this will show good ol' Mr. Brooks that, oh, I don't know, his kid is someone he should keep better track of? I get that it's technically his hotel, but he doesn't actually work here and has no clue what we go through. This isn't a playground for spoiled, rich teens. Or at least it shouldn't be."

River finally recognized the gravelly voice. It was the general manager, Mr. Chandler. The person he was talking to, Boat Shoes, sounded nervous, but was still trying hard to be agreeable. "You're not wrong . . . But man, that's so messed up."

"Well, sometimes these rich douchebags gotta learn the hard way."

River felt sick as she watched both the general manager's loafers and Boat Shoes disappear from view. As soon as their voices had faded away, she picked up her phone and finally read her mom's frantic messages:

We saw the storm reports, but planes are grounded and no boats are leaving the mainland.

I'll be there as soon as I can to get you.

Are you okay baby?

Please tell me you're okay.

She tried to send a message back. The weak bar of service was still there, but the signal must not have been strong enough. She kept getting a red exclamation point, and the *Message Not Delivered* alert.

"Fuck," River whispered. If her mom couldn't make it to her, River had to make sure she made it back home. Alive.

River took a deep breath and flipped into fixer mode.

Ant couldn't have drowned by accident—that much River knew. It seemed more and more likely that someone had done this to him.

Someone murdered him.

Someone who was still on this island.

Step one, figure out what happened to Ant so it wouldn't happen to her. Step two, find a way to get off the island.

She opened her notes app and typed *SUSPECTS/MOTIVES*, and then: *General Manager: hates Ant's whole family, mentioned him being "taken care of,"* and *Noelle: argued with Ant by the pool.*

She didn't think Noelle would do something this brutal, but the similarities between the bad things happening here and what had happened last year with Key were making her question everything.

Key.

Her phone was still clinging to that single bar of signal, so River rushed to read the messages from Lo_KeyKeisha.

I know you know what really happened last year, River. And I know you're lying about it.

Tell everyone the truth.

Or I'll tell the whole school you're the person behind MANIfest the Mess.

River's palms got clammy and her throat went dry. No one could *ever* find out it'd been Dana Reynolds's daughter kicking up all that unnecessary dirt. And while these messages couldn't possibly be from a dead girl, had someone hacked Key's old account?

She navigated back to her videos. They must've been cached in her history or something because she was able to play the last one. In it, the voiceover mentioned Keisha. And told a truth about her she wanted no one to know. In the video, River had painted her nails a deep, complicated scarlet with a black sheen. She knew the color was called Riotous Rose. But the longer she watched, the more it looked like blood.

PRESENT DAY

QUINTIN "QUATRO" McCALLUM IV

April 6
4:42 p.m.

FOR THE LIFE of him, Quatro couldn't seem to pull his eyes away from the IV tube. Up and down and up and down, his focus ran from where the plastic snake hung from the butt end of the transparent pouch that was a little over half-full of clear liquid, down the surprisingly long length of the tube itself (though why it was surprising, he wasn't quite sure), and right into the back of his hand, where it was taped down and covered over. Each time he got to the bottom and realized there was no watching the substance actually enter his body, he'd let his gaze travel back to the top.

Again.

And again.

It was official: he'd lost it.

Why the hell was this stupid thing even *in* his hand? What were they forcing inside him?

It was kinda messed up, he thought. That someone could just

shove whatever they wanted straight into his bloodstream. And yeah: he'd put an, uhh . . . *illicit* thing or two in there himself through ingestion or whatever. But that was different, wasn't it? With this, he hadn't consented.

He had to get outta there. The room felt too small. Stuffy. Where the hell even was he? And where were his . . . the people who'd been with him? Even the thought of the word *friends* after everything that happened made Quatro feel like the walls around him were beginning to spin.

Though there was River. Where was she? Was she okay? Quatro eyeballed the bag of fluid again and then stared at the entry point just beyond his wrist. Shouldn't be *too* hard to get it out. He'd popped his shoulder back into place a time or two after taking hard hits on the football field. Pulling a needle out of his skin—one that, as far as he was concerned, shouldn't even be there—would be light work. Especially with no one there to stop him.

Just as he reached to remove the fabric-ish tape that held the tube in place, a nurse walked into the room carrying a silver tray. It didn't hit Quatro that he was hoping it contained food—*when was the last time he'd eaten?*—until she set it down, and he saw the line of empty tubes with different colored rubber tops. There were four of them: red, green, purple, and black.

"All right, young man," the nurse said, pulling on a pair of gloves with a *snap* like in the movies. "I'll need that free arm, please."

"For what?"

He didn't *mean* to sound like a grade-A asshole—didn't realize he did until the words were out of his mouth, in fact—but all these storms and explosions and dead bodies (plural!), etc., etc., etc.? It was too damn much.

Her eyes flashed for a split second, but she responded kindly. "I need to get some vials of blood from you, sweetheart—"

"Blood?" The panic began as it always did: a wavy, blue-toned light at the edges of his vision as a low hum filled his head. If they tested his blood and found . . . They couldn't. No one could know he'd been juicing. It would ruin everything. "The hell you need blood for?"

"Just gotta run some tests. Make sure you're—"

"I didn't do anything or touch anybody and I'm not sick," Quatro said, fingers creeping back toward the IV port in his opposite hand. "I shouldn't even be here. I want to go home."

She saw what he was trying to do and gently touched his forearm. "You were severely dehydrated, love. That bag of fluid is getting you back on track." She stared into his eyes, trying to get him to see sense.

Didn't work, though. "I don't wanna be here," he said, picking at the tape. It was stickier than he'd expected.

"Young man, please don't do that," she pleaded, a warning in her voice.

"Just let me go!" He scratched at it more fervently.

"All right, now," she said. "You keep that up, and I'll have to have you restrained. The police ordered a toxicology report—"

"*Why*, though?"

It was all too much. All of it.

To his surprise, she leaned in close. "You came in here on the verge of alcohol poisoning, young man. You're lucky to even be *lucid* right now. The officers will be in here any minute to ask you questions, and I'd like to be gone by the time they come. So if you would allow me to do my job—"

"Knock, knock," came a male voice from the doorway. "I'm Detective Franco. I'd like to ask you a few questions."

Quatro watched as the nurse let her shoulders drop. He felt a little bad now, but not enough to cooperate with her taking—and then testing—his blood.

"Hey, where is River?" he asked the detective. "River Reynolds? Where is she?"

The jackass smirked. "That your girlfriend?"

"Where is she, man?"

"I'm gonna be asking the questions here, young man—"

"Can y'all stop calling me that shit, please?" Because he knew. He knew the more they said it, even with the *young* attached, the more inclined they were to treat him like an adult. Which he was not. And honestly wasn't ready to be. Obviously.

Not that my "readiness" actually matters, he thought.

The detective took three slow steps closer to the bed. This close, Quatro could see his peeling, sunburned nose; his puke-green eyes. Quatro's heart raced, and he tried not to watch the beats accelerate on the monitor.

"What do you remember about that first night on the island?"

"I already told the other cops on the island that. Why are y'all asking me again, man?"

"I'm double-checking their notes and firming up some of the details. You're in our jurisdiction now. Failure to cooperate with this investigation isn't a good look for you—"

"You know what else ain't a good look? A pile of dead bodies at a luxury establishment! *And* interrogating me—a kid!—without a lawyer present," Quatro snapped. "I don't wanna talk about that shit no more! You ever seen *your* friend's dead body?" He needed to calm down. He was losing control, and if he kept talking, he would say too much.

Just like Noelle had.

"Yo, who you need to be talking to is Noelle Clarke. *Everyone* who was there will tell you she's got a nasty habit of stabbing those she claims to love in the back."

The detective's eyebrows knitted together. "What are you insinuating?"

"I'm not insinuating a damn thing. I'm telling you straight up." Too late to turn back now, so Quatro pushed ahead. "Noelle is who you should be questioning," he said. "She was so pressed about that dinner the first night and getting credit for the menu. Maybe she put something in the food. Maybe she drugged Ant. Maybe she drugged *all* of us."

Quatro watched the detective's green eyes narrow, the recognition of precisely who Quatro's dad happened to be, now present. His suspicious gaze shifted to the IV stand on Quatro's left side, then to the tray of empty blood vials on the other (Quatro almost wanted to thank the guy for thwarting the whole blood-theft-for-nonconsensual-drug-testing thing). He was making things up about Noelle, but he didn't care. She'd broken the pact. Nothing wrong with him planting the seed that any drugs in his system were put there by her (because he knew that eventually they *would* get his blood, and there was a lot in it).

Honestly, for all he knew, he was right about her drugging Ant. Certainly wouldn't put it past her. "Go find her," he said. "Ask her about the drugs. Ask her about it all. She's the one who loves to talk when she should be keeping her mouth shut."

THE WEEK BEFORE:

TUESDAY

CHAPTER NINE

NOELLE

5:11 a.m.

THE SCENT OF Ant's aftershave chased Noelle through his suite as she fumbled in the dark. The sun wouldn't rise for another hour, and she was too afraid to use the last of her cell phone battery to light her path. She'd have to make do from memory and a bit of stormy moonglow from the skylights as she desperately collected all the things she'd left up here yesterday. She couldn't let anyone find anything related to her in Ant's room.

The rain streaked the windows, and its steady rhythm provided cover for her movements.

"You're a fucking nightmare," she mumbled to herself, parroting the phrase Chef Donaldson used to say to her when she'd get overly excited and open the oven too fast during dessert service and ruin a tray of chocolate soufflés, or get too in-the-zone with plating and forget the caramel on the stove.

Why did you even let your ex-friends run you out of your room that you also paid for? Why don't you have a backbone? Why can't you ever stand up for yourself?

"What the hell is *wrong* with you, Noelle?" she said to herself, shoving her stupid items in the duffel bag under her arm. "How did you even get yourself into this shit in the first place?"

She remembered sneaking into lounges and clubs with Key's fake IDs, their dresses stuck to them like sausage casings and both wearing so much makeup (done by Key, of course) that Noelle felt battered in brown buttermilk and dipped in colored flour and glitter.

They'd have a blast, but Noelle had always been hopeless talking to non–family member boys she didn't already know (aka any boy who wasn't Dwayne or Quatro).

Until Ant.

Noelle could remember the day she met Anthony Brooks as easily as the ingredients in her favorite brown-butter pie. A student front-office aide had plucked her from environmental science lab, and she'd been grateful to escape analyzing more sediment layers beneath a microscope. It had been the one time she hadn't resented or been embarrassed to be the daughter of Principal Clarke.

She'd spotted him through her mother's office windows, his tall frame too big for her high-backed armchairs. She'd thought he looked like a giant in a stuffy British dollhouse.

"My sweet pea," her mother had exclaimed as she crossed the threshold.

Noelle cringed at the use of her childhood nickname. The little pea in her parents' pod. The only pea. Their baby who survived after the others didn't make it to term.

"This is our newest junior, Anthony Brooks, and I'd like you to show him around. Give him our signature welcome."

Ant had smiled at Noelle, his eyebrows lifting with mischief, and his eyes locked on her as her mother tapped her elegant nails along her mahogany desk and rattled off the laundry list of things for Noelle to do: show him the junior wing and his locker; give him a school tour and help him familiarize himself with the locations of his classes, paying special attention to the athletic center and pool; allow him to shadow her for the day; and, most especially, introduce him to her friends—the Six.

Well, the remaining Five.

This meant Anthony Brooks, or his parents, were important and of value to her mother. Noelle had wondered why but wasn't the type to disobey either of her parents, who she thought of in terms of the pecking order from her father's fine-dining kitchen: her mother was executive chef of their household with her father second-in-command as sous chef. Other than occasionally sneaking out to party—which she only did when sleeping over at Key's and very much at Key's urging—Noelle was an ideal daughter.

Ant hadn't said a word to her as she led him through the impressive Thurgood Marshall Academy campus and into the junior wing. He'd let her pontificate about the state-of-the-art gym and Olympic-sized pool and the Michelin-star quality of the food in the cafeteria, with menus set by her father and their family's restaurant.

He hadn't uttered a word until they'd reached his locker. Eight away from hers in alphabetical order. She'd shown him how to use his lock and praised him as he learned quickly.

"You're pretty special here, huh?" he finally said.

Noelle pursed her lips, trying desperately not to bite them. "I don't understand what you mean." She did, but she'd never been good at receiving compliments.

"Just meant I noticed people move out of your way in the halls or nod at you. They want your attention, or maybe it's your approval."

Noelle shrugged, feeling equal parts embarrassed and proud—and also like a fraud. Then she let her gaze drop to a mark on the floor, trying to separate herself from the contradictory emotions. She knew that it was a leftover effect from Key. Her best friend had been the one everyone actually wanted attention from. Noelle included, if she was honest.

He'd lifted her chin, startling her back to the present. His dark eyes were intense. "It's like you're the key to how everything works around here."

The word *key* felt like a hot poker, as if he'd heard the whisper of Keisha's nickname in her thoughts. "I guess" was all she could muster.

He smirked and dropped his hand, shoving it into his pocket. "You know, your mom said you had to look out for me," he said.

She froze at first. He was flirting with her, wasn't he? But what if he wasn't . . . How could she be sure?

But then she shook it off, and tried to channel how Key would've reacted, batting her eyes and adding a lilt to her voice. "Did she, now?"

"Should've written it in stone or made a blood pact. Then you'd have to respect it." He took her hand. She froze, not knowing what to do. The first boy to ever do so. It gave her a full-body shiver. "Point being: I'll stick close to you. I'm guessing you've got all the luck, too." He winked, and she hated herself for liking the warmth of his attention when she'd felt cold for so long after the loss of Key.

By the end of the day, Ant had slid into the open spot in her friend group. And in the weeks and months to follow, he'd filled the silent spaces of her life: his DMs and text messages flooded her phone (which she absolutely loved), her empty weekends filled with stuff he invited her to, and the hole in her heart felt on the mend. Didn't hurt that he'd also become the life of the party at school. Ant had helped her solve every problem she'd faced, from removing a damaging video from a gossip blog of her getting a little too drunk while out in the city with her friends, to tracking down the person sending her nasty messages and trying to force her into speaking about Key as a way to heal. Sometimes she forgot he hadn't been an original member of the Six, there with them from the very start. For Noelle, Ant had unlocked the old rhythm of her fragile friend group almost as if *he'd* been the missing key.

Noelle hustled to the suite's bathroom to grab her mousse and hair gel but froze in front of the mirror, her reflection obscured by condensation as if someone had just taken a shower. Her heart plummeted with fear as she slowly turned to gaze back at the shower and braced to find someone behind the glass.

"Hello?" she whispered, taking a hesitant step forward and discovering the shower empty. Her whole body shook with panic. Nobody was supposed to come in here, staff included. The general manager had been clear. She snatched a nearby towel from the rack, ignoring the fact that she shouldn't touch anything in the suite. She'd seen enough movies. This was a crime scene. But she wiped away the condensation, then resumed her task.

You need to get the fuck out of here, Noelle, she thought, grabbing the last of her things and trying to push away the memory of Chef Donaldson's voice reminding her that she was a prize idiot who made stupid decisions under pressure. She hated how frequently the man's voice popped into her mind.

As she tiptoed to the bedroom, she heard the door creak open. Blood drained from her face, and she darted back inside the bathroom, then searched for a place to hide. She crouched inside the wardrobe among fluffy robes and extra towels. She held her breath and squeezed her eyes shut. As she listened to footsteps getting closer and closer, the walls closed in, sending her on a mental loop she didn't want to revisit.

As Noelle clutched her knees to her chest and anxious sweat drenched her skin, the bathroom wardrobe morphed into a time machine. Her mind whisked her back to her first kiss . . . to a memory she *shouldn't obsess over while on her healing journey,* according to her therapist. But the warm wooden walls tucked her inside that memory with Key. They'd both barely turned ten, one right after the other, while on a long joint family vacation in the south of France. They'd been running through the villa to their parents' chagrin, trying to avoid Key's pesky younger siblings, but also because Key promised a surprise. She always had something to show Noelle.

"This way." Key led Noelle up a winding staircase to the chambre de bonne. Noelle followed as she'd always done. Key's loose curls bounced down her back, touches of blond finding their way through the light brown like ribbons of sunlight. "Shhh."

Noelle tiptoed as best she could, the beautiful old house betraying their footsteps and secret plan to get away from everyone.

Key stopped abruptly and Noelle crashed into her back. Key glanced over her shoulder, her eyes intense, their different colors more pronounced with the skylight window overhead. "Do you trust me?"

"Of course." Noelle hated when Key asked her questions like this—questions she already knew the answer to.

Key grinned slowly and deliberately, then yanked Noelle forward and into the large wardrobe in the room. Beneath the thin cotton dresses of the woman who owned the house, Key had arranged an uncanny assortment of objects: Band-Aids, a Swiss Army Knife, lip gloss, wildflowers, and a Polaroid camera.

"What is all of this?" Noelle tried to soak it up in the subtle darkness, only a sliver of light finding its way into the wardrobe. Key tangled her ever-growing legs in Noelle's as they crouched inside the tight space.

"We're going to have a blood marriage," she'd said so matter-of-factly she could've been telling Noelle they were venturing out to the bee hives near the lavender fields at the edge of the property.

"A what?" Noelle had gazed at her like she always had when Key suggested one wild thing after another.

"A blood marriage, so we'll always be friends." She grabbed two dresses from above and forced Noelle to undress and put one of them on. They turned their backs to each other, shielding their small bodies as they changed out of their summer shorts and tank tops and into the oversized frilly dresses of a French woman who spent her summers in Geneva and rented out her beautiful old house. Noelle pretended to know what marriage was aside from the fact that she knew her parents had a happy one, and she'd just attended her first wedding, and liked that it involved pretty dresses and pink flowers and all the guests being happy. She'd loved watching her favorite cousin get married last month.

"I need a hat," Noelle had said, digging into one of the striped boxes in the wardrobe. Her cousin's husband had worn a top hat. He'd looked ridiculous, but she'd loved it. She found a red wool winter beanie, a baseball cap, a visor, and a floppy beach hat. She chose the visor.

"I need heels!" Key had said, jumping out of the wardrobe and returning a moment later with big white heels that swallowed her small feet.

In the closet, Key painted Noelle's mouth with the lip gloss. When they were sufficiently dressed, Noelle snapped open the Swiss Army Knife. There were a million gadgets in there—a magnifying glass and a corkscrew and tiny scissors and a bottle opener. And a knife. Small and sharp and so silvery and shiny Noelle wondered if it had ever been used before. "Do you blood marry me?" Key said, holding the knife over Noelle's small pointer finger.

She wasn't even shaking. If someone did that to her now, she'd be so scared. But back then, she wasn't scared of anything as long as Key was by her side.

"I do," Noelle had said.

The pain of Key splitting Noelle's skin was the screaming kind. Hot and throat-closing. She'd made a brand-new noise, a combination between a hum and a scream emanating from the back of her throat. She hadn't realized her eyes were closed until the cutting was over.

"Your turn—hurry," Key had said.

Noelle had started to wrap her hand around her bloody finger, to stop the bleeding and the throbbing, but Key swatted her hand away. "Wait, wait, we have to rub our blood together, to become blood married. Do it, do it." She handed over her Swiss Army Knife and her own forefinger, but she kept her eyes open.

"I can't do it," Noelle said.

Key sighed. "Come on, it's fine," she said. "Don't you want to be together forever? Don't you want us to be special?"

Noelle nodded. And kept nodding as she took the knife in her hands, because it was what she'd wanted most of all in the whole world—Key and her to be connected forever. But it would require hurting her.

"Do it, *now*!" Key ordered.

It only took a quick poke at the skin and a small movement drew the tiniest line of blood from one side of her finger to the other. Key didn't make a noise. Her pretty eyes glazed over momentarily, and Noelle loved watching the one blue and one green eye change. She swallowed, and Noelle could see the bit of pain travel in a gulp down her throat.

Key grabbed Noelle's bleeding finger and pressed it hard against her bleeding finger, moving them in tiny circles against each other to mix up the blood, then she leaned forward, kissing Noelle.

The taste of Key's cherry lip gloss made her lips tingle because of how much she always bit them, but it didn't stop her best friend from continuing to press her mouth against hers. Noelle's pulse raced and her imagination painted a picture of them doing everything together always.

And Noelle had tried to keep Key after that. Blood married and secretly more than just friends ever since.

A male voice snatched Noelle back to the present, erasing the bittersweet heartache of her memory with Key. The heat of the wardrobe and the bathroom suffocated her once more. Sweat beaded across her nose.

"We gotta find it," one voice said.

She craned to listen and tried to identify who was in the bedroom. The rustle of clothes and the opening and closing of drawers drowned out some of their conversation. Who was in there? How had they gotten a key? She didn't dare open the wardrobe any farther or peek her head out for fear of getting caught. She'd look just as guilty as whoever was going through Ant's stuff right now no matter how she tried to explain why she was there.

"Where could it be?" came a second voice.

An exasperated sigh echoed. "Maybe it was on him."

"While swimming? Nah. It's gotta be here."

Noelle tried to decipher the voices as they grew closer and closer to the bathroom. Was it one of the male staff members, perhaps? Or maybe Quatro or Dwayne? But what would they need from Ant's room? They were whispering so she couldn't identify them despite all the years of knowing them. But the same question circled her brain on a loop. She tried to remember anything Ant might've said about what he and the boys were up to, but adrenaline and fear erased all coherent and logical thoughts. Her ears flooded with her anxious pulse and a desire to get out of there as soon as possible.

"The wallet isn't here!"

A hot flash rushed through her. Wallet? What did they want with Ant's wallet?

Then she thought maybe it wasn't her male friends after all. They wouldn't need money from him. As she craned to listen even harder, her duffel bag dropped with a plunk. She clasped a hand over her mouth and didn't move, bracing for the footsteps to enter the bathroom and discover her hiding spot, but instead, she heard the two people scurry out and the click of the door closing.

She counted to fifty, then left the suite. She couldn't chance them returning. If she forgot something, she'd have to explain it later.

Once in the hall, she walked as fast as she could without running or letting her footsteps echo. She headed for the staircase. When she rounded the corner, she smacked straight into Dwayne.

"Whoa!" She fell backward and he caught her.

"Ummm . . . you good?" he asked, his warmth surprising her. Sweat collected at his temples and he tried to wipe it away.

She righted herself, smoothed out her dress, and squared her shoulders, bracing for meanness from him. "Fine."

His eyebrows lifted.

Before he could ask her what she was doing up this early or on the fifth floor, she asked him: "What are you doing up this early?"

He rubbed his face and shook his head. "I couldn't sleep. I can't stop thinking about Ade's body," he said, his breath now ragged and fear marring his face. "I've been pacing every floor just to stay calm . . ."

Her stomach twisted. "You think someone hurt him on purpose, don't you?"

"I don't know what to think, but first Ant and then Ade? What are the chances of two back-to-back freak accidents?"

CALLUM BROWN

Private Security for Kuzimu Island
10:38 a.m.

THE WINDS SLAPPED around the entire mangrove forest. This never-ending storm might ruin it all.

Callum mopped his forehead with a handkerchief as he crept along the small, muddy road from Vista Village on the leeward side to Kuzimu Horizons. He had to pull over and stop every few minutes so he and his coworker Brent could clear enough debris to get through with the resort's SUV. All the main perimeter roads had been washed out, and with no emergency services and disaster relief crews to come through, it was their job to clear a single viable path to the other side of the island.

The drive usually only took about half an hour. This island was one of the smaller ones in the Florida Keys. It was why he'd liked it and had come to work security for the sleepy little resort town. The most trouble was drunken fights or fussy women who lost their earrings while shopping at the small stores. He got paid to be in paradise.

"Glenn's got hell on his hands, doesn't he?" Brent said while throwing thick leaves and branches off the road. They'd been working around the clock but there was still debris everywhere.

"Yeah." Callum stared up, the sky would reopen any minute, and they still had over a mile to go. "He didn't plan on this storm at all."

"Does it change things?" Brent grunted out as he rolled a large mangrove tree trunk, then waved at him for help. "My back isn't as young as yours. Help me out here."

Callum ignored his question as they heaved the heavy wood out of the way. "We have to take statements and close off the crime scene until the storm passes and the cops from Islamorada come through. They've got their hands full with all the problems caused by the storm."

Brent rubbed his palms together before climbing back into the open-air vehicle. "This should be fun." He flashed Callum a sadistic smile. "It's been over a decade since I've gotten to investigate a murder . . ." He droned on about his days in the Key West police department before he retired and took security gigs at luxury resorts to pass the time and keep his mind sharp. Callum sensed he fucked with people in his day; he knew the type. Drunk on power. Relishing the ability to make people do whatever he said just because he'd issued the order.

"I wonder how bloody it was. The grislier the better," Brent added. "Adds to the excitement. I'm telling you, it's better than the movies."

Yes, Callum thought, this should be a nice disruption of their boring routine. A real chance to play hero. Or flex a little. He needed to blow off steam. Tourism had been slow with Kuzimu under construction with renovations. Not many women coming through. But he knew he could count on that fussy romance writer. He'd been trying to get her to pay attention to him every time she was in town, but she'd brushed him off, teasing him.

Maybe this week would be different.

He revved the SUV engine trying to outpace the storm clouds gathering overhead.

It'd been so long since real trouble had come to the island, and he planned to enjoy every minute of it.

CHAPTER TEN

SYDNEY

11:57 a.m.

"YOU GOT SOMETHING to confess? You confess it to God. Do not confess it to the police. Understand me?"

Sydney dug her nails into her palms and nodded at her security guard. They'd been doing this—prepping for Sydney's upcoming police questioning—for over an hour. Not that it was helping to make her feel any less nervous.

Prescott paced from the hotel room door to the windows. Briefly, she sat down next to Sydney on the bed, but she immediately sprang back up again.

Sydney had never seen her this rattled, not even a few months ago when there'd been a credible threat against her mom at a rally. If Sydney wasn't so worried for herself, she'd feel bad for the woman. Coaching her protectee on how not to incriminate herself during a murder investigation likely wasn't what she signed up for.

"My mom won't let me talk to the police without a lawyer present," Sydney said, thinking back to all the times when her mother had impressed this upon her. She could see her mother's face right this instant—lips pursed, eyes narrowed, the only wrinkle she had showing itself across her forehead with the ultimate seriousness. "If you ever find yourself, or your friends, in any kind of trouble, you call me, and you say nothing. If you can't get ahold of me, you have our family lawyer Devin Halloway's number in your phone. Anyone at his practice will be available to you at all times."

But Sydney couldn't contact her mother right now, and she didn't know if she'd actually be able to get herself or her friends out of this situation as easily as her mother made it sound.

"You aren't going to talk to them. You're going to say nothing but what I've told you—and your mother has told you—your entire life. We want to be on record as showing that you're cooperating in some regard like the others by sitting for the interrogation at least," Prescott said. "So repeat it back to me."

Sydney suppressed the urge to tell her she'd had enough. What she really needed—the thing that was going to settle her nerves the most—was for Prescott to leave so that she could keep trying to get Ant's phone to turn on.

"Let me hear you say it," Prescott prompted.

"Confess to God, not to the police," Sydney said, and somehow managed not to sigh in frustration.

Prescott paced some more. "No matter what they say, they're not your friends. I'm telling you this now because, though I'll be in the room with you, I can't speak on your behalf. Cops are trained in psychological coercion. They might downplay how much trouble you're in to get you to relax. They might take the good-cop route and promise to make all your problems go away. They might lie about the evidence and—"

Sydney shook her head sharply. "They can't do that—"

Prescott cut her off. "I used to be a cop. Trust me when I say police lie all the time. If a cop is talking, best assume they're lying."

Sydney swallowed past the stone of fear in her throat.

"Now also repeat the line your mother taught you: 'No comment, and I will not answer your questions without my attorney present.' Don't smile. Don't pal around. Cops assume everybody is guilty. The friendlier you are, the more suspicious they are." She stopped pacing and stared hard at Sydney. "Do you understand?"

"I understand," Sydney said. Then, quickly, before Prescott could dispense more advice, she asked, "Have you been able to reach my mom?"

Prescott didn't bother to answer. They both knew that her mother would've found a way to be here already if she knew what was going on.

"Okay, it's almost time," Prescott said, and walked to the door. "I'll be right behind you. Freshen yourself up and be ready in ten minutes."

As soon as she was gone, Sydney slumped back onto the bed and tried to quell her rising panic. She fingered the cross around her neck and said a quick prayer. Then she took one long inhale in: she could do this. One long exhale out: she *had* to do this.

She allowed herself one more breath before quietly locking the door's dead bolt. The last thing she needed was for Prescott to catch her with evidence.

Sydney opened the safe, took out Ant's phone, and clutched it flat against her chest. "God, if you let this thing turn on, I promise to stop questioning you," she whispered.

What was it her grandmother used to say? *Everybody finds God on their deathbed.*

Sydney pressed the power button.

Nothing.

She pressed three more times.

Still nothing.

Ugh, why wasn't it working? Weren't these things supposed to be waterproof? Or were they just water-resistant? She swore her little brother had swum with his phone to take snorkeling photos on their last beach trip. Blow-drying it earlier hadn't helped. Maybe she could find some rice back in the kitchen. That was supposed to help dry things out, right? But the thought of going back there, being so close to Ant's body again, made her nauseous. Should she ask Prescott for help? No. The woman would ask questions *and* tell her mother, and then the whole situation would be out of Sydney's control.

Sydney's decision to ask Ant for help with the Dwayne situation had been driven by pure desperation. And all of it had been provoked by a breakfast she'd had with her mother all those weeks ago.

"It's been seventeen days since I asked you to work on that special project," her mother said. She sat down across from Sydney at the small table in their breakfast nook. Her designer pantsuit for the day was a classic pale pink. Her hair was slicked back into a tight bun, and her makeup was so expertly done it looked like she wasn't wearing any at all. Sometimes Sydney couldn't tell whether her mom was getting dressed for a political rally or church.

Sydney pushed away her cereal bowl. This conversation was going to ruin her appetite.

"You've been spending so much time with Dwayne, I would've expected results by now," her mother said.

"*You're* the one who asked me to spend time with him," Sydney said, knowing she sounded too defensive.

Her mother tilted her head and simply stared. Looking at her mother was like looking at an older version of herself. They had the same warm brown skin with pink undertones. The same clear brown eyes that could shift from joy to anger in a flash. The same high, sharp cheekbones that made them look both beautiful and fierce.

Sydney tried to hold her mother's gaze while keeping her expression neutral, but as always, her mother saw too much.

"That time is supposed to be in service of our campaign, not in service of your crush."

Sydney shook her head. "I don't have a—"

But her mother held a hand up. "Have you found anything we can use?"

Sydney looked down at her hands. "He doesn't talk about his dad much. I don't think I'm going to find anything."

Her mother's look was withering. "You know better than that.

Everybody has secrets." She stood and smoothed her hands down her suit. "And never forget, that man betrayed me. He betrayed our entire family. He would not be governor without me. And how does he repay me? By running against me. No. It will not stand. I will bury him." She closed her eyes briefly and cleared her throat. "Ten minutes ago I got our latest internal polling results. This race is closer than it has any right to be. I know what I asked you to do is not easy, but we *all* have to sacrifice to achieve this. As a family, we've been working toward this for years, and I won't allow that vile betrayer to snatch it out from under us." She squeezed Sydney's hand briefly. "Do not let me or your father or your brother down. Get your head in the game and get this thing done. Get it done now." She let go of Sydney's hand and left.

Up until a couple of weeks ago, Sydney wouldn't have thought to ask Ant for help. In fact, up until then—when he helped her with something else—she'd barely paid him any attention at all. She'd known things about him, of course. He was the kind of rich that even other rich kids envied. Somehow, he'd befriended all the school's factions: the nerds, jocks, art geeks, and theater kids. He was even in with Dwayne and Quatro. Even though the boys claimed he was one of them almost immediately, Sydney had held him at a distance. Ever since her mom declared her candidacy, her mantra was *No new friends.* It was too hard to know who was trustworthy versus who was out for access to power.

Two weeks ago, though, he'd slipped under her guard. She'd just gotten her grade on the second big calculus test of the year. She'd failed. Again. She was on track to failing the class. Her mother was going to be livid.

Ant had come up to her before she could swipe away her sudden tears.

"You good?" he'd asked.

"I'm fine," she said, and gave him hard eyes that dared him to comment on her crying.

He laughed lightly. "I know you don't like me much, but Imma keep you on my favorite-people list anyway."

She folded her arms tight across her chest. "And why's that?"

"My man Dwayne says you're good people. Says you're one of his favorite people in the world," he said.

Immediately she'd softened. "He said that?"

"Sure did," he said with a nod and a grin. "From that little smile you got going, I can see you feel the same."

Sydney shifted her face back to neutral but relaxed a bit. If Dwayne trusted him, maybe she could too. She told him about her calculus grade. If she couldn't get to at least a B, her mother was going to lose her damn mind. "She says honesty is the best policy, that lying is a sin before God, but I've seen her do all kinds of things to make sure she looks the way she's supposed to look for her constituents. So, what really matters? The truth, or what people think is the truth?"

Ant had looked at her for a beat, then reached into his backpack for his laptop. Two minutes later, he turned the computer to show her the screen: her average in the class was a C+.

"Why not bump it all the way to a B?" she'd asked.

"You gotta work for it a little, Syd," he'd said with a wink and a smile before he took off.

So, the day after her mother told Sydney to get her head in the game and find some dirt on Dwayne or Dwayne's dad, she'd gone to Ant for help. Behind the stadium bleachers at the end of the school day, Sydney told him everything in a flood of words. For a full thirty seconds he didn't say anything at all. Had she made a mistake and trusted the wrong person? But then he started talking and surprised her. He wasn't judgmental or sneering. He said he understood about having parents who made impossible demands. He told her not to worry, that he'd find something on Dwayne, and that none of it would blow back on her. Dwayne would never know the real reason she was staying so close by his side these days.

"Don't feel bad," Ant said. "Sometimes you have to do the wrong thing for the right reason." It sounded like something her mom would say behind closed doors.

Hearing him say that eased her guilt, made her feel that maybe everything would work itself out. How wrong she'd been.

Any hopes Sydney had of the interrogation going smoothly died the moment she entered First Light. Someone—the island security?—had rearranged the furniture to make it look as intimidating as possible. Everything had been pushed to the edges of the room. A single table remained in the center of the room with just three chairs, two on one side and one on the other. The cops (or private security officers? What sort of jurisdiction did these guys even have?)—two of them, both white and balding—were seated next to each other. When had they even arrived?

Instead of greeting her, they just scowled. Their eyes tracked her every movement. Thank God Prescott was right behind her.

Sydney reminded herself she hadn't done anything wrong. Well, not the thing they might have thought she'd done wrong, anyway. And she wasn't going to be answering any questions without the family lawyer present. She clasped her hands together and tried not to fidget. She didn't want them to see how afraid she was. She focused on appearing perfect. *That* she'd had plenty of practice doing.

"I know who you are," the younger one said.

Sydney eyed him, wary. What he really meant was he knew who her mother was, and he didn't like her or her politics. It didn't matter to him that Sydney was a private citizen who was not running for public office. All some people ever saw when they looked at her was her mother and her mother's politics.

He leaned back, laced his fingers behind his head. His name tag said *Callum Brown, Security*. "She's the one always talking about defunding the police, right?"

She looked back at Prescott, but her face betrayed nothing. Sydney's stomach twisted, but she steeled herself and didn't say anything. The wind picked up again and dark clouds rolled in, further making her feel like she was in some sort of horror film.

A slow, nasty smile crawled across his face. "Mommy's not gonna be so high and mighty when it comes out her daughter killed someone."

Sydney's heart slammed into her chest. "That's not true! I didn't kill anyone." Then she covered her mouth. "No comment."

He laughed. "The truth doesn't matter," he said. "I'm surprised your mommy didn't teach you that already."

"Are you even real cops?" Sydney asked.

Behind her, Prescott cleared her throat.

"Have a seat, Ms. Davis," said the older cop, sweeping away her question. He waited for her to sit before continuing on: "We only have two questions for you. Then you can be on your way."

Sydney resisted the urge to press her hand to her chest. Her heart felt like it was trying to escape through her rib cage.

The older security guard slid his phone in front of her and pressed record in an app. "First question: Were you and the victim friends?"

It was such an innocuous question. It should've been an easy one to answer without lying. Up until two days ago, Sydney's answer would've been *yes*. But then Ant texted her and changed everything.

ANTHONY:

Got what you needed

And it's good

Very very good

Your mom will have this thing in the bag

SYDNEY:

!!!!!

What is it?!

ANTHONY:

Whoa now

Not so fast

BIG finds mean BIG rewards

Imma need a BIG favor

SYDNEY:

Wtf?!

You didn't say ANYTHING about a favor

ANTHONY:

Just a little quid pro quo, Syd

Your mom would understand

Unless you want me to take what I found to the DC press?

Might have to let it slip that your mom asked you to do opposition research on one of your friends AND that you agreed to do it

We won't even need to mention those score changes in calc

That was when Sydney lost it. She texted him back saying things she wasn't proud of. Vicious, angry things. Things that could be construed as threatening. That was why she needed to get into Ant's phone. So she could find out exactly what he had on Dwayne. And to erase all her incriminating text messages to him. She needed to cover her tracks. Cover up the stupidest thing she'd ever done.

"This is not a hard question, Miss Davis," the older cop prompted. "Were you and the victim friends or not?"

"No comment," Sydney said, hating how small her voice was. She coughed, trying to summon her regular tone.

His eyebrow lifted. "So this is the game we're going to play?"

"Must've been the hooking-up kind of friends," the younger cop said with a sneer. He leaned forward and slammed his palm on the table. "That's what happened, isn't it? You two got into some sort of lover's spat and things got out of control."

"No!" Sydney said hotly. "I mean . . . No comment!" She had to get control of herself. But Sydney hated when people lied about her more than anything else. Being the kid of a politician meant so many lies circulated online and in the papers about her, her family, her friends, and even her pets. Her dog, Sunshine, had been called a predator by a tabloid just two weeks ago.

"Know what I think?" he began, but the older cop cleared his throat. It was obviously a signal because the younger cop immediately stopped talking. He leaned back in his chair. His sneer remained in place.

The older cop took over again. "Just one more question, Miss Davis. Where were you on Sunday night?"

Sydney did her best to pull herself together. "No comment."

They exchanged a look she couldn't decipher.

"You're sure you don't have anything you need to confess?" the older cop asked.

"I think that's enough." Prescott finally spoke up. "Her family lawyer isn't present, and she's a minor, so she doesn't need to say anything to you."

The fake cops shook their heads, and they dismissed her with an order to "Send the next one in."

"Good job," Prescott said as they walked out. But then they bumped right into Dwayne. He took one look at Sydney's face and pulled her into his arms. Something about the way he smelled always reminded her of an early spring morning when leaves were just starting to blossom once again. It made her feel like only good things were on the horizon. The tears she'd been holding in spilled out. Dwayne hugged her even closer.

"Don't worry," he whispered. "We'll get through this together."

More than she wanted anything, Sydney wanted to believe him. She looked up into his eyes. Had they always been this beautiful? It wasn't the color, though the glittering black of them was stunning. It was the sincerity in them. The goodness.

He palmed her cheek and wiped away her tears. "I'll find you afterward," he said. "Should be quick because it's going to be a no comment for me." He winked at her, and she offered him a weak smile.

Sydney watched him walk into the restaurant, followed by Johnson, and she stood there for a few seconds after the door closed. One of those sudden obliterating silences descended on the hallway, as if all life had dropped out of the world. She couldn't even hear the hurricane above them anymore. The long corridor dimmed and everything around Sydney seemed unfamiliar. How, exactly, had she gotten here, to this place on the verge of both having and losing everything she ever wanted?

CHAPTER ELEVEN

RIVER

1:24 p.m.

IT WAS HOT.

The sun was finally out again now that the storm had paused for a few minutes. The sky was a shade of crystal clear cerulean that reminded River of La La Lapis, a nail color she'd been obsessed with last year. She'd done a series of manicures featuring only blue polish on MANIfest the Mess, and her followers loved it.

She hadn't been able to stop thinking about receiving those messages—or really *threats*—from Key's old accounts. It was almost time for her to be questioned by the resort's security officers, and as she walked from her room, she began to sweat. And not just because of the weather.

It was gonna be hard to control the narrative when she couldn't even control her sweat glands.

When she got to the Dawn wing, the hallway was empty. She didn't know what she'd expected . . . a handful of nosy staff hoping to listen in? Frowning people in official-looking uniforms? But there was no one.

She could hear voices coming through the doorway to First Light, and before she even had a chance to cross the threshold, Dwayne appeared, looking frazzled and dazed, Johnson standing like a shadow behind him.

"Guess you're up," Dwayne said, handing her a weak smile, and when she walked inside, she was still alone. None of her other friends in sight.

As she sat in the warm restaurant, gross rings of moisture grew under her arms and around the collar of her tank top. There were a few folders on one of the tables, the edges of their enclosed pages peeking out of the openings. She wanted to flip through them, see what might be inside.

It was almost as humid inside as it had been out on the beach, and River was nervous. River frequently choked on tests even after studying all night. And also stumbled through oral presentations that she was completely prepared for. She just hated being put on the spot; she was too desperate to be perfect to handle even the *hint* of scrutiny. It was why MANIfest the Mess had been so great: she could say whatever she wanted without anyone knowing she was River Reynolds.

But now she'd have to speak to the guards or whatever. They'd be looking at her, wanting something from her. On top of that was the growing suspicion that something was really wrong—that what had happened to Ant wasn't an accident. She'd have to become Dana's Daughter to get through it.

She thought of Sydney and Dwayne, and then of Noelle and Quintin.

Everyone was acting weird.

Everyone seemed like they had something to hide.

The trust between them now was fragile. And the more she thought about it, the sicker she felt. River had watched and listened to everyone, and it was starting to seem like each one of her friends had a motive for wanting Ant dead, which was the last thing she wanted to believe. They'd been friends for years and she didn't want to lose them, but she could no longer deny the truth: they'd been headed for disaster since Key's death last year.

She looked around. She listened. There was still no sign of the officers who were supposed to be questioning her.

Before she lost her nerve, she opened the folder right in front of her. She meticulously snapped photo after photo of what looked like interview notes, moving the papers and folder as little as possible. She flipped the last page and caught a glimpse of something that made her slam the folder shut.

A photo of a lifeless body, the light of the flash bouncing back at the lens off a chain.

Just like that, she was beside the pool the day before, in the glimmering, after-storm morning.

She remembered the bellhop diving in to drag Ant out; remembered how heavy he looked. Then, without deciding to, she remembered Key. How *she'd* looked after they'd pulled *her* from the pool at that stupid gala none of them actually wanted to be at. The way her head flopped lifelessly to the side. The tips of her fingers were wrinkled, like she'd been pickled—sunk in cold liquid for a little too long.

The photo of Ant made River feel faint, and so nauseated she turned her head away from the table and took three quick breaths to settle her stomach.

She slammed the folders closed and referenced the first photo she'd taken to return them as closely as she could to their previous positions, suddenly wondering if the cops had planted the folders on purpose—left them there to see what she might do. They could be watching her right now, she realized, looking up and around.

Dana's Daughter would've thought of this possibility.

Damn it.

They walked in only a minute or so later. Tall, bald white men in dark uniforms. They had serious, tanned faces, their mouths in hard, straight lines. And River felt her heartbeat quicken the instant she saw them. Part of her hadn't believed they were real.

As they approached, she couldn't help but think of the last time she'd been this close to law enforcement: the night Key died. She lowered her phone into her lap and, even though anxiety and guilt gnawed at her from the inside out, she smiled sweetly at them both.

"Good afternoon, officers," she said, shedding Real River like snakeskin.

The interview wasn't as awful as she'd expected. They asked about her relationship with Ant, where she was the night before he was found in the pool, how long she'd known him. They asked about her friendships with the other kids on the island, and she answered mostly with honesty. She knew her mother would have told her to say nothing, but without Dana or an attorney here, she thought cooperating was the smartest choice.

If she answered nothing, they'd only have more questions, and she needed their eyes focused on someone or even everyone else.

She stayed calm. Or at least that was what they'd write in their little notebooks.

"You were the one who discovered the body, is that correct?" one asked.

The phrase *the body* rang in her head like an alarm.

He was a kid. He was her friend.

And now he was just *the body*.

Fingers of heat crept along her neck. She needed to remain cool, to cooperate. But she looked up sharply and was met with empty eyes. How cold these men were. How disconnected they seemed to be from what it meant to be human. The least they could do was use his name.

She took a deep breath. "His name is Anthony," she corrected them fiercely.

The one on the right nodded. "That's right. Anthony."

"And no. I didn't discover him," she said, satisfied. "I believe a couple of the others did, but can't say for sure as I wasn't present. By the time I reached the pool, he'd been removed from the water."

"What time was it?" asked the one on the left. "And who were you with?"

She told them everything as they nodded and jotted notes. Then they let her go.

Now, as she walked back out into the heat, she could smell another round of the storm headed their way. She shrugged and opened her Notes app to look at her list of suspects and motives.

Would the officers put everything together the way things seemed to be coming together for River? She was worried they wouldn't. This place didn't exactly seem like a breeding ground for competent police. And weren't they just security guards, anyway? At no point did they seem to be worried that she'd looked through their notes—either she'd put them back perfectly or they hadn't noticed or cared about anything she'd left askew.

Which was bothersome to River. If they missed something, who would they try to pin things on? How would they actually figure out who killed Ant . . . and Captain Diallo?

She updated her own list based on what she'd seen in their notes and felt more confused than ever.

SUSPECTS/MOTIVES

General Manager: hates Ant's whole family

Noelle: argued with Ant at the pool, but never came back to the room

Quintin: is an angry, drunken mess. And seems to be hiding something, even from me. (Did Ant have something on him? What could it be?)

Dwayne: seemed stressed and upset when he left the restaurant after being questioned. Was something going on between Ant and Sydney? Is Dwayne pissed about it?

Possible it really was an accident and not a murder?

What about Captain Diallo? How does he fit?

River scanned her notes for the hundredth time. She noticed she didn't have anything down about Sydney, but she knew Sydney, didn't she? Her best friend wouldn't have done something like this without River's knowledge . . . right?

Something going down between Noelle and Ant seemed the most plausible. But River didn't think Noelle was strong enough to hurt Ant—physically or emotionally. Plus, Noelle needed Ant. Without him, she would be adrift because the rest of the crew didn't want anything to do with her right now. Would she really do something that would alienate her even more? Noelle hated being alone.

River took the long way to the Sunset wing walking along the beach. This was so ridiculous. Her friends weren't murderers. Honestly, why would any of them even need to get rid of him? They all came from families that had the kind of money to make things disappear.

But she needed to think like Dana's Daughter right now. She thought about how her mother could decipher the hint of a half-truth or excavate a motive with minimal effort, as if she'd been born a human lie detector.

River picked up a few seashells from the litter-scattered sand. She turned one over in her hands, and in the sun its underside was the same pearly opal as her old signature nail color. She hadn't worn Borrowed Light since she'd painted all her friends' nails the same color the night of the gala when everything went sideways. Sydney had been the one who'd wanted their nails to match. So they had.

But seeing the shade gleam from Key's lifeless fingertips had made River never want to wear it again.

Just then, as she passed the charred and ruined arrival dock, she saw a few members of the resort's staff wearing gloves and picking over the yacht's wreckage. She still couldn't believe the boat had exploded. They were all holding small plastic bags and putting bits and pieces of the mess inside it. Collecting evidence? River wondered. But why? As it started to drizzle, she saw them point toward the Dawn wing and head back inside.

River wiped a few raindrops from her brow before letting the shell fall soundlessly into the sand, then she shielded her eyes and looked out over the water. A nearly flat line of blue greeted her, despite the events of the past few days. She wondered if figuring out the truth about Ant would make endless waves ripple through their lives or keep things as they were: eerily calm.

At least on the surface.

Because she wondered if figuring out what happened to Ant could save her from whoever was threatening to reveal the truth about *her*.

STARLIE PARSONS

Chef

4:22 p.m.

STARLIE PARSONS WAS grateful the kitchen still had power, because it meant she could still cook. And Starlie desperately needed to cook. When her panic disorder was in danger of flaring up and spiraling out of control, the only thing that calmed her was the predictability of an ordered kitchen, the weight of a skillet in her hand, the heat of a stove's flames licking at her fingers.

She hadn't heard from or seen her son since the storm Sunday night, but he'd told her he was going to head to Vista Village to meet a friend for a drink when he got off. There was no cell service, no power, no way for him to make it back to the resort or to reach her, so she was just trying to trust that he was okay.

Still, her legs were tingling, pins and needles snaking up past her kneecaps. She popped her daily dose of meds, tied up her waist-length box braids, and opened the fridge to survey the offerings. She was avoiding the walk-in freezer, where they'd put . . . the body . . . She was trying her hardest to forget it was there.

Starlie knew she'd have to ration what was left of the perishables.

With the storm damage preventing or delaying deliveries indefinitely, they needed to be smart. So she decided to make chili. Pantry items like grains and legumes they ordered in bulk every month, and she knew from her weekly inventory that they had plenty of beans and lentils to get them through the worst of this. Foods like those stuck to the ribs and would keep everyone feeling full longer.

She heaved two seven-quart Dutch ovens onto the stovetop and turned on the burners.

Though she'd worked everywhere from diners to pubs, bistros to bars and grills, and had held dozens of positions in fine-dining restaurants over the years, she'd lost them all. At nearly fifty-five, she had more varied experience than lots of people in the industry, but panic attacks that left her trembling so hard she couldn't hold a paring knife steady didn't go well with fast-paced kitchens, where presentation needed to be flawless and impatient food critics couldn't be kept waiting. Four months ago, for the first time in her life, she'd been having a hard time finding a job. She'd thought this place would be the perfect solution. She'd get to do what she loved—cook—but at an island resort where everything moved a little more slowly and everyone would be on vacation. She could spend her downtime reading the cozy mysteries she loved. Though the kitchen didn't have the full staff she'd grown used to in her last position (sous chef at Red Bone, a Michelin-starred soul-food restaurant in Washington, DC, with a warlord for a chef de cuisine), she had begun to feel happy here. Until this week.

Starlie jumped at the sound of the swinging door, but it was just

Cruz, the bellhop, his bronze skin looking as smooth as the caramel she drizzled onto her signature mascarpone cheesecake cookies. "What you making, Chef?" he asked.

"Chili," she said, hoping he didn't get too close. His scent was a mix of citrus and salt water, and she notoriously had trouble with brown-skinned men who smelled delicious.

"Nice. Make it extra spicy for me," he said, and winked. He *always* winked. Starlie wondered how his thick paintbrush lashes weren't permanently tangled as much as he did that.

She could feel her cheeks heat, but she hoped he wouldn't notice. He was part of the reason she'd been happier the past few weeks, though she wasn't yet sure if he was just a huge flirt or if he was really interested. She swallowed hard, grabbed a pepper, and promised she would before he swept out of the kitchen, taking his mile-long lashes with him.

Starlie had had a strange feeling about the kids as soon as they'd arrived on the island and she'd seen how they were treating Noelle, and she'd told her son, Orion, as much. Starlie had always been anxious, but she hadn't felt vibes this off since she'd worked under that maniac Chef Donaldson. She browned the ground chuck in a separate pan and added the presoaked beans to the big pot with veggie stock she'd made the night before. As she did, she could feel the meds begin to take effect—her shoulders lowered slowly away from her ears and her heart rate slowed. But her mind was still spinning.

Anthony Brooks couldn't really be dead, could he? Her interview with the cops that morning had gone smoothly because she'd been in the kitchen all night and had been seen by nearly every other member of the staff—a clear and concise alibi. She hadn't seen the body, wrapped up at the back of the walk-in, but had tried to text her son about what happened as soon as she heard.

She glanced at her phone: *Message Send Failure* still flashed red as a storm warning.

What she didn't tell the cops, though, was that she'd known Ant's father, Kelvin Brooks, since she was thirteen because her brother was his roommate in college. She didn't tell them Kelvin had given her this job. And she didn't tell them that Kelvin had always been a bit scheme-y, a bit desperate to feel important, a bit greedy. She wondered if it was possible that something else, something darker, was going on.

As Starlie pulled the spices she needed from the neatly arranged lazy Susan, she thought, *Why would Kelvin want to be responsible for six (basically unsupervised) kids visiting his resort?* That many kids in one place would seem like a bad idea even if they weren't on an island—even if the kids weren't these particular kids. She seasoned the pot and returned the spices to their places, rotating them until the labels winked at her just as Cruz had.

Starlie pressed a few garlic cloves with the flat of her knife and rubbed them over several thick slices of neatly arranged baguette before drizzling everything with oil and sliding the whole sheet of bread into the waiting oven, an additional bulb of garlic in its center to roast as the bread toasted. Now came the worst part of cooking a passive meal like chili: when it was out of her hands. She set a timer, sat down, and opened the latest mystery she was in the middle of reading.

Just as she finished a new chapter, there was the sound of voices, the bang of the kitchen's doors opening again. She turned, smiling, expecting to see Cruz, but instead it was those fake cops. They beelined for the walk-in. They must have come for the body.

CHAPTER TWELVE

DWAYNE

7:13 p.m.

DWAYNE KNEW THAT being a skillful wielder of words was what made a good politician. One needed to have a stone-cold poker face, nerves of steel, an extensive vocabulary, and a mind that moved quick enough to spit out a correct-sounding answer for every question lobbed your way.

To an outsider, what had always set Dwayne apart from the rest of the Six was his seemingly straitlaced persona. In fact, even said childhood friends stayed clowning him for his "accountant-dad aura." Which he never minded. Being the so-called nerd of the group helped him fly under the radar.

Because except for when it came to Sydney, Dwayne was typically calm, cool, and collected.

Even when he'd spotted Ant's body, he'd done his best to keep it calm, cool, and collected.

Just like he'd done after Keisha's death.

The lies had poured out of him like water when the cops had

questioned him back then. He'd sat beside his family lawyer and told them what they wanted to hear, needed to hear:

"No, sir, I have no idea where Keisha would've gotten drugs from."

"No, sir, I can't think of a reason that someone would want to kill her."

"No, sir, I don't believe there was foul play."

Over and over, and he'd never broken a sweat.

But as Dwayne paced in his darkening hotel bedroom, his heart thumping like it did when he knew he had to convincingly argue a position he didn't believe in for Model UN, he could feel the cracks in his composure thickening and spreading. He'd never been on ice this thin.

Snatches of light trickled in through the shades as the sun set on another stormy day in hell. All Dwayne wanted to do was slip into Ant's room, find the stash they were supposed to be selling off to the Kuzimu staff members, then find Sydney and hole up with her until help arrived.

Only quick thinking on his part had saved him from being caught trying to get into Ant's room. But planting the seed in Noelle's head that maybe there was a serial killer on the loose had succeeded in distracting her from the real reason Dwayne had gone to floor five. And even though Dwayne didn't believe it when he said it, once he'd put it in Noelle's head, he hadn't been able to stop theorizing himself.

Did it bother him that he didn't know why *she'd* been up there and that he hadn't gotten the opportunity to ask why?

Definitely.

But of paramount importance right now was keeping himself off all radars—present and past.

He really wished he'd found that stash. He would never have told Ant—or anyone, for that matter: even in a legal state, the governor's son couldn't be caught in possession of a substance that was still illicit on a societal level (despite coming straight from God's green earth), and he certainly couldn't be seen under the influence of it—but Dwayne would occasionally skim a bit of the product to test it out. Make sure it calmed the nerves like he told his customers as a selling point.

He could use a little tester right now.

And as idiotic as he knew it was, Dwayne also wanted to see how much he could sell. Especially with everyone on the island in distress.

That was Dwayne's problem. He was addicted to risk. Could rarely resist seeing how close he could get to an inferno without getting burned. He hated to admit it, but the more he thought about it, the more he realized the tendency was part of the reason he couldn't leave Sydney alone. He wanted her because he wasn't supposed to.

At least initially.

Now he wasn't sure about anything. It surprised him to no end, but ever since his questioning with "officers" here at the resort—even though it had ended his night with Sydney, Dwayne couldn't have been more grateful that he'd passed out early the night Ant died—all he could think about was Keisha. And what he'd done.

I told her to stop drinking.

Whenever Dwayne thought about Key, that phrase played on a loop in his head. Dwayne had said it multiple times that night . . .

Key, please stop drinking.

But she hadn't listened. She never listened. It was his least favorite thing about her, that spirit of unnecessary defiance, that refusal to let anyone tell her what to do and her lack of concern for other people's feelings.

If Dwayne was honest, he'd always cared too much about his image. To the point where he'd kept a massive secret from his closest friends.

I told her to stop drinking.

Keisha finding out about that first little side hustle Dwayne was running—top-secret, high-table-minimum card games the highest rollers from their overwrought school would gather to play—was one of the worst things to ever happen. Because, as was her custom, she promised not to tell a soul, then weaponized the knowledge.

It started with some new "party pill" Key had heard about and wanted to try . . . and her knowledge that one of Dwayne's card-playing regulars had access to it. Dwayne had refused at first—not only for the sake of avoiding liability in case something bad happened, but also because at no point did he want to risk being caught with the stuff.

But she'd told him that if he *didn't* get it for her, she'd leak his "little card-shark shenanigans" to one of her "tabloid connections," and the possibility that she might was enough to make him fall in line and get her what she wanted.

I told her to stop drinking.

That was the sole warning the supplier gave him when he purchased the pill: "Under no circumstances should this thing be taken with alcohol."

But Key didn't listen. She never, ever listened.

Key's death had been ruled an accident largely due to the toxicology report. And Dwayne had been the one to give her the drugs. A fact that's haunting him now.

He shut the game ring down the morning after Keisha's death despite the fact that her death would set him free to expand the enterprise.

It didn't take long for him to miss the money.

His hand found his phone; the lack of cell service and Wi-Fi made it impossible for him to obsessively check his bank account three to four times a day. He clenched his jaw. He couldn't even place his game bets this week either.

One thing Dwayne did appreciate about his father was that so long as (1) his son didn't ask *him* for money, and (2) the First Son of Maryland stayed out of overt trouble, no questions were asked.

Dwayne was sure his dad not being all up in his business had something to do with plausible deniability, but Dwayne didn't hate it. Or at least he *used* to not hate it. He wasn't so sure now with things as out of hand as they'd gotten.

He glanced down at the phone screen, believing for a moment that the mere thought of his dad might miraculously give him a bar of service. Had Dad tried to call? Was he seeking Dwayne out at the very moment? Probably not. Same way he hadn't asked much about this trip. Honestly, it seemed to Dwayne that the moment Johnson had been assigned to accompany Dwayne on the trip, his father had checked out entirely.

Which was interesting. Because Dwayne knew without question or doubt that Governor Harris was *not* fond of Anthony Brooks.

Dwayne paused his pacing at the window. It faced the center of the resort and those three infinity pools. Rain pounded the clear blue surface, and he hoped it had erased any traces of Ant's blood.

When Ant first showed up at Thurgood Marshall, everything about him screamed *gently conspicuous consumption*. His clothes, his car, his shoes, his chain, even his haircut. Dwayne knew on sight that Ant was someone his father would call "new money." Governor Harris despised new money. "It's such a blatant waste of limited resources," he would say.

But Dwayne liked Anthony's understated-but-overpriced style. Dwayne never saw a logo on anything Ant wore, but he didn't need to: even without conspicuous labels, everything associated with Ant *looked* expensive. Which seemed to lend itself to a brand of confidence that made heads turn and crowds part and girls swoon. Ant was a guy who commanded respect. And it's not that Dwayne wanted to *emulate* the guy . . . He just wanted the world to respond to him—as himself—the way it responded to Anthony Brooks.

How Ant found out about Dwayne's previous money-making activity Dwayne would never know because Ant would never tell him. What Dwayne *did* know was that Ant had the uncanny ability to pop up at the precise right time with offers Dwayne couldn't seem to refuse.

"So, how you making your bread these days, man?" Ant asked out of the blue one random Friday in October. They were sitting in the stands at the varsity football game, watching Quatro take hit after hit after hit after hit down on the field.

"Huh?" Dwayne had heard the question, but it hadn't quite registered. Especially since his boy kept getting pummeled. "Yeesh!" he said, cringing as yet another defender broke through Thurgood's offensive line and tackled Quatro like he'd insulted the big guy's grandma. Of course the crowd went wild as the receiver caught the pass Quatro threw just before the defender plowed him down like a lone stalk of wheat in an open pasture. It seemed so unfair to Dwayne—the provider taking the heat while the receiver got the glory.

"Damn, I might need to talk to your boy, too," Ant went on. "Man's got skills without question, but it looks like he could use a little help out there. Anyway . . ."

Dwayne gulped, inexplicably nervous about what might come out of Ant's mouth next. It was impossible to explain what it felt like to be around Anthony Brooks. The guy just had this . . . aura.

Dwayne cleared his throat.

"Your games are missed, man," Ant said then.

Dwayne locked onto the fifty-yard line. Blinked. Blinked. Blinked. "Not sure I know what you mean, man." Though of course he did.

Ant just laughed. "Yeah, all right," he'd said. "How's that cash flow, though?"

Dwayne hadn't said a word to that.

"That's what I figured," Ant went on. "I know how it is, man. Trust me—"

"You know how *what* is, Anthony?" The presumption had begun to grate.

"Oh shit, he hit me with the full government name!" Ant replied. "Look, Imma shoot you straight—"

"That would be greatly appreciated, friend."

Ant had turned to Dwayne and smiled then. There was a glint in his eye that made Dwayne's pulse speed.

"We're a lot alike, man," Ant said. "High-potential young Black men with more access to resources—academic, financial, *and* human—than most will have in their entire lives."

Dwayne's eyes narrowed. "Go on."

"And yet it don't *feel* like it, right?" Ant said. "Because it's not technically *ours*. All that supposed 'access' comes with mad caveats because we gotta rely on our parents to actually *do* anything with it."

Dwayne's fingertips began to tingle.

"From what I heard, you had quite the enterprise going around here. One of your former regulars described it to me as a well-oiled machine."

At that, Dwayne smiled. He really did miss his card games, and not just because of the money. The camaraderie had also been very real. The ritual of it had felt like his own private fraternity.

"Obviously won't ask you to confirm or deny anything," Ant continued, "but I'll say this: if you got the kinda juice these guys are saying you do, I have a replacement initiative you might be interested in. Shit, I only know about your previous endeavor because a number of *your* guys have become *my* patrons."

"Sounds like you're doing pretty good on your own, man," Dwayne replied, a little stung. "What could you possibly need *me* for?"

At that, Ant draped an arm over Dwayne's shoulders and motioned to the crowd around them. "We're on your turf, champ," he said. "This market is hot, and it's time to scale . . . but I'm still too new. Can't level up around here on my own."

"Hmm."

"Look, I got the product. You got the people *and* the pull. I've been watching you, man. We could really go places together; you feel me?"

And though Dwayne didn't wind up agreeing in that moment, said "replacement initiative" eventually netted him more in the first few months of business than his card game had in more than a year. Because Ant had been right: people admired Dwayne, so they trusted him. What was more, contrary to his expectations, once word about his latest endeavor got around in the right circles, his peers seemed to respect him *more*, not less.

Did he sometimes feel guilty about what he had going on? Definitely. In fact, he felt the worst when he learned his clients referred to his product as "that F.S. flower."

As in First Son.

It shook him a little bit, knowing his activities were being connected to his dad's Very Important Job, even if only in a peripheral way. And he almost quit.

But Dwayne didn't sell high-quality cannabis because he needed money. He did it for the rush. And to feel free. He did it because he needed to be something other than the Governor's Eldest Child and Only Son.

What was he gonna do now with his business partner gone?

Dwayne dove back into his over-plush California king bed and stared up at the unnecessarily ornate ceiling above and shook his head.

Ant was *dead*.

As in deceased.

Gone.

Kaput.

Never coming back . . . And all Dwayne could think about was how he would get his supply? What the hell was *wrong* with him?

Who had he become?

He needed to get some air.

Dwayne exited his bedroom and crossed the common area in three strides, but the moment he reached for the suite's doorknob, he heard "SHIT!" shouted from inside Quatro's bedroom.

He rushed over and opened his best friend's door. "You good—"

But Quatro wasn't good. At all.

And now neither was Dwayne. The boys locked eyes, and then both looked down at the object on the floor at the foot of Quatro's bed.

"Umm . . . Quatro?"

"Yeah?"

"How did you—?"

"Don't even ask, man."

"Mmmm . . ."

Quatro kicked the thing, and it fell onto its side with a thud. The monogrammed luggage tag stared up at them: *AMB.*

It was one of Ant's suitcases.

"So, what's inside?" Dwayne asked.

"Couldn't tell you," Quatro replied. "It's locked."

MS. GLORIA PLATT

Front Desk Manager

9:26 p.m.

MS. GLORIA TYPED her little emails as fast as her perfectly manicured nails would allow. She'd been able to type ninety-seven words per minute in her heyday as a secretary. She even won a prize for it back in the day—back when those sorts of things were new. It always killed her she couldn't consistently get it to 100. Now she struggled to keep up with the ever-changing software.

But she was on a mission tonight.

She leaned forward, glancing left and right down the expansive hallway in the Dawn wing. Empty. Just how she needed it. Those kids had listened to hateful Mr. Chandler after all and stayed in their suites. They reminded her of her own grandkids in Tallahassee. Regret pooled in her stomach, like it did after she ate the sweets she knew she wasn't supposed to because of her *sugar*, and she wished she was with those knucklehead boys and adorable girls right now instead of needing to take this job in her seventies to help pay for their college educations.

But she'd soon get enough money to be able to quit and spend the rest of her life back at her mama's home on the porch basking in the sun. Making sweet tea and baking cookies for her babies. She glanced at the ceiling. The skylight was the best part of her desk. She imagined that sun shining down on her, warming her skin and leaving behind more freckles. She hummed for a second, the dream filling in over the crackle and boom of thunder and lightning.

The plinking melody of falling rain snapped her back to reality. There was no sun. Only dark clouds. Which set the tone for the week. She had work to do and fast. Paranoia made the arthritis in her hands worse. Or maybe it was the content of the emails she was frantically typing.

SUBJECT LINE: THE TRUTH FOR SALE.

She told her side of the story. Well, as much as she could so that it would be valuable. Her grandson would know what to do with it.

"Now, Ms. Gloria, what do you think you're doing?" came a voice from behind her.

As she swiveled in her chair and spotted the glint of one of Chef Starlie's sharp butcher knives, she clutched her literal pearls. Her late husband had given them to her for their thirtieth wedding anniversary. Her heart squeezed with terror, then it tripped over itself in her chest . . .

And stopped beating altogether.

As Ms. Gloria keeled over, dead at her desk, the knife wielder lowered the useless weapon.

"Huh," the voice said. "Well, I guess that's that."

The rain continued to fall as the door slid shut.

PRESENT DAY

BRADLEY JOHNSON

April 6
5:27 p.m.

BRADLEY JOHNSON HAD seen a lot in his time on the force. Enough that he knew his politics didn't always line up with his appearance. People saw him, an old white dude, a former cop, a *suit,* and they expected him to stand for certain things. But there was lots about him that was complicated.

One: he liked to hunt, but he also knew *it was the guns.*

Two: while he hoped he was one of the good ones, he knew communities needed more than cops to prosper.

Three: Prescott had more guts than he did, maybe precisely because she hadn't seen everything he had. Bodies and buildings littered with bullet holes. Car crashes where only the jaws of life could claw out survivors. Bad people doing impossibly bad things.

So when the detective walked into the hospital room and saw him, Bradley knew what he was thinking. He could see it in the way the detective's shoulders seemed to relax; the way a small knowing smile immediately crossed his lips. Bradley knew that look—body language that seemed to say: *Finally, a guy on my side. Someone who cares about what I care about. Someone who is gonna give me some answers.*

But the truth was Bradley was still trying to figure out how so much had gone so wrong so quickly—and on his watch. He was supposed to be better than this—he was supposed to be one of the best. Instead, he was still puzzling over how much he had missed, and *how*, and *why*. Had he spent so much time checking out Prescott's ass or trying to impress her with stories from his golden years that he'd fucked up? Or would this fiasco have gone down in exactly the same way no matter what? Was one of these kids a bad apple? After spending the week with them, he'd heard and seen enough to know they all had secrets. People had died, and while he'd only been sent—was only being paid—to protect one person, he couldn't help but feel like some, if not all of it, was his fault.

THE WEEK BEFORE:

WEDNESDAY

CHAPTER THIRTEEN

RIVER

4:12 a.m.

RIVER SLIPPED OUT of her room while the moon was still high.

It was that in-between time, not quite night, just barely morning, when the whole world felt like it was holding its breath, waiting for something to happen.

But River couldn't wait.

She eased the door shut behind her, careful not to make too much noise despite the fact that both Sydney's and Noelle's respective bedroom doors were closed. River had spent most of the night repainting her nails a placid shade of blue, light as its name—Aqua Atmosphere—trying to calm the way her mind kept running in circles:

Ant.

The threatening messages.

Her shady friends.

The yacht explosion.

The laptop.

That device haunted her almost as much as the last time she'd seen Ant alive, as if her brain had decided to watch last night's pool party scene on repeat. Lately, his words at the pool buzzed through her thoughts. He seemed so eager to find out who was behind MANIfest the Mess . . . though River didn't really think he was doing it for the reward.

She might have been imagining it, but it seemed as if his eyes had flitted from his phone to her, and lingered as he spoke, like he already knew the truth.

Was she just being paranoid? He'd been playing DJ that night, and she and Sydney had just walked over to the pool, catching the tail end of their conversation. Maybe he was only looking around? It felt ridiculous and impossible, but it also seemed like the perfect way for everything that happened with MANIfest and Key to come full circle.

River knew Dana Reynolds would not tolerate her daughter being investigated for anything, let alone a gossip site that caused real harm and could be connected to not one but *two* dead kids. Her mother's reputation as a fixer would not survive if her own daughter was embroiled in a scandal as wild as this one, which meant her mother's business, and River's whole life and livelihood, were at stake.

Since finding the phone felt much closer to impossible, and since it would be the device anyone investigating his death would want to locate first, River knew she had to find that damn laptop. Besides, if she erased anything in the cloud that connected her to

MANIfest the Mess on the laptop, it would disappear from the phone too.

About an hour ago, as lightning struck outside, the memory had struck her: the last place she'd seen Ant with his laptop was on the yacht. The staff had abandoned collecting debris from the yacht explosion once it started raining. There was a chance they hadn't found the laptop, which meant there was a chance she could find it instead.

She left her room with a singular plan: to search the wreckage.

And as she crept down the open-air hallway, River marveled at how foreboding the sky looked, even with the sun down. There was no sight of the moon or stars due to the opaque storm clouds, which looked heavy as a weighted blanket, and she knew the sky could open up at any minute. She needed to get to the pier, and fast. Hopefully the staff and those guards hadn't done too much digging around.

Once out from under the cover of the buildings, she slipped past the second pool—a much smaller one none of them had visited, but something about it gave her the creeps—and continued down the stairs to the beach. She took the path toward the Dawn wing, ducking behind planters and abandoned luggage carts that the hurricane winds had blown over. And then she heard footsteps. A flashlight beam swept across the path ahead of her.

Shit.

She froze. There was nowhere to hide.

Stay still.

The beam got closer. The footsteps louder.

River couldn't breathe—

"Callum, what are you doing, man?"

The light shifted away from the path as Callum (River guessed) turned toward the sound of the voice that had spoken to him.

"Thought I saw something creeping around on the beach."

"We don't got time for that shit, man. Prolly a sea turtle. Come on."

Callum cursed under his breath and turned around.

River exhaled slowly and forced herself to keep going.

Once she made it inside Dawn wing, she spotted a housekeeping cart parked just outside a supply closet. Which was perfect. She swiped a pair of latex gloves from a box on the top of the cart and stuffed them into her pocket before easing back outside.

River could smell the rain coming. As she scrambled down the final stretch of sand to the pier, she could see that the storm had truly left its mark everywhere—palm trees uprooted, debris scattered across the beach, lounge chairs overturned and half buried in sand.

But that damage was nothing compared to the wreckage of Anthony's dad's yacht.

Her sneakers sank into the wet sand as she approached the pier, carefully stepping around splintered wood, twisted metal, and shattered glass. What was left of the yacht lay in ruins, half-sunken, still smoldering, ribbons of smoke curling into the early morning air. The ocean had spit out most of it, leaving a constellation of tattered objects across the shoreline and beneath the pier's legs.

River pulled on the gloves she'd swiped from the housekeeping cart, and tugged them snugly over her fingers, thankful they did the triple duty of protecting her skin, keeping her hands from getting dirty, and preventing fingerprints.

Keep your hands clean even when you're getting them dirty, her mom would say.

As she put a hand out to steady herself while stepping into the yacht's charred shell, River randomly remembered the look on Quatro's face when she'd taught him about gloves and bleach. How adorably stunned he'd looked as she talked about wiping down surfaces and the way his mouth fell open when she mentioned never leaving DNA behind. This was back when they . . .

She swallowed and shook the thought away. She had a laptop to find.

River crouched low and picked through the debris. Every now and then, the wind would shift, sending the chemical scents of fuel and burned fiberglass mixed with salt water straight into her nose. She kept her hands steady as she flipped over a jagged piece of wood. It looked like part of the deck, where she and her friends had been drinking and pretending not to think about Key.

No laptop there.

She pushed aside broken glass, reached beneath a charred railing, dug through a pile of scorched seat cushions. Every time her fingers found something solid, her breath caught.

But it was never the laptop.

The longer she went without finding it, the more frantically she searched, shoving pieces of wreckage out of her way and no longer bothering to be quiet. She had to find that laptop. Or at least evidence that it had been destroyed. A piece of ash-covered chrome, a handful of keyboard letters . . .

She froze.

A few feet in front of her, wedged between two large pieces of wreckage . . . it wasn't the laptop.

But a travel case.

The blast and the storm had already done most of the work: the metal casing was dented and scorched, and the lock barely held on. She knew the laptop wouldn't be inside because the safe wasn't big enough. But still . . . She tugged at the lock. With a snap, the latch broke free and the lid creaked open.

Inside? Drugs, cash, a phone.

And a bracelet.

River pulled it out. And stopped breathing.

It looked just like one Keisha never took off.

Why the hell is Key's bracelet in Anthony's safe?

Anthony had started at their school after everything that happened with Keisha. After the tragedy, the whispers, the memorials, the investigation, the toxicology reports. After the whole thing had been ruled an accident and everyone had started pretending to move on. As far as River knew, Ant only knew of Key through secondhand stories of the Six's so-called ringleader. Had he gotten this bracelet from Noelle? And even if he had, why would he keep it?

River stared at it. It was the first time she'd let herself think about Key in a year.

In an instant she was back there. Her thoughts plunged into the deep as though pulled by an undertow.

Down into the night after the gala.

The indoor pool glowed neon blue in the dark. It was closed to hotel guests, but the Six didn't dare turn the lights on. The last thing they needed was to get caught.

But River didn't feel right.

It wasn't even the fact that they'd snuck in against all hotel protocol using a key Noelle had swiped from her dad's restaurant—which was connected to the hotel. Nor was it the plethora of contraband—liquor, pre-rolls, edibles—they had with them. She just . . . felt off in her body. The music they were listening to sounded way too loud—she could swear the bass was vibrating through her like a second heartbeat—and the blended aroma of chlorine and weed was making River's stomach churn.

Key sprawled across a lounge chair, laughing way too hard at something that wasn't actually funny. Her silver charm bracelet glinted in the soft overhead light.

She was the furthest gone of them all. To the point that River wondered if she'd had something the rest of them hadn't. She moved and spoke as though in some sort of euphoric haze the rest of the group didn't have access to. River knew she wasn't the only one who'd noticed because Dwayne kept cutting his eyes to Key as though watching over her.

They'd both told her to slow down, Dwayne and River had. "Key, please slow down," River said when Keisha reached for her fourth tequila shot.

The response had cut River (though she would never admit it): "Jesus, Riv, why are you *always* so uptight? Loosen up and have some goddamn fun for once in your life!"

"It's not even about that—"

"So what's it about?" Key put a joint to her lips and lit it. "Certainly can't be about getting in 'trouble.' Doesn't Mommy get all sorts of bad people out of terrible things without a scratch? You'll be fine."

The party kept going, and Key kept going too.

More drinks.

More drugs.

More dancing.

More laughing.

More. More. More.

River desperately wanted to leave but knew she couldn't. That wasn't how the Six did things. It was one for all and all for one. If one was in some shit (usually Key), they all were.

She was kind of getting sick of it, River was. Being dragged into or held to things she didn't want to do simply because Key had made a decision for them all. It'd been Key's idea to pull this little sneak-off-to-the-closed-and-therefore-off-limits-pool stunt.

River cut her eyes to Quintin. He was totally checked out, his girlfriend's antics so commonplace to him, he couldn't be bothered to care. River wondered what Key had on him to make him stick around.

River hated the way Key had overtaken MANIfest the Mess, pushing her to post more and more scandalous things. It made what River was doing feel less and less harmless with each passing day. Especially with the rumors she was hearing about her latest target—a girl who, according to Key, "let her little crush get out of control and flirted with Quatro." Key had poked around for dirt and come up with something involving a youth pastor. And in typical Key fashion, when River initially refused to use the intel—it was a hair too slippery for River's liking—Key threatened to expose River as the site's owner.

The only time River hated herself more than when she pushed *post* was when she heard that the girl's absence from school after the post went live had more to do with a bottle of swallowed pills than with her embarrassment.

Of course, Key had just shrugged. "I mean, she kinda earned it."

Key turned the music up louder.

"Keisha, you really gotta chill," Dwayne said, looking around. "We *cannot* get caught in here with all this shit."

"Yeah, yeah, yeah. I'm sure Daddy would be sooooo upset." Key waved away his concern.

"God, why is she being like this?" Sydney had appeared at River's side.

"You mean other than making other people feel bad being her entire personality at this point?" River replied. She stared out over the eerily still water.

"I mean, touché." Sydney peeked in Keisha's direction. She had her eyes closed and was bopping along to the music (that, yes, was far too loud). "Doesn't it seem a little . . . intensified, though?"

Dwayne waved Sydney over, and they disappeared into the changing rooms, probably to make out.

"Quatro, I need another driiiiiiink!" Keisha called out then.

"No, the hell you don't," came Quintin's reply.

"Whatever, I'll get it myself."

As Key stood shakily, Noelle left the pool area, looking mildly frantic.

River glanced at Quintin like *get your girl*. "You drank it all."

"Sit down, you can barely walk. I'll go get more." Quintin stalked into the hall, clearly pissed and unable to resist Key's demands. River's eyes followed him.

Suddenly, they were alone together, and Key watched her every move. "You think I don't see that you want him, Riv?"

The next stretch of time was a black hole in River's memory (she'd had fewer intoxicants than Keisha, but still too much). One minute she was stepping toward Key, and the next she was in the hallway hearing someone screaming.

Noelle.

Screaming Keisha's name.

Keisha who was . . . no longer with them.

But it wasn't just Keisha's death that haunted River. It was what came right after. They had to move fast. Wipe down surfaces, toss out bottles, scrub away every single trace of what had happened. Everyone did their part: followed her instructions to a T, every move straight from Dana Reynolds's playbook.

Tampering with a crime scene was illegal, but as her mom would say, "Legality only matters if you get caught." By the time the cops arrived, it looked like nothing more than a hangout gone horribly wrong.

They'd been so, so careful.

But then Noelle had blabbed to that damn reporter.

And despite the fact that the article hadn't dropped before they'd made their way to Ant's yacht—River had been checking religiously—now, staring at Keisha's bracelet, something cold and sharp clawed at River's insides.

What if she and Quintin had missed something? What if the cops found evidence that led back to them? All it would take was one loose end. One thing they didn't clean up well enough.

One mistake.

River's stomach churned. She stuffed the bracelet, the drugs, the cash, and the phone back in the travel case and snapped the lid shut like that would somehow contain the mess. Which of course, it didn't.

She glanced around. There wasn't another soul in sight.

Once again, she had to move, and leaving this safe wasn't an option. It held too much evidence, and evidence was dangerous in the wrong hands.

Control the narrative or the narrative will control you.

Control the evidence or the evidence will control you.

The rain forced her to ditch the computer mission. River hoisted the safe into her arms and made her way out of the metal shell, across the sand, and back toward the resort. She did her best to move just as quickly as she had come, dodging security guards, ducking behind items big enough to hide her and her quarry, and staying on the beach path back to the Sunset wing and her room.

As she entered the third-floor hallway, she froze. Prescott had found her post. River gulped, her anxious brain spinning the lies she'd need to tell about why she was up so early and why she was carrying a strange case in her arms. Sweat streamed down her entire body and not even the warning wind of the approaching storm could cool her. She had to think fast. She had to get past Prescott without raising any alarms and without inspiring any questions. She had to get this thing hidden in her room.

River scanned the ground. She spotted a broken shutter frame and picked it up, chucking it down to the second floor. The noise boomed. She watched Prescott tromp toward the sound, signaling for River to run.

She darted back down to the second floor and ran as fast as she could to the opposite side of the hallway and the other set of staircases. She leaped up them three at a time and entered the third floor from the other side. Prescott was nowhere to be seen. She ran like Quatro did on the field and shot inside her room just as the guard reentered the hall.

Sydney's and Noelle's bedroom doors were still shut. Good.

River closed the front door behind her as quietly as possible and crossed the room to the common-room closet. Neither of the other girls had even opened it. Her dirty laundry was piled up inside, right next to the neatly folded towels. The housekeeper had stocked them up after River had puked her guts out the other night, like the woman expected her to need them again.

Right now, River would rather have a hangover than this mess. Her chest heaved from all the running and all the worry.

She placed the travel case on top of the safe the resort supplied. Then she straightened and shut the closet door.

She tried to take a few calming breaths, but they didn't work.

She was panicking.

She had to get out of the room—get away from the bracelet and what it could mean.

She turned away from the closet and saw that the sun was rising. She'd go for a run. It would help clear her head and calm her down. She wished she could go see Quintin. She wished she could call her mother. She wished she was anywhere except stuck on this island with too many questions and no answers at all.

CHAPTER FOURTEEN

SYDNEY

8:58 a.m.

IN ANOTHER LIFE, what she and Dwayne would be doing alone in his room on his bed would be different. In that life—better and less complicated than this one—they'd start off by flirting. She'd be shy and awkward, but not because she lacked experience. She'd had two long-ish term boyfriends before, and she wasn't a virgin even though her mother didn't—couldn't—know that. The awkwardness would be because she'd never liked anyone the way she liked Dwayne.

With other guys she wasn't nervous or self-conscious. There was no need to be. She never let them see or date the real her, just the too-good-for-you version of herself she'd cultivated over the years. At first, it'd been fun to see herself through their eyes. It was fun to be adored. Those guys treated her like they couldn't believe their luck, like they'd won something expensive they'd always wanted but didn't quite deserve. They didn't really love her. Hard experience taught her that most people weren't to be trusted. So many of them wanted access to her mother's power. Or to claim her body like it was a prize.

But she'd known Dwayne basically her whole life. He wasn't trying to get power or fame. If anything, he wanted less of both.

In that other, better life, Dwayne would be awkward, too, but maybe a little more confident. He'd do the thing where he'd tease her about some habit of hers: the way she fiddled with the beads in her locs when she got nervous or the way she got an incurable case of the hiccups when she giggled too much. Then he'd move closer to her. The bed would shift, and she'd place a steadying hand between them on the mattress. He'd tangle his fingers into hers. She'd look up into his bright black eyes and then down at his soft, waiting lips. And when he said, "Syd," she'd hear the desire in his voice that matched her own.

"Sydney," Dwayne said again. "You with me?"

Sydney straightened. They were not living in a better, less complicated life. They were living in this one. And the thing she and Dwayne were doing alone in his room on his bed was trying to figure out a way off this godforsaken island.

She looked back down at the tourist map he'd gotten from the front desk display. The resort was on the windward side of the small island, then the center filled with a mangrove forest and one road connecting Kuzimu to Vista Village on the leeward side. She spotted the clinic, shops, and security center, and the small port. If they could get there, then she could hopefully reach her parents and have them send a boat for her from Key West. What she and

Dwayne needed to do was figure out a way to get themselves from here to there.

Dwayne tapped the tiny village with his finger. "Let's hope this port is okay. And for sure they're not under any kind of lockdown, unless they got dead bodies turning up everywhere too."

Sydney frowned at him. He didn't usually make jokes like that.

"Sorry." He swiped his hand down his face. "This is some crazy shit."

"We'll get through this," she said with more confidence than she felt. He was always trying to make her feel better. It was only right that she returned the favor.

He gave her a half smile that said he understood what she was doing and appreciated it.

She looked back down at the map. The overwhelming urge to confess overtook her. He deserved to know the truth. She opened her mouth but closed it again.

"What?" he asked.

But she was too afraid of losing him to do it. Instead, she said, "You remember that book *Just Mercy* from Mr. Nelson's class?"

"The Bryan Stevenson one? What about it?" he asked.

"There's that part when he says that people are better than the worst thing they've ever done. You think that's true?"

Dwayne tilted his head back against the headboard and closed his eyes. For a long time, he didn't say anything. Sydney looked over at the window. Late-morning sun washed bands of pale yellow light through the blinds. A temporary break in the rain . . . and this nightmare. But seeing the sun felt like a tease along with the fact that she could hear birds and wind rustling through leaves. It was hard to believe that the rest of the world carried on normally even when you felt like it was upside down. It didn't bring cell service or a rescue. No one in the outside world knew what was happening to them.

Maybe Dwayne's closed eyes made her brave, but she shifted closer to him and put her head on his shoulder. As always, he smelled beautiful—earthy and vaguely floral.

"Imma be honest with you, Sydney. I don't know," he said. "Some people do some repugnant shit." He looked down at her. "One thing I'm sure of, though: I'd forgive you anything."

She met his eyes and felt caught, but in a good way, like he'd keep her safe. It was time to be brave. She decided to trust that he meant it when he said he'd forgive her anything. She'd explain what her mom had coerced her to do, and about Ant. She'd tell him how much she regretted it, and how she'd never do something like that again.

She'd tell him how she felt about him.

"Dwayne—" she said.

That's as far as she got before the pounding on the door began.

"Dwayne! Open up!" a voice yelled. "It's River. Is Syd in there with you? I need to talk to her."

Dwayne sprang from the bed and rushed to the door. River came in like a storm, drenched in sweat, like she'd been running for her life.

She pushed past him, eyes on Sydney. "I need to talk to you . . . alone."

Sydney nodded and mouthed "I'm sorry" to Dwayne.

"I'll be right here," he said.

Outside in the hallway, River was frantic in a way that she rarely ever was. River usually had every hair in her neat braids in place; every button on her shirts fastened up to her neck, every skirt she wore wrinkle-free, and shoes that were always spotless. And her mood was usually as buttoned up as her appearance. One of the things Sydney loved most about her was the way she kept her cool when everybody else lost their minds.

But right now, River's eyes were wild, her hair was frizzing around her face like a mane, and her clothes were damp and dirty, like she'd been playing in mud on purpose.

"What happened to you?" Sydney asked.

"I went on a run," River replied, but she was on the verge of hyperventilating, not breathing easy, like someone who had just gone jogging.

Sydney clasped River's hand. "Hey, breathe with me." She sucked in a long breath and locked eyes with River until she did the same. Then she let her eyes cut toward Prescott as a reminder to River to keep her mouth shut about whatever this was because they didn't need the security guard asking questions—they both knew Prescott's lips were basically glued to Sydney's mother's ear.

"Now breathe out through your mouth." Again she demonstrated and waited for River to do it.

It was a few more breaths before River was calm enough to talk. "I found something," she said, voice shaking.

Sydney stepped closer. "What is it?"

River shook her head, checked left and right down the hallway. "Not here." She took off. Every time she got to a corner, she slowed to a walk in case someone was around the bend. She didn't want to raise any suspicions. Any *more* suspicions.

They raced down the hall, hitting the staircase. Prescott tailed them, shouting about slowing down, but that didn't deter either of them.

They reached the door to their room. River's hand shook so hard Sydney had to take her key card and swipe them inside. Sydney apologized to Prescott before closing the door. She ushered River over to the bed and sat beside her. "Tell me what's going on."

River wrapped her arms around her waist. "This morning I went out to the dock. To the boat."

"Why?" Sydney couldn't help the shock in her voice. "What if someone saw you?"

This kind of carelessness wasn't like her at all. Which meant that River was keeping secrets of her own.

"Just listen," River said. "I found a travel case. I think it was Ant's." She clenched and unclenched her hands. "It was all messed up, but there was some stuff inside."

"Like what?"

"Drugs, some cash, a burner phone." She twisted her hands together. "And a bracelet that looks just like Key's."

The small hairs at the back of Sydney's neck tingled. "Why would he have that?"

River shook her head. "That's what I want to know."

Sydney understood that from River's point of view, the bracelet was the most significant thing she'd found. And it *was* important. It didn't make any kind of sense for Ant to have a bracelet of a dead girl he didn't even know.

But it was the burner phone that Sydney was most interested in. What if *that* phone was the one she really needed? Burner phone for burner activities, right? She knew she wasn't making complete sense. There was still the matter of the nasty texts she'd sent to Ant. Those were probably on his main phone, the one in her safe. But what if this burner phone had all the opposition research on Dwayne? If she could get on there, she could erase it, could erase anything connecting it to her and her mom. Without that evidence, her mean texts to Ant couldn't prove anything, right?

She needed to see that phone. Now.

"Where'd you put the stuff?" she asked River.

"In the closet," she said. "On top of the safe."

Sydney frowned at her. "*Inside* the safe, you mean?"

River shook her head. "No, I—"

Sydney bolted over to the closet and flung open the door. River's and Sydney's clothes were crumpled into a pile in the back corner. There was nothing else in the closet. The travel case was gone. From behind her, River gasped. She pushed past Sydney. "I left it right there."

The part of Sydney that had been best friends with River for most of her life wanted to comfort her. But another part, the part desperate to save her own skin, and her mother, and any chance of a relationship with Dwayne was angry.

River wrung her hands together. "I locked our room! I didn't think—"

Sydney exploded. "You didn't think at all! How could you just leave it sitting there? Your mom would never ever do something so stupid!"

Tears brimmed in her eyes. Sydney had never spoken to her like this before, not in the thirteen years she'd known her.

"Why would Ant have a bracelet that was Keisha's?" River asked.

Sydney paced in circles. "We'll never know now that everything's gone."

River dropped her head into her hands and sobbed.

Sydney knew she'd gone too far. River's greatest insecurity was that she'd never be able to live up to her mother's achievements and expectations. And Sydney had pressed her finger on that bruise.

Sydney watched River cry. She knew she should apologize. She should put her arms around River and comfort her. But something inside her clenched and wouldn't release. She watched her friend fall apart for a few seconds more.

Then she left, letting the door slam behind her. The sound reverberated like the thunderclaps filling the rapidly darkening skies. Halfway down the hall, it occurred to Sydney that she was more like her mother than she thought she was.

CHAPTER FIFTEEN

NOELLE

11:21 a.m.

SYDNEY'S LOCS WERE the first things Noelle noticed about her when they were six years old. Now they were long and jet black, with cowrie shells dangling from them at different points along their length. They teased onlookers, making you want to touch them, run your fingers over each and every perfect one.

Every time Noelle saw Sydney, she was reminded of when she'd first found a shell like the ones in Sydney's hair. She'd been on a different beach, Trunk Bay on the island of St. John in the US Virgin Islands, with her family. Noelle's aunt had smiled as she explained what the shells meant in Mali, where she was from: wealth, protection, and power. Noelle knew the shells were also used as currency in Mali and other parts of the world—that they could be traded for services and goods—and it made her wonder if Sydney knew she was, quite literally, wearing money (the way other people wore flowers) in her hair.

Sydney, who was even richer than Noelle (if she was in an admitting mood), and who wielded her beauty like a weapon, like Key used to, didn't need the shells to possess what they represented. She already had it all. She had everything Noelle had lost. And it was strange for Noelle to be watching her, feeling like her whole life was on the line and everything she'd worked so hard for might be at risk because Sydney, who already had everything, wanted even more.

Noelle used to be bad at lying until she'd met Key. She'd watched her dead best friend face any obstacle that might stop her from reaching a goal, transforming her voice and her expression into a new version of herself, one that would get exactly what she wanted. Noelle pretended to be her as she stepped out of her hiding spot once Sydney disappeared inside their suite.

"Prescott," Noelle said, smiling as she approached her. "The general manager was looking for you. He asked that if I saw you, I'd tell you to come to his office right away."

Prescott frowned. "Did he say what it was about?"

Noelle shook her head and shrugged. "Nope, which is what made me think it must be important."

Prescott looked at her watch, and then lifted her hand as if to knock. Noelle stopped her. "I'm going in there, so I can let her know you'll be right back."

The security guard nodded. "That would be great, Miss Clarke. Thank you." It was still weird that the security guards called them all miss and mister, like they were adults. "No problem," Noelle replied.

She waited until Prescott disappeared down the stairs to press her ear against the door. It sounded like Sydney was yelling and River was . . . crying? Then it sounded like one of them was heading in her direction.

Noelle raced to the end of the hall and tucked herself away behind a column as best she could in the open-air breezeway. She saw Sydney exit the room. "Prescott," she called out, but as soon as she realized she was free of her detail, she stormed down the hall in the opposite direction.

Noelle followed her, keeping a safe distance between them. There was only one place Sydney could be headed: Dwayne and Quatro's room.

If something had been happening between Ant and Sydney, there would've been signs. Noelle prided herself on noticing every tiny detail about the people around her. Noelle's mother always said, "Details are what make a person. Be sure to always pay attention!" But maybe she'd missed something. That wouldn't happen again. She waited until she couldn't hear the clacking of the shells in Sydney's hair before she followed her, creeping down the same hallway, and then up the stairs to the fourth floor, hoping the ocean's crashing waves and the storm winds would hide the sound of her footsteps.

Noelle wasn't sure what her goal should be with this little mission, or even what she was looking for; she just had a feeling in her gut that she couldn't ignore; that her ex-friends would take the first opportunity to screw her over if they could, and they were all plotting something.

She heard a door open, a deep voice she recognized as Dwayne's mumbling something she couldn't hear, and then the door closing. Noelle had assumed Johnson would be posted up in front of Dwayne's door, but surprisingly he wasn't.

She tiptoed farther down the hall and pressed her ear against Quatro and Dwayne's door this time. She could hear Sydney and

Dwayne talking in hushed, rushed voices about getting off the island, and Noelle couldn't come up with a reason they'd plan an escape that didn't include everyone except one: guilt. If Sydney was somehow involved with what happened to Ant, getting off the island as quickly as possible would definitely be her priority. And Dwayne would want it too—to protect her. It made perfect sense. Noelle listened harder when things went quiet.

The hallways were dead silent since the resort was so deserted, so she even tried to breathe quietly, afraid of being overheard by Sydney and Dwayne. Before she could hear more, she heard footsteps—it had to be Johnson returning to his post.

She looked around for somewhere to hide, heart racing, and saw an emergency-exit stairwell about ten feet away. She ran to the door, which was emblazoned with a sign that warned an alarm would sound if opened. With the power out, she figured it wouldn't, but she still held her breath as she turned the knob. The door eased open soundlessly and she slipped through it, leaving it cracked so she could still hear anything that happened in the hallway. She inhaled and exhaled through her nose, willing her heart to slow down.

What had Sydney been yelling about? And why had River been crying? And though Noelle knew they all wanted to get off this godforsaken island, Sydney seemed especially desperate and was the only one who seemed to be making actual plans to escape. Could it be about Ant? The storm? Or maybe it was all too much when combined with the anniversary of what had happened to Key.

Noelle jammed her eyes shut, not wanting to summon images of Keisha's face or any moment the night she died.

"You good?"

She jumped.

The deep, melancholic voice pulled Noelle out of her memories. She hadn't even heard Dwayne approaching, but now here he was, standing right in front of her. She opened the door further and saw Johnson lurking just a few feet behind him.

"Yeah, yeah," she said, blinking. "Jesus. Where the hell did you come from?"

He looked up and then down the hall. "My room is right over there. What are you doing just standing out here like this? You know there's all this shady shit going down on this resort. It's not safe."

"Yeah," Noelle heard herself say again, stupidly. "Yeah, no. I know you're right. I was, um, looking for River or Sydney. I went for a walk, just to get some air and locked myself out of the room."

Dwayne frowned, like he didn't believe her. "Your room isn't even on this floor."

"No, I know. I thought both of them might be up here."

He shoved his hands in his pockets, and his eyes softened the tiniest bit. "Sydney's in my room, but I don't know where River went."

Noelle nodded, then cleared her throat the way Key did before she prepared to charm someone to get them to answer her questions or give her what she wanted. "Are *you* good?" she asked him, making sure to widen her eyes the way Key always told her to in order to look pitiful and vulnerable.

Dwayne looked at the floor and rubbed the back of his neck. "Not really," he said. "I wanna get the hell out of here."

When he looked back up at Noelle, his eyes were hard again,

like he was worried he'd said too much. "You should probably get back to your room. River's likely in there. I don't think anyone should be wandering around this place alone."

"So why are you?" Noelle asked.

Dwayne let out a dark laugh. He pointed behind him to Johnson, who was surveying the hall.

"I'm not." He turned and headed back in the direction of his room. "Watch yourself, Noelle," he said over his shoulder. Which sounded vaguely like a threat. "You fucked everybody when you spoke to that reporter. We won't forget that."

The hairs on Noelle's arms stood on end.

Noelle decided to take Dwayne's advice and head back to her room, but on the way, she bumped straight into a flustered Prescott and the half-baked lie she'd told earlier.

"I couldn't find the general manager anywhere," Prescott said, her cheeks flushed and sweaty. "You sure he was looking for me?"

"I'm pretty sure," Noelle said, looking down at her phone just so she didn't have to make eye contact with her. "Did you check in the Dawn wing?"

"Why don't we head back over there together, Miss Clarke?" she said, like she knew she'd be catching Noelle in a lie. "Sydney is in Dwayne's room, according to Johnson, so I have a few minutes."

Noelle knew she couldn't say no, because then she would be admitting her deception. "Sure!" she chirped, even though her stomach churned.

At least I'm not alone, Noelle thought as she and the security guard began the walk from Sunset to Dawn. They were quiet as they walked, only the occasional static from Prescott's two-way radio piercing the silence.

They heard the voices as soon as they got close to the building. Shouting, cursing, pleading. Prescott immediately stepped in front of Noelle, as if to protect her, but they both continued to creep forward.

Through the glass doors of the Dawn wing, Noelle could see that the general manager had the concierge pressed against the wall. The concierge—a squat Black man with kind eyes in a collared shirt, khakis, and boat shoes—was much shorter than the general manager, who towered over him, gesticulating wildly in his face.

"I don't think we should go any closer," Prescott said. "Let's head back to Sunset."

But Noelle hated injustice about as much as she hated an overcooked egg.

"Shouldn't we do something?" she asked Prescott. "What if he hurts him?"

"Shhhhh! Keep your voice down," Prescott chided in a harsh whisper.

But her warning came too late, and Noelle's voice must have carried more than she thought.

The general manager turned—still red-faced and furious—and looked right at her.

PATRICK JAMES "P.J." MORGAN

Head of Guest Services, Concierge Extraordinaire

3:54 p.m.

PATRICK JAMES MORGAN knew he'd written his death sentence when he'd agreed to come work this week. He'd known it was the end. He'd sold his soul for a few extra dollars. That's why, in the hospitality suite where his office was, he kissed the cross around his neck as he scribbled away at his desk. He didn't have enough to leave behind in a will, but he could write down his confession, his sins, all the same.

He'd done all the worst ones: been proud and greedy, jealous and lazy. But this list would include other vices too. He wanted to be free of his wrongdoings, and while there was no church on this island, time was running out. He glanced at his boat shoes where they sat by the door. They had been a gift from Mr. Brooks, instead of the bonus he'd asked for. But none of that mattered now. He turned his attention back to the notebook in front of him.

The paper would be his confessional. The pen his priest.

Bless me, Father, for I have sinned.

I have lied.

I have stolen.

I have not been generous of heart.

I have gossiped and planned to do harm.

I have done harm.

I have been afraid and have wished evil upon those that have made me afraid.

I have borrowed and never repaid my debts.

I have not prayed, and when I should have come to the Lord or the Church for help, I went to people. Bad people.

When he heard the hidden staff door slide open, he knew he was getting what he deserved. He slid the paper into the desk, hiding it inside his Bible. When the real cops arrived, they'd find it, probably soaked with his blood, but it would all be there.

He slowly made the sign of the cross with his fingers, touching his forehead, his chest, and both shoulders. He kissed his cross necklace one final time.

He didn't even flinch when he felt the knife at his back. He didn't fight as the perpetrator pulled it out and eased it back in, like he was cutting bread for communion. His blood spilled like wine.

CHAPTER SIXTEEN

QUATRO

7:26 p.m.

THE KNOCK ON the door scared the shit out of Quatro. He was alone in the room when it came; where Dwayne had gone off to, Quatro didn't know. Nor did he really care. It was nice having the room to himself for a minute.

He'd been in the same spot for hours. Sprawled across the bed on his back, staring up at the ceiling as if all he needed to do was find the right constellations of plaster swoops and bumps to get the answers he needed. He'd avoided drinking all day—largely because of how hungover he'd been when he woke up that morning, but whatever. He was sober and still. He needed his brain to work, to puzzle this whole thing out.

So when the knock came, it almost shook him out of his skin.

He crept over to the door and attempted to look through the peephole. Of course, the thing was filthy, and he couldn't see much more than nondescript blotches of color. There'd been no housekeeping since they'd arrived, and the storm had blown dirt and sand everywhere, leaving the walls, doors, and hallways a mess.

He sighed and shook his head. How this spring break was actively making itself *worse* than the last one was beyond him.

Another knock. More urgent this time.

Quiet as he could, he hooked the chain hanging on the doorframe into the slot screwed to the back of the door. If nothing else, it would create a minor barrier to entry . . . you know, just in case the person outside his room happened to be the same one who'd murdered Ant. And they were coming for him next.

More knocking. He turned the handle and pulled the door open just enough to see who was there. River stood, fist frozen in midair like she was giving a Black Power salute.

Their eyes met. He saw the look of desperation in hers.

"Oh, shit," he said. "One sec, okay?" He pushed the door closed to remove the chain, snatched it open, wrapped an arm around her waist to pull her inside, then shut the door again before turning the deadbolt *and* putting the chain back. The idea of Dwayne waltzing in while he was alone with River—who, on sight, made him feel like football spirals were being thrown back and forth in his stomach—made him more panicky than the idea of someone finding out why his game had improved so drastically last season.

Without really thinking about it, he took her soft hand and led her into his bedroom to sit at the foot of his bed. "Your eyes are red," he said. "You been crying? What's wrong?"

She looked away from him and pulled her hand back. "I really just wanna go home," she said. "This place is . . . I need to get off this island and as far away from this *resort* and everything attached to it as soon as possible."

Quatro nodded. There was something she wasn't telling him. He could feel it. Knew it as surely as he knew her favorite color (lavender) and greatest fear (failure).

"I hear you," he replied, deciding not to pry. There was a part of him that was afraid to know. He couldn't stand the sadness in her eyes and wanted to kiss her, to make it go away, to make them both feel better, to transport them away from this hellhole.

"Do you think Ant knew Key?" River asked, seemingly out of nowhere.

"Huh?" Quatro turned to look at her. (There was definitely something she wasn't telling him.) "What would make you say that?"

She looked down at her hands in her lap and shrugged. Her eyelashes were a mile long. "I dunno," she said. "Sometimes I just feel like she's haunting us? The fact that he was found dead on *her* death anniversary is too weird."

"And you think that means they knew each other?" He wasn't following her logic, but he didn't want to shut her down when she was this anxious.

"Not necessarily, I just . . ." She shook her head as though to clear it. "I have no idea what I'm talking about. Ant was just sorta different, wasn't he? He had this *way* about him. Like, how are we even all here right now, Quintin? How'd he even get *in* the Six? The more I think about him being gone, the more I realize how little I actually knew him . . . and here I am on his dad's private island? Which I got to by way of a yacht that's since been blown up?"

When she put it like that . . .

"None of this seems real, is what I guess I'm saying."

"Ant had something on me," Quatro admitted. Why he was telling her, he didn't know, but having it out there (though he didn't plan to tell her his *whole* secret) was more of a relief than he expected.

"Really?" She looked up into his eyes. "What was it?"

He shook his head. "Can't tell you that part."

She laughed, and the sound of it hit Quatro's ears like wind chimes.

Yeah, Quatro really needed to get off this island. He wanted to kiss her. But a(nother) kid had *died*. Exactly a year after his . . . He shook his head.

"Not to be morbid, but he's dead now, right? So whatever he had on you died with him." She bit her bottom lip. "Didn't it?"

Quatro hadn't considered this. In a way, she was right. Even if those cops did get into Ant's suitcase, it's not like what he'd brought for Quatro would have Quatro's name on it.

But getting caught wasn't really the problem in Quatro's case. His issue was that—well, he still *needed* the supplements. If he stopped taking them now, there would be a noticeable change in his athletic performance once training started after spring break. And his dad tracked him: he'd notice because his trainer would document it in their workout reports, and Dad would comment on it and ask a million questions about it.

Yes, with Ant gone, Quatro would have to wean off: he didn't know of any other way to get more, and he wasn't about to get caught looking for it. Ant had made it easy. But quitting cold turkey . . . Yeah, nah. He couldn't do that. He'd read enough about these steroids to know that the body crash was potentially as harmful as using them.

He had to get those pills.

Which meant getting the suitcase key. Which meant checking Ant's pockets. Which meant contact with Ant's dead body.

But it was what it was, was it not?

"You okay over there?" River said, cutting into Quatro's thoughts.

"Huh?"

"You didn't answer my question."

"Oh," Quatro replied. "Sorry. Got a little lost in thought."

"Okay, well, don't you think—"

"Hey, listen." Quatro stared into her eyes, trying to show as much confidence and self-assuredness as he could. "There's something I gotta run and do real quick. You can totally stay in here if you feel safer—bed's all yours if you want to lie down or something—just know Dwayne could be back any minute, so keep my room door closed."

"I'm coming with you," she said.

"What? No, River." He shook his head. "This isn't . . . Nah. You can't—"

"Quintin, please," she pleaded. "I can't be alone right now. I'm scared. Please don't leave me by myself. My head's a mess."

Quatro put his head in his hands. There was no way he could let her in on her what he was doing because there was no way he could tell her why. And she would definitely ask why.

On the other hand, though, it wouldn't be a bad idea to have a lookout. Especially one like River, who was quick and smart and pretty. Who had been trained by a mother who did this sort of thing. And it wasn't like they hadn't worked together on something just as terrible before. He drummed his fingers on his leg, not wanting to think about the two of them cleaning up the mess of Key's death. The smell of bleach would haunt him forever.

He lifted her chin so she could see directly into his eyes. The seriousness. The intensity. Just like that night a year ago when they'd stood beside Key's body and made a terrible decision they could never take back.

"You can't ask any questions," he said. "That's the stipulation: no matter where we're going or what I ask you to do, you can't ask any questions."

She nodded. He felt the memory of Key and what they'd done slide and stretch into the silence between them, a twisted buried treasure wrenching itself from the depths of a dark ocean and resurfacing in the light.

"Understood." She stood up, dusted off the front of her shorts-bodysuit thing, and extended a hand to help Quatro to his feet (not that he needed the assistance). "River Reynolds, reporting for duty." And she gave him a salute.

He took in her face, so eager to help him. So willing to trust.

His eyes drifted to her lips. He'd always loved the look of River's lips, the way they curved into a heart shape. A perfect, kissable mouth.

They needed to move fast before he did something stupid. He planted the softest kiss on her forehead. Just like he had the night they'd cleaned up the indoor pool area after Key's accident. They were back doing something they shouldn't once again. Maybe she was his twin flame. Always with him at the scene of every crime and when he did the worst things.

"Let's go," he said, pulling her toward the exit.

They had one very close call: after running into precisely zero people for the bulk of the journey from the Sunset wing to the Dawn wing, as they crept down the final stretch, they heard an exchange of shouts from the restaurant—which they had to pass through to get to the kitchen. They barely managed to slip into what turned out to be a janitorial closet (very small and dimly lit by a high, rectangular window at the back) before the shouters stepped into the hallway . . . still shouting.

"Who do you think that is?" River whispered. The volume of the voices was steady—the people involved in the argument must've been standing still now—and they sounded masculine, but it was impossible to make out what either person was saying.

Quatro looked down to find River gazing at him expectantly. Like whatever he said, she would trust implicitly. Which he knew wasn't like her at all. River Reynolds was nothing if not (healthily) skeptical. Seeing her face so open made Quatro feel a collision of sensations and emotions so intense, he got a little dizzy.

There was a loud *thud* outside the door, and River gasped and threw her arms around Quatro's waist as she buried her face in his chest.

Man, did it feel amazing to be her strength.

They stayed like that, all wrapped up, as the voices got louder before beginning to fade. At which point she loosened her grip so she could pull back to see his face. Never in his life had Quatro wanted to kiss someone so badly. Timing was shit, but—

"Do you think they're gone now?" River said, shattering the trance to pieces.

It needed to happen. He knew it did. But there was no denying the ache of disappointment. "You're not supposed to ask any questions," he said then, tapping her on the chin.

He turned and opened the closet door a crack. Then wider.

The hallway was empty. "Come on." He took her hand.

As they approached the entrance to First Light, River pulled him back. "Let me go first," she said.

Quatro shook his head. "Come on now, Riv. I can't protect you if you throw yourself in the line of fire—"

"It'll be easier for me to pull the damsel-in-distress card if there's someone in there. You know my mom taught me to cry on cue when I was six. Trust me on this one." And she stepped in front of him.

Which, by some miracle, wound up being unnecessary: whoever they'd heard arguing (and what was that *thump* they'd heard?) had apparently been alone in the restaurant before coming out of it. There wasn't a soul in there now. Quatro hoped the same would be true for the kitchen.

And it was. When they reached the door to the walk-in freezer (was he really about to go through with searching the pockets of a dead body?), he asked River to post up outside while he went in. "If you hear anybody coming, knock three times," he told her.

"Okay."

He tiptoed inside and hustled to the back. He held his breath and opened the big metal door. Seeing the shelves with food still on them shot a chill down Quatro's back that had nothing to do with the low temperature of the space. It was just the thought that he might've eaten something that had been stored in here with . . .

He needed to find Ant's body and get out of there fast.

He looked all around. Checked every nook and cranny and corner.

Ant was nowhere to be found.

Where the hell had the body gone? Had the security guards moved him?

He felt the three faint knocks more than he heard them and quickly jetted for the door. When he was about ten feet away, it opened, and he froze. River's head appeared. "Come on, come on, come on, come on," she whisper-shouted. "Somebody is coming!"

He bolted out, shut the freezer, and got just far enough away from it as the general manager stormed into the kitchen with the chef on his tail. Starlie, he remembered from her name tag their first night. River was holding something behind her back, but he couldn't tell what it was.

It took a second for the general manager to notice them, but when he did . . . "What the hell are you two doing in here, huh? You punk kids think that just because—"

"Are you kids all right?" Starlie cut in. "I know it has to be difficult being so restricted when you're supposed to be on spring break and something tragic has happened, but you really gotta get to your rooms. The winds are picking up again. Another wave of the storm is on top of us. It's dangerous."

"We're sorry," River replied, dropping her head in the cutest fake remorse he'd ever seen. "We just . . . well, we got hungry." She held up a bagged loaf of brioche in one hand and a jar of Nutella in the other one.

The general manager turned so red, he looked like he was going to combust. "GET THE HELL OUTTA HERE RIGHT NOW!" he shouted.

"Mr. Chandler—" Chef Starlie started.

"Hey, man, you don't gotta yell at her like that." Quatro took a step toward the guy. "Perhaps it's slipped your memory, but we're *paying* guests at this little establishment you're doing a terrible job of running during this crisis—"

"Let's just go, Quatro." River pulled at his hand.

She didn't let go until they were all the way back in the Sunset wing approaching the door to his suite . . . at which point she turned around and collapsed against him, silently crying. "I want to go home, Quintin," she whined into his chest.

As he wrapped his arms around her shoulders to comfort her, the door to his suite opened and Johnson stepped out. At first, the guy looked startled to see them standing there—*and of course he did*, Quatro thought. *We probably look like one of them couples who can't bear to be apart from each other.*

But the guard recovered quickly. "You two need to get into your *separate*, *assigned* rooms immediately, lock the door with both dead bolt and chain, and stay there until further notice."

"Why?" Quatro couldn't help but ask. "What's happening? Is there an update?"

The security guard looked back and forth between them, eyes narrowing. Quatro had no idea how to interpret the dude's expression, and that made him more than a little nervous. First they'd overheard an argument (with a *thud*!), then Ant's body wasn't where it was supposed to be. As far as he knew, it was being kept there because no one could get to the island to retrieve it. (Had that changed?) Then the general manager was clearly buggin', and now they were being told to go lock themselves in and not come out. What the hell was going on?

"You heard what I said, Mr. McCallum," Johnson replied. "Now go in that room and do as instructed before I have you arrested. I'm sure Ms. Reynolds knows her way back to her room, correct?" He looked at River.

Who looked at Quatro. And for a few beats, time seemed to stand still. Who did this guy think he was?

"Is Dwayne even in there?" Quatro realized he hadn't seen his best friend in hours.

"You need to get inside and lock the door now," Johnson barked, spittle collecting in the corners of his mouth. "It's an emergency."

Quatro raised an eyebrow and took a step closer to the man. "I don't answer to you, bruh. Go find Dwayne if you want to boss someone around."

Johnson scowled. "We're trying to protect *all* of you—"

"Protect us from what? More rain?"

The guard's professional veneer cracked. "We're not doing this for shits and giggles, you little asshole," he said right in Quatro's face. "Someone else is dead!"

Quatro stopped breathing and looked at River, who didn't look like she was breathing either.

"The front desk lady, Gloria—" Johnson began.

"Move." Quatro grabbed River and pulled her into the suite, then shut the door in the security guard's face.

"Might not be a bad idea for you to stay here with me tonight, River," Quatro said.

She nodded and leaned into him. "I think I'd be too nervous to be anywhere else."

The relief that flooded Quatro's system at the thought that River wouldn't leave his sight almost made his knees buckle.

But then something else hit him harder: there might be a killer on the loose.

GLENN CHANDLER

General Manager
8:49 p.m.

GLENN HAD BEEN a general manager for over twenty years. He was often praised for running a tight ship and working well under pressure. Whether it was stepping behind the grill when a chef fell ill, fixing almost anything with a hot glue gun, or fashioning bed sheets into decorative curtains for a wedding, he'd dealt with it all. He'd handled it all.

But in all that time he'd never had to deal with a dead body.

Sure, there had been close calls. A Jet Ski accident here, an overdose there, blood that ruined countless white towels. But a dead body was something far more intense. Above his pay grade.

Glenn checked the time. He had a small window to potentially steal away for an hour or two. He'd been running nonstop for four days straight, since the arrival of that group of teenagers guaranteed to wreak havoc across the resort before the storm swooped in and worsened it. He hadn't had a full night's sleep since. If he was honest, he hadn't had one since he'd agreed to come back to

Kuzimu. The renovations weren't done, and the whole place felt like a mess.

He stood guard in front of the kitchen, where the resort's not even two-month-old walk-in freezer had been converted to a morgue. He used the bar as a sort of command center for the staff, doling out assignments, keeping the place marginally operational.

He'd never wanted to be a general manager of a hotel, especially this one. Rich people disgusted him. But it came naturally to him, and the salary sustained his wife and three children, enough to deal with the snobs and their offspring. The Florida Keys was an expensive place to raise a family, but it had been his wife's dream. And working here had given him the money he desperately needed to make that come true. He'd do anything (and he really meant *anything*) for his wife. Beg, borrow, steal, and worse. Since the power had gone out, he'd had no contact with Zenny, the love of his life, and their latest baby.

"Boss." Cruz ran in, sweat dripping down his light brown face. "The coroner is here from Vista Village. They had to clear the roads again. Trees down."

"Already?" He checked the time. If they worked fast, he could still sneak away and check on Zenny on the leeward side. He doubted she had any electricity, and he worried whether she'd listened and gotten food like he'd told her to on Saturday when the forecasted path of the storm had changed to include the island. He'd take the resort SUV through the mangroves and bring her some of Chef Starlie's chili when the rain paused again. "Fine. Show him in."

Glenn adjusted his tie, the collar of his shirt damp. He told himself that when it was all over, he would buy several new shirts. With the additional money from overtime for this arrangement, he'd be able to do what he liked. He'd be billing Mr. Brooks triple time for this bullshit.

The coroner walked in with a flashlight, clearly out of breath, with Cruz, the bellhop, trailing behind. "I'm Mr. Redding." He shook Glenn's hand with an aggression reserved only for someone new on the job. "So. Where is he?" The man blotted his tanned cheeks.

"In the freezer. We tried to keep him as cold as possible, but the generator has been struggling for the past twenty-four hours."

"You did the right thing. Is there anywhere I can move him for a proper inspection?"

Glenn's jaw ticked, checking the time again. "I'd prefer to not contaminate another area on the resort. Nor alarm the guests."

"Well, we can move him into another space, away from any window." He removed his straw hat. "I'll need help lifting him onto the gurney."

Glenn steeled himself, then turned to Cruz. "Go get George and Lamar. We'll take him into the sundry shop."

Cruz hesitated, but then he must have realized he'd have to do the dirty work if the other two didn't, and vanished.

When the two men arrived, they took top and tail of the body, penguin-walking him out of the freezer and onto the gurney, which the coroner pushed down the hall and into the sundry shop for better lighting. The body was still covered, and the shrouded shelves around them gave the whole space a crypt-like feel.

"Gawf! He smells awful." The coroner gagged. "Was there no air circulating in that freezer?"

He probably smelled like this before, Glenn almost said aloud.

"And where's security?" The coroner's eyebrows lifted. "Have they been able to get in touch with Islamorada's police department? Is the satellite phone working? Ours in the village wasn't. I thought I'd have more luck here."

"No, and no," Glenn replied, his eyes cutting to Cruz and Lamar.

The coroner turned his attention back to the body. "There is significant bloating," he muttered as he glanced over the body. "He must've been in the water for a few hours."

Glenn gulped sips of air, trying to avoid looking at the corpse, questioning every decision he'd made that had led to this moment. He felt like *he* was drowning. Was it all worth it? He couldn't stop thinking about how the Brookses were a rotten family full of rotten secrets that put him in this predicament. Now there were several dead bodies to deal with.

He was sick of dealing with it all.

PRESENT DAY

SYDNEY DAVIS

April 6
6:55 p.m.

SYDNEY COULD NOT stop crying long enough to even catch her breath. She heaved. Her chest burned, like someone had lit a match inside her. Her throat was clogged and raw. Her eyes were red and swollen.

At first Detective Franco had been cajoling, even sympathetic. He gave her a box of tissues and let her go to the bathroom to splash cold water on her face. But it'd been over an hour now, and she was still inconsolable. Her tears endlessly ran down her cheeks like the rain along the hospital room window.

"Ms. Davis, the sooner you answer my questions, the sooner you can get out of here," he said, voice hard and impatient. "What happened and when? Paint me a picture of the trip."

Sydney nodded over and over and pressed her palms to her eyes. If her mom were here, she'd get Sydney to stop crying by sheer force of will. If her mom were here, they wouldn't be interrogating her. And since she wasn't, Sydney still knew she wasn't supposed to talk to this man without a lawyer present, but part of her just wanted it all over with. She'd be in trouble either way—whether she broke her mother's rule about talking to officials without the family lawyer or herself present, or if she told the truth. The weight of it sat on her chest, and she wanted to be free of it as soon as possible.

She squeezed her eyes shut, sucked down huge gulps of air, and tried to calm herself down. She could do this. Had to do this.

Before she could speak, a door banged open, and another detective came stalking in. He tossed something—a cell phone—that landed with a smack on the table in front of her. Sydney flinched. It was Ant's burner phone in an evidence bag.

"You'll never believe whose prints we found on this," the gruff man said. He pinned the phone in place with his finger. He leaned toward Sydney. "And you'll never believe what we found on it."

And that was it. Her tears became a flood. Like her body was trying to purge a poison, but the poison had spread too far, and too deep. Maybe the poison was a part of her. Maybe the poison *was* her, and no prayer or promise or greater power could save her from herself.

THE WEEK BEFORE:

THURSDAY

GEORGE WONG

Groundskeeper

12:26 a.m.

GEORGE MOST DEFINITELY had *not* signed up for this week of nightmares. Chasing tarps down the beach, cleaning up spilled paint, collecting broken cobblestones and shattered shutters, lifting dead bodies . . . and now, delivering room service. But he wanted to be a team player. He knew Mr. Chandler would reward him when the time came. A pay raise and a new title, head of maintenance and grounds, would do.

He hobbled down the path from the Dawn wing with the tray for the fussy writer who always had demands, even after midnight. Over the past five years or so, he'd spent time in her signature suite fixing all the small things that irritated her. If she didn't spend so much time indoors, she wouldn't notice the tiny crack in the sofa's armrest or the spot on the wall that needed a paint refresh. He felt relieved that she was in the finished part of the resort this time. His walkie-talkie had been noticeably quiet about fixing things in room 140 this week. He wouldn't have been able to handle it anyway, with all that was going on.

George felt lucky her suite door was on the first floor. He set the tray down, hoping she wouldn't be mad about her food on the floor like this and went to knock, but the door was slightly ajar. "Hello?"

No answer.

He took another step into the dark room. "I have your midnight snack, Ms. Sabine, from Chef Starlie. I can leave it out here in the living room or bring it to you." He was used to hearing her click away at her old-fashioned typewriter, so the silence felt eerie. Wrong.

His whole body went cold as he turned the corner. The tray tumbled from his hands, the chai and cookies spilling all over his feet.

Sabine sat at the little desk facing the window, ribbons of blood cascading down her slender brown neck and staining her nightgown and the teal typewriter she used to write her stories.

The knife and the hand wielding it glinted in a sliver of moonlight. George flinched at the sight of it and the figure shrouded by the shadowy room.

"Are you going to do what's asked of you, George?" came a voice George was trying to pretend he didn't recognize.

George nodded. He wanted to run, but his feet were pinned beneath the tray and frozen by fear. "Why . . . why would you do that?"

"No witnesses," the voice replied. "She wasn't supposed to be here this week."

He gulped. And he wasn't supposed to be in this room right now. The concierge should've brought this tray, but P.J. was also dead. His stomach twisted. What had he gotten himself into?

"Be ready when the time comes, George. Don't end up like her."

"Okay . . . okay . . . yes . . . yes . . . I will," he stammered.

CHAPTER SEVENTEEN

NOELLE

6:52 a.m.

AS THE MORNING sun crept through the window, Noelle watched her ex-friends Quatro and River pace back and forth, mumbling. Her mind slipped in and out of lingering dreams of her hustling on her father's cook line in the expansive Red Bone kitchens. She struggled to stay present after such a rough night of sleep. She still couldn't believe someone had died in the room next to them. No, someone was murdered in the room next to them.

Quatro's deep voice, the panic-laced baritone, swept her back to Chef Donaldson stomping behind her during brunch service as she dipped her ladle in a vinegar bath to fetch perfectly poached eggs.

She drifted back into half sleep and memory. "Did you test that water temperature, Noelle?" he'd shout. "Or use the special vinegar from the back shelf? Or, lemme guess: you used the one I told you not to like a fucking idiot."

Before she was ever able to answer, she'd get hit with another command or insult, his breath so close to her neck the soft hair at the nape would lift.

"You think you're special because of your father! Because you're a Clarke? You think I'm going to take it easy on you? That you deserve slack?" he'd whisper. She used to think he'd made a bull's-eye out of her, and he'd been determined to never miss an opportunity to remind her that no matter how many teen baking competitions she'd won, she was *nothing* in this kitchen. It was *his* kitchen that he ran to impress her father. He'd even perfected her father's claim to fame, the Red Bone special from which the restaurant had gotten its name: slow-roasted marrow bones presented with a scarlet drizzle of pomegranate reduction. She could almost feel his lips again, and she rolled her shoulder as she tumbled deeper down the rabbit hole of memory, his voice a cacophony of her failures and her shame.

"Noelle!"

"Noelle!"

A hand jerked her shoulder and she jumped, thinking about Chef Donaldson's pale white hands. But as she blinked, her father's kitchen disappeared, and her surroundings sharpened into view.

The resort room.

Storm clouds now rolling in outside the window.

The reality of the murder of her boyfriend.

River glared down at her. Irritation replaced Noelle's anxiety. Key had been the only person able to ease her out of her "dissociative moments," as her therapist called them.

"I asked you a question." River's eyes narrowed as if they had the ability to search inside her. "What's going on with you?"

"Sorry, what?" Noelle glared back. *Pull it together*, Noelle thought. *You're going to blow it.*

"You said you heard Sydney say something, then you spaced out like a weirdo," River said as Quatro flashed her a look.

Noelle fussed with one of her long twists and told herself not to bite her bottom lip. "Oh yeah, okay, so I overheard Sydney, like I said." She ignored River and continued. "Sydney and Dwayne are trying to find a way off the island." Noelle's thoughts raced alongside her heart as she recounted what she'd overheard outside Dwayne's room yesterday morning. She'd gone to try to talk to him and figure out if his was one of the two voices she'd heard back in Ant's room. She'd had a plan to force the information out of him because of something Ant had told her.

Noelle could still feel the weight of the red and blue chips in her hands as she'd arranged them on the plush green game table in Dwayne's basement three weeks ago. It had been his turn to host their signature parties while his parents attended a fundraising dinner in New York City. She was lucky to be there. Her friends were pissed with her for talking with that pesky reporter about Key's death, so she did her best to be useful, and the one thing she knew how to do without question was throw a good party. Key had molded her. The three rules were thus:

The right place.

The right people.

The right prep.

And she'd always provide the most delicious sweets. She'd gazed over at her dessert table, the macaron tower having turned out better than expected. As she admired her handiwork, she watched Dwayne and Ant in each other's faces. Veins bulged out of Dwayne's warm brown neck as they stood eye to eye. Dwayne yanked Ant's collar, bunching up his gold chain until Ant brushed him off. She'd never seen Dwayne like this before. He was mostly super chill.

Dwayne grumbled, then stormed upstairs.

Noelle eased over and helped smooth out his now crumpled neckline. "What was that about?"

"You know how he is," Ant replied, trying to mask his anger.

"About the card games?" Noelle asked. Sweat beaded on his temples and she could almost feel the anger radiating off him like steam from a freshly cracked loaf of sourdough straight from the oven.

"What is it?" She kept her voice soft, feeling more like Key than herself. Key would always fold her voice in half when she'd want answers out of someone. Even her.

Ant sneered "He's bugging. We always had a plan. A set amount we'd planned to make off these games, then be done with it. Now he's getting all scared and trying to change it up." The anger made his tongue loose. "And it's looking like he's trying to cut me out. Something's got him shook, but I'm *not* having it. I don't care about these people's parents. Fuck that."

"It'll be all right," she'd whispered, then craned up to plant a gentle kiss on his cheek. She relished being needed again after Key's death. How many thousands of times had Noelle pulled Key into a closet to kiss her, or hold her hand when she'd spiral, or tangle their legs together in bed, with Key's head on her chest, letting her heartbeat calm Key's erratic one when she'd flip out? Not uttering a word until each thrum matched.

Noelle could handle pressure. Her father's kitchen had ensured that.

"He can't cut me out." Ant balled his fists. "I really helped get this shit going. Got him twice as many people wanting in on these games."

Noelle nibbled her bottom lip as she gazed up at her beautiful boyfriend. Her first one ever. The only person she'd kissed aside from Key. "I can make sure he won't do that," she said, tucking smug confidence into her voice as Dwayne's biggest secret from the night Key died tangled with hers and tickled the tip of her tongue.

Ant leaned down and kissed her forehead. "I knew you'd be the key to my success here. My lucky charm."

The *Key*.

It gave her a chill to hear that word from Ant's perfect mouth, but Noelle let his praise fill the dark, empty part of her and rebury her secret, tucking it deep down below her stomach.

"So that's it?" River's voice held a sharp exasperation that pierced Noelle's memory. "Did they have a plan? How the heck do they think we can leave? Will we all be able to go? Why didn't Sydney tell me?"

Her questions hit Noelle one after the other, the last one landing with a note of hurt. Noelle opened and closed her mouth, realizing she hadn't stayed around long enough outside Dwayne's door—a fact she conveniently left out of the story—to hear the rest of the plan. "I'm not sure," she said.

And just like that, Noelle watched River lose interest in her the way she always did, typing on her phone while Quatro continued to pace. Was River writing down what she'd just said? It wasn't like anyone had Wi-Fi or phone service. "What are you doing?"

"Where were you yesterday?" River asked, looking up from her phone. "I was looking for you everywhere. Came back to the room, then went to the restaurant too."

"God, River. Not this again. I just needed a little room to breathe."

"So you went where, exactly?"

Noelle tried not to sweat. "I found this little cove down by the water." The heat of the non-air-conditioned room coupled with the wet, muggy breeze from the open window and the big lie she'd just told made her feel like it was a thousand degrees. Noelle gritted her teeth as River lobbed another question at her, setting her nerves ablaze to the point where the words went in one ear and out the other.

"Why are you interrogating me like you're those security guards?"

River stepped closer and closer to Noelle; her anger—that Noelle didn't understand—was as wild as the rain starting to fall in heavy sheets. "You're acting just how you used to back when Key was still alive. Shady as hell. All these secrets. All these half-truths." Her voice got even louder. "All the times—"

Quatro grabbed River, pulling her into a hug. "She's not worth it, boo," he said. River's small frame disappeared into Quatro's large arms, and she burst into tears. "You're just scared." He eyed Noelle like *she'd* done something wrong.

Noelle shook, an earthquake of rage vibrating through every part of her body as she watched. A chill settled in her stomach with the realization that she didn't have anyone to comfort her like that in this moment.

Not Key.

Not Ant.

The rage inside her boiled over, all the frustration of being on the outside of her friend group these past few weeks loose and ready to find a target: River. "Why are you trying to blame me for everything? Caught up in these pointless details instead of helping to figure out how to get us all off this fucking island and back home? Unless you're trying to make it seem like I'm always to blame for everything that goes wrong in this group. You think you're in charge now. You and Sydney. Maybe *you're* the one with something to hide . . ."

River peeked her head around Quatro's massive torso. Her eyes narrowed. Noelle braced for a nasty response and balled her fists.

"Because I know, okay?" River spat.

"You know *what*?" Noelle challenged.

"I know you were the last person to see Key still alive!"

Quatro gaped at Noelle, the shock dropping his mouth open.

The words crashed into Noelle's chest, but she stood her ground. Her pulse thundered. She felt like a shaken bottle of champagne ready to explode. A hot lump grew in her throat, threatening to choke her. Tears welled in her eyes. She tried to blink them away along with the image of Key's dead face storming into her mind. The glazed reflection in her one blue and one green eye as they bulged and rolled back the moment the life left them.

"Fuck you!" Noelle screamed. "I loved her and you know that!

You're just trying to cover your own asses. Both of you are!" Uncontrollable sobs rattled her body, the tremors of the angry earthquake now transformed to grief. Her head turned into a weightless balloon ready to drift off. Black-and-white spots freckled her vision.

She felt Quatro catch her and lead her to the bed before she could collapse.

"Look, both of you!" he shouted. "This ain't the time to talk about Key." He put his huge hand in the air. "Key is *gone*, okay? And now there's someone killing people! We need to get the fuck off this island alive. Nothing else matters."

Alive.

That word burned a pit in Noelle's stomach. There were so many days and nights over the last year when she didn't know if she was in fact still living. The person she loved the most, her best friend and her secret love, dead and buried. Now Ant. And when everyone should be working together to get out of this, she was still public enemy number one, no matter what. Cast out and hated. They'd probably leave her behind if they could.

Noelle whispered a promise to herself . . . she wouldn't be treated like shit anymore or left behind.

She wouldn't be underestimated.

She *would* stay alive.

And they'd regret the way they'd treated her.

CHAPTER EIGHTEEN

RIVER

10:02 a.m.

RIVER WAS SHAKING as she stepped into the hall. She didn't want to leave Quintin's side—not after what he'd told her last night. From the tight way he'd held on to her in bed, she didn't think Quintin planned to let her out of his sight—which was why she'd waited until he dozed off to sneak away.

It had felt impossible to sleep last night knowing a killer could be among them, that he or she could be anywhere or anyone. And it was terrifying to be moving through the resort on her own.

But River had to go. Now that she knew Dwayne wanted off the island, River was almost certain he would find a way to make it happen. And he'd definitely be taking Sydney with him. River hadn't thought any of them would leave in secret—and she'd especially never expected Sydney to leave her—but people were getting desperate. She needed to make sure she knew everyone's next move—even her best friend's.

After Quintin had stopped her from coming for Noelle this

morning, they were both even more exhausted. She still wanted to punch Noelle in the throat, which was another reason she needed to get out of their room. Noelle was just sitting there, feeling sorry for herself, looking pathetic, like she was the only victim in all this.

And it made River want to scream.

So she'd gotten into bed with Quintin about twenty minutes ago, telling him that it might be easier for them both to sleep in the light of day. His hazelwood-and-honey scent was a comfort, but as soon as he started snoring, she made her escape, knowing this might be her only opportunity to do what she needed to do. Sydney was somewhere with Dwayne, and River needed to know what they were up to.

The hallway was quiet and creepy, and River jumped at every tiny noise she heard. Doors closing or opening, the sound of crashing waves, the rough roaring wind, even her own footsteps made her shoulders shoot up to her ears. She definitely hadn't inherited her mother's steeliness. She moved quickly and silently toward Dwayne and Quintin's room, rehearsing what she'd say. She had to be calm, even though she didn't feel calm at all. She had to somehow get Sydney or Dwayne to bring up getting off the island all on their own because she, River, wasn't supposed to know about the plan.

But before she even got to the fourth floor, she heard voices.

"We're planning to hire a boat, sir," she heard someone say.

She froze and looked up and down the long hall for a place to tuck in. There was nowhere to hide. She pressed her body hard against the wall and stood stock-still trying to decipher whether the voices were moving toward or away from her.

The loud wind carried their voices off with it. She was breathless with gratitude after listening for a few seconds and realizing they were standing still.

"We were able to reach your parents via the satellite phone in the general manager's office. They've been terrified, watching the slow path of the hurricane on the news, and are throwing all their weight behind getting you out of here."

River unconsciously leaned forward, as if those few inches would help her better overhear the conversation. She wasn't sure who was speaking, and she was too afraid to move any closer to see.

"What kind of boat?" a different voice asked. And River recognized this one as Dwayne's immediately. It was rumbling and low, like distant thunder before the rain.

"We aren't sure yet, sir. It will depend on what can be found. It's been difficult locating one nearby that wasn't damaged by the storm and is safe enough to withstand the rough waters."

"Just get us to Islamorada. Isn't that the closest island?"

"Yes."

"Well, just make sure it's big and sturdy enough. Sydney needs to get out of here, too, and I doubt she'll leave without River. River won't go without Quatro, and if boats are this difficult to find, we might all have to make some hard decisions."

Hard decisions? River frowned and repeated the words to herself. How could Dwayne consider leaving without them all? Was he as afraid as River and Quintin had been last night, or did he have some other reason for wanting to get out of here? Why would he want to leave anyone behind?

They were the Six . . . or so she'd thought. But now it was everyone for themselves.

Without thinking, River continued down the hallway and stepped out of the shadows to stand right in front of Dwayne and Johnson. She filled with adrenaline, giving her more courage than she'd ever had before.

She looked Dwayne dead in the eye and swallowed the fear that bloomed inside her like a black hole before it could get to her nerve. "What do you mean by 'hard decisions'?" she asked.

Dwayne looked both surprised to see her and a little pissed off, but he was trying to hide it.

"And," River continued, "you know Sydney won't leave without me. So what lie are you planning to tell her?"

River had been holding herself together all week, but she was getting closer and closer to falling apart. Johnson looked shaken, but Dwayne's face had adjusted since she'd caught him by surprise. He smiled and calmly placed a hand on her shoulder.

"Whoa, whoa, whoa," he said. "I know this has been a wild-ass week, but don't jump to any conclusions here."

"I'm just repeating what you said," River replied. "How is that jumping to conclusions? You're willing to sacrifice the rest of us to save yourself? That's so fucked up, Dwayne."

Dwayne shook his head. "River, that's not what's happening."

"Then what the hell is going on?" River cried. She looked at Johnson again, who looked at Dwayne.

"What you didn't hear," Dwayne said, "is that we'd have to decide who'd be leaving the island *first*," he said. "This boat, if it's too small to take all of us, we'll have to go in shifts. Me and Sydney with our security guards and then everyone else. No one is getting left behind."

"We have to get from the resort to the other side of the island. That pier is intact," Johnson explained. "So, we'll take the resort SUV through the forest and pray the road isn't blocked with mangrove trees like the general manager said."

"How many can fit in the SUV?" she pressed.

"A driver and passenger, so the security guards then three or maybe four in the back seat if we squeeze," Dwayne replied.

"Then let us go first," she said. "If you plan to get to the village then send the car back as you wait for the boat, why not let me, Quintin, and Noelle go first?"

Dwayne swallowed hard. Blinked a few times. And in those seconds, River realized that she didn't know Dwayne at all. But she should have. Because this was what entitled people did in the end, and she'd been dealing with them her whole life through her mother's clients. They always chose themselves.

Always.

Now it made sense why Dwayne fit perfectly with Sydney—he was just like her. And they were both just like Key.

When Key had walked in on River making one of her MANIfest the Mess videos, River had been excited to tell Key about it. "Oh, it's just this thing I do online, kinda like a diary. But it's anonymous. No one knows it's me making the videos, which is why I can say anything."

Key sat down beside River on her bed, found the MANIfest account on her own phone, and scrolled through the videos. "This is so cool," Key said. "You could literally say whatever you wanted and get away with it."

River shrugged. "I mean, I guess I could. I'm not really saying anything I need to 'get away with,' though. Just talking about dumb shit no one really cares about."

"Yeah," Key said. "But that's what I mean. You could be saying more. What if you made a video about Jocelyn Pierre? That bitch is always trying to make me look like an idiot in debate."

"Really? I'm in AP History with her, and I'm pretty sure she cheats on, like, every exam."

Key's eyes went wide. River was still getting used to their odd, alluring colors. "Yes. That's the kind of shit I'm talking about, Riv! Make a video about her."

So they did. River had thought it was funny, outing this girl who everyone knew was kind of bitchy, who pretended to know everything but cheated her way through most of her tests. Not that she would've admitted it then, but it also felt good to make Key happy. To make her dote on her. Except where River had thought it was only a fun, one-off prank, Key kept coming over, kept telling her to make videos about different kids. And River obliged. Key was that persuasive. And like she did with her mother, River had craved Key's approval. She kinda hated herself for it, too.

Soon anyone who did anything Key didn't like was on the chopping block. After a video about Ty Bryant went viral—River told the camera he'd punched a hole in the locker room wall after the basketball team lost their championship game, and *Did anyone think the bruise on his girlfriend's arm might be from him too?* (it wasn't), while she painted her nails a shade of seafoam green that was much softer than the lies she was telling—she told Key she didn't want to make any more videos.

"If you stop now," Key told her, "I'll tell everyone you're the creator of MANIfest. And everyone will know it's true. All they'll have to do is look at your nails."

So River didn't stop. And the rest of the Six knew because, River found out, Key had already told them for collateral. The girl loved power and she had something on everyone, so they all looked the other way and let Key use her until the guilt was literally making River sick.

So River came up with an exit strategy.

A way out. River posted a video revealing all the worst things about Key.

She could never have predicted that Key would die the same night she posted it.

"Well, it'll be my boat," Dwayne said with a shrug; his voice piercing the thick memory of Key. Even in death, she was a hard person to erase. "So I'll definitely be on the first trip out of here. And there's no way I'm leaving without Sydney. And our security guards legally can't leave us, so . . ."

At that moment, she thought of the creepy messages from Lo_KeyKeisha and realized they could be from any of them. They all were as fucked up as Key had been. And they all had something to hide.

"Okay," she said to Dwayne. "Well, let me know what the plan is. I hope, for all our sakes, we get out of here soon. All of us."

As River walked away from him, she felt her throat get tight and her eyes fill with tears. But she also felt like she was getting closer and closer to the truth. She still had so many questions, but she knew one thing for sure: she couldn't trust anyone on this island.

WILLA PRESCOTT

Executive Protection Security Guard for Sydney Davis

3:12 p.m.

WHEN SHE WAS given this assignment, Willa Prescott had known it would be difficult. She'd joined the force ten years earlier, after graduating from Stanford with a criminal justice degree, and had been working in personal protection for the last five. A lot of people would say that's not very much experience. In law enforcement, everyone wanted to brag about being on the force for more than fifteen. (She didn't get why you suddenly became legit after fifteen years of service, but she tried not to dwell on it.) One thing she'd learned in the last few years was that kids are always harder assignments than adults.

Johnson had been in personal protection for the last eight years, but had been a cop for seven years before that. Fifteen years exactly. And he liked to brag about it. Prescott tried not to look as annoyed as she felt when he wouldn't shut up about his *years on the force*, but she didn't know how successful she'd been at pretending. He also knew a kid assignment would be hard. But what Willa thinks neither of them had anticipated was how hard it would be to watch a teenager in a place like this with five *other* kids.

With friends, Prescott thought. She had underestimated how much the hormones of five additional teens would affect her assignment, and Sydney had been extremely unpredictable the last few days. Not to mention everything else that had happened.

In school, Willa had taken a class that was all about noticing patterns. They talked about patterns in nature, patterns of behavior, and literal patterns, like polka dots and stripes. And what it all had come down to was *something happening more than once, with some regularity.*

So she'd known when they hit rough air on the flight, rough water on the yacht, and then had a rough reception at the resort, that this week wouldn't go as planned.

Patterns. They were everywhere. And Willa always noticed them. It was why she was such a good security detail.

There were patterns on this island too. Death and destruction and people behaving strangely, like Chandler—and the rest of the staff—but especially Chandler.

But she hadn't been able to put the puzzle together. Something was missing, and she wished she could ask one of her professors if they could see the bigger picture she was sure she wasn't seeing.

Someone was lying. That much she knew. And Glenn Chandler seemed like the best bet.

In his office, she would look for the key to the SUV. She left her post, left her assignment unguarded and unsafe, to look for a way off this island. She found out about the SUV because of a pattern too. The literal tracks in the mud around the property being the biggest one, but people would disappear and reappear with supplies too heavy to carry. She eased Glenn's door open, but inside she found much more than keys.

"Oh my God," someone said from behind her, and she turned. She'd been afraid it was Chandler, catching her in the act. But it wasn't. From where she was standing with the door open, anyone walking by would be able to see past her into the office. "Is he . . . dead?"

She turned back. The body on Chandler's office floor wasn't him either.

Back at her post, where Willa was pretending she'd never left, that she'd seen nothing in the last hour but the other side of the hallway even as she felt sick to her stomach, she heard something. Her nervous system went into full alert, activated like she was a robot programmed to react to the subtlest movements. She gently bent her knees, placed her hand over her gun, and turned toward the sound. Johnson came swaggering down the hall just behind Dwayne. She nodded at them both once they were closer.

Dwayne went in, leaving her alone with Johnson.

"Prescott," he said in greeting. "Nice night. Reminds me of a night back in 2010 . . ."

Maybe that's why it's fifteen years, Willa thought with a smile. Maybe in five years she wouldn't be referencing school or classes or professors. Maybe after fifteen years she'd have done enough to reference the field. Maybe she'd be referencing her time on this island. All she'd seen. All she'd done.

Johnson droned on and Willa zoned out. When she tuned back in he was still talking, but she decided to shut him up for once.

"There's another body," she said. And when he barely reacted, she tried not to either.

"Here's what we need to do . . ." he said, but before he'd outlined even half of his plan, she'd already decided: *she'd* be the one to find a way out of here.

Maybe it really was about experience. Or maybe this—her insecurity, his ego—was all because she was a woman. And no matter what she did, and no matter how many years she dedicated her life to this work, no matter how many bodies she saw or lives she saved, she'd always be compared to the men standing next to her. Either way, she was determined to do her job. To protect Sydney and the other kids too. To get them to safety.

It had to be her.

CHAPTER NINETEEN

SYDNEY

9:47 p.m.

"THIS ONE HAS bandages, gloves, eye wash, antibiotic packets, antiseptic towelettes, gauze, alcohol wipes, burn cream, and dressing," Sydney said as she opened up the wall-mounted first aid kit. It'd been easy for her and Dwayne to break into the resort's small infirmary. The power outage meant none of the keypad entries were working.

"Come on, Sydney," Dwayne said from the doorway behind her. He was on lookout duty. "You really think we need all that? We're getting on a boat, not going to war."

Sydney eyed him. Something was for sure bothering him. He never took that hard-edged tone with her. Still, her own irritation spiked. She was exhausted and afraid, and she needed everybody to get their head in the game.

She stopped dropping supplies into the duffel bag at her feet and spun around to face him. "Ant is dead! Not two days ago, his yacht exploded! And someone is out there picking people off at this resort one by one! But you think I'm being too cautious by getting us some damn bandages?" She was being louder than she should be. What if someone heard her? The stress of everything was overwhelming.

Dwayne sighed and rubbed his hand down his face. "My bad," he said. "You're right. With how things are going, we can't be too prepared."

Sydney let go of her irritation. She didn't want a fight with Dwayne, especially not after the one she'd had with River.

"Let me just get a few more things," she said, and went back to filling the duffel with more supplies.

Two more minutes passed. "I think we're good now," Dwayne said, gently this time.

Sydney looked down at the bag. He was right. She'd packed enough for more than just her, Dwayne, River, and Quatro. It would take a catastrophe for them to need all these supplies.

"I'm nervous," she admitted.

Dwayne reassured her. "The ride won't be too bad." She knew he'd assumed she was talking about the car ride through the mangroves.

She shook her head. "River and me got into it before," she confessed.

"About what?"

She shook her head. If she told him about their argument, she'd have to tell him about Ant's safe, and, in particular, why she was so interested in the contents. No way was she ready for that conversation. "Just dumb stuff."

"You guys will work it out," he said. "Anyway, you need to do it. The ride will be long and tense enough without any drama."

She nodded, knowing he was right.

Back in Dwayne's suite, Sydney emptied the duffel at the foot of his bed. She shrugged off the confused look he gave her. "Just double-checking."

He watched her silently for a few seconds.

"I really needed to do something," she said. "The stress is—"

"A lot," Dwayne finished her sentence. He stretched himself out on the bed, back against the headboard. "Come sit by me."

She repacked the duffel and then went to him.

"You ever think about what our lives would be like if our parents weren't our parents?" Dwayne asked.

"Like, if they weren't so . . . public, you mean?"

"Might be nice to be anonymous."

Sydney closed her eyes and let herself imagine it. No ever-present reporters and cameras. No editorials about her mother, or their family, or the historic nature of her candidacy. No fundraisers or Get Out the Vote events or endless church services where she had to sit perfectly still. No editorials in *Teen Vogue* or *Seventeen*. No need to always be aware of what she was saying and who she was saying it to. No need to have a security guard everywhere she went.

She imagined getting lost with Dwayne in some European city. They'd turn a corner and find a charming plaza filled with people talking, laughing, dancing, eating. *Being.* None of it curated. All of it real and true and—above everything else—private. Dwayne would take her hand and twirl her around. Her cute kitten heels would get stuck in cobblestone. She'd kick them off and leave them behind.

But kitten heels, especially the type she liked, didn't cost *nothing*. One of the things her mom's career and fame brought was money. Money for that trip to some charming European city. Money to be able to afford to sit in the front row of the cute restaurant on the plaza. To take private tours of famous museums. And flying commercial, even in first class, was so much more tedious than flying private.

She looked at Dwayne and wondered what answer he wanted from her. With him, she didn't want to pretend to be someone else.

She took a chance. "Could we be anonymous *and* still be rich?"

Dwayne threw his head back and laughed.

Sydney wanted to put her hand on his chest, feel his laughter in her body. "I love the way you laugh," she said.

"Yeah? What do you like about it?" He was staring at her. His voice was low and inviting.

"It's so—" She cast about for the right word. His laugh was like watching a helium balloon, newly released, drift up into the sky. "It's so free," she said.

He shifted closer, just enough to make Sydney feel brave enough to touch him. She cupped his face with her hand. He closed his eyes, turned his face into her palm, and kissed it.

"I've been waiting to do that," he said quietly.

"Me too," she whispered back.

He tilted his face closer to hers. She let the moment hover there for just a second. She wanted to capture it, crystallize it into something she could hold on to and treasure when times got hard. For when she needed something to remind her of one perfect and true thing.

Finally, she closed her eyes and let the distance between them disappear. He kissed the way he laughed. Sydney let herself get swept up and away.

There was a place inside her that was always buzzing, always on the lookout and wary. But kissing Dwayne made it go quiet. Sometime during that first kiss, Sydney admitted to herself that she was in love with him and that he was in love with her, too. No matter what happened next, they'd find a way to be together. What they had was special, maybe even the forever kind of special.

Once they'd started kissing, Sydney couldn't make herself stop. Why would she do anything else when she could be doing this? But they had to. Prescott and Johnson were taking the SUV tomorrow. She had to pack and apologize to River. Not to mention she needed to find that travel case that River had managed to lose . . .

"Dwayne," she said against his lips. "I gotta go back to my room and—"

"Just one more," he said with a groan. He kissed her again, and she lost herself for another minute.

Later, he was the one to stop. "Jesus, Sydney, you're killing me." He got off the bed. "If we stay in here, we're going to—"

Sydney hugged herself and smiled. It was nice to know he was feeling the same chaotic, needy energy that she was.

Dwayne bit down on his lip and palmed the back of his neck. "With you and me, it has to be right, okay?"

She understood what he was trying to say. He was telling her he loved her. That their first time together needed to be under better circumstances than these.

She smiled so hard her face hurt. "Okay, let me just fix my face before I go." A little lipstick touch-up was probably a good idea. She didn't want anyone guessing what had happened between her and Dwayne. Wanted to treasure it privately for a while longer.

In the bathroom, Sydney examined herself in the mirror. Her eyes were bright and clear. Her cheeks were warm. Had she ever felt so happy? It was like she was glowing. Who needed fancy, expensive serums when you had love? She touched her cheeks and suppressed a squeal. She felt brand-new, in a good way.

The feeling didn't last. In the mirror she saw the reflection of something metallic hiding just behind the shower curtain. Dread piled in her stomach. She swallowed hard. Immediately, she knew what it was. Didn't want to know but knew anyway. It was the safe River had found. She had no doubt. But it couldn't have been Dwayne who'd taken it. She'd barely left his side since before it went missing. So that meant it had to be one of the others . . . but who?

As quietly as she could, Sydney eased the curtain aside. Was Ant's phone still in the safe? Should she risk taking them? No—someone would know she'd taken them. How would she explain that? Not that Dwayne would have a right to demand answers. Clearly, he had secrets, too. A more conspiracy-minded part of her wondered if Dwayne already knew what she'd asked Ant to do. What if Dwayne had been doing his own opposition research? What if he'd discovered her dealings with Ant, and that discovery had given him exactly the ammunition he needed to take her and her mother down?

She stared down at the safe, trapped between what-ifs and indecision. Should she confront everyone? Confess? Take Ant's burner phone and deal with the consequences later? She looked back at her reflection in the mirror. Was it just a minute ago that she'd been so warm? So shimmery with possibility? Now she felt cold and flat, all her possible futures narrowed down to whatever she decided to do next.

LAMAR KINGSLEY

Bartender
11:21 p.m.

FOR THE LIFE of him, Lamar Kingsley couldn't seem to count.

Actually, that wasn't true. He could *count*, he just . . . couldn't *keep* count. Where was that inventory list again? And which spirit was he on?

Crap.

He knew those damn kids had been in his storeroom, taking things they didn't have the gumption to steal straight from the bar—surely led by that brat Anthony, who, if questioned about it, would make a "joke": *No worries, Lamar, my man. Put it on my dad's tab.* Like the countless other times bottles had gone missing while the kid was on the island.

The one time Lamar had attempted to take the issue to Mr. Brooks—you know, the *dad* in question—the rich prick wouldn't even allow Lamar to get the sentence out. "If this is about my son," he'd said, holding a hand up, "I don't wanna hear it. This place is as much his as it is mine. He's my legacy made flesh. Just do what you were hired to do."

Assholes, father and son alike.

Eventually, Mr. Chandler started docking the missing bottles from Lamar's check. ("Sorry, pal," he'd said. "A general manager's job ain't always fun, but I have to keep this ship tight.") Which felt unfair . . . though it did put an end to Lamar sneaking bottles out himself to party with Cruz and Callum after hours in the staff quarters whenever the kid was around.

The dark symbols on the white sheet of paper staring up at him from one of the shelves blurred into focus. Ah, there was his inventory list. He was on the rums.

"Hey, Lamar, need four mezcal margs in the restaurant, please," came a voice through the walkie-talkie sitting on a different shelf.

Mr. Chandler.

How inhumane this guy was, huh? Forcing Lamar to keep making drinks for the security guards who shouldn't even be drinking on the clock—which it was presumed *he* would do stone sober (Ha! If only they knew!)—while this nightmare unfolded around him. Like *he* didn't have a heart (and a kid of his own!) and wasn't all shaken up.

Didn't help that no one was *paying* for these drinks he was being ordered to make around the clock, it felt like. And his fellow staff members never tipped him. More damn bottles *he* was going to be held responsible for. He just knew it. He'd have to talk to Chandler about it.

Man, he hated this job. He hadn't *always* hated it, but he sure did now. Summer used to pay for a year of him getting to be able to work on his real passion: detailing and restoring vintage cars. But not this week.

That big payday couldn't come quickly enough. He'd been wary about getting involved at first, but now he couldn't be more thankful he'd made the impulsive decision to take on his role and say yes to working this week before the resort even reopened to the larger public. He just had to keep his head down and stay true to his role. Not much longer—or so he hoped.

He sighed and started counting the whiskey bottles.

Where was Cruz, and what was he doing right now? He'd watched the guy boss the kids around a little more forcefully than he should have—despite it being totally warranted, in Lamar's humble opinion. Lamar totally got where his buddy was coming from and would also love nothing else than to lay into the little rich punks. Show 'em who's really in charge.

Not that the person in charge was Lamar. But those brats couldn't keep treating the staff the way they did, could they? It was unacceptable.

Just a little while longer. Then he would be free.

Seventeen . . . eighteen . . . nineteen . . . twenty—wait . . . That one in the back there . . . had he counted it already?

Crap!

Lamar shook his head to try and clear it.

Actually, forget it.

He headed to the bar to make the margaritas. Including a fifth one for himself while he was at it. As far as he was concerned, he deserved it for putting up with this shit.

He'd need liquid courage for what came next anyway.

PRESENT DAY

RIVER REYNOLDS

April 6
8:01 p.m.

HE WOULDN'T ANSWER the damn phone. If only he would answer the damn phone.

River wasn't sure what pissed her off more—the fact that the detective kept ignoring her mother's calls or that she was stuck in this hospital being "interrogated" in the first place.

She bit down on her lip as the nurse dabbed alcohol against the gash above her left eyebrow. The stitches would come next—six of them, according to the doctor. She was a kind-looking older woman with sun-kissed lines etched around her eyes. She'd likely seen her fair share of chaos over the years, but River doubted she'd ever seen a bunch of wealthy Black kids corralled into the hospital, separated, and interrogated over a series of murders.

"This will sting a bit," the doctor murmured, but River barely heard her. Her focus was laser sharp on the detective's phone buzzing on the metal table, her mother's number lighting up the screen. If he had even an ounce of common sense, he would've known *not* to ignore a call from Dana Reynolds.

But the detective seemed completely unfazed by his phone. He was far more interested in the backpack lying beside it.

"This yours?" he asked casually, like it was merely a piece of lost luggage and not potential evidence that could destroy her life.

River kept her mouth shut. She was a young Black girl without an attorney or a legal guardian present—she was fresh meat in a pool of sharks. She'd be a fool to answer him.

She noticed the slight curl of his lips—a smirk. "Bird got your tongue?"

River nearly rolled her eyes. He couldn't even get his clichés right. "Cat," she muttered under her breath. "The phrase is 'cat got your tongue.'"

"So you can speak," he said smugly. "Well then, I'm Detective Franco, and you're River Reynolds, yes?"

River stayed silent, even as the doctor pierced her skin with a needle containing local anesthetic before starting the stitches she knew she needed, sending a sharp jolt of pain through her brow.

"It will take a few minutes to get numb. I'll be right back," the doctor told her.

The detective unzipped a backpack and began pulling out evidence bags: a phone charger, a water bottle with her initials engraved on its silver surface, a piece of twisted metal she couldn't identify, and then finally . . . *it.* The waterlogged, battered laptop that wasn't hers. That she'd been looking for. It held the one blemish that could shatter her perfect image.

The detective set the ruined laptop on the metal table, his green eyes narrowing as if he'd cornered his prey. River thought the sunburn on his nose looked like it hurt. "Is any of this yours?"

"The water bottle," she said calmly. She was Dana's Daughter in this moment, through and through.

River schooled her expression to something unreadable, just as her mother had taught her clients to do. "The eyes can betray you, even when your lips don't," Dana always said.

The detective leaned in close, his breath reeking of coffee. "You know," he said, as if he was letting her in on a secret, "we've got ways to recover whatever is on the hard drive. So if there's something you don't want us to find out, now's your chance to come clean."

River gripped the edge of the hospital bed and thunder roared outside. Another buzz filled the room, competing with the sounds of the storm. The phone vibrated, Dana's number appearing for the millionth time.

"She's not going to stop." River motioned toward the angry ringing phone.

He clicked the call, not breaking eye contact. "And neither will I. Not until one of you tells the truth."

Control the narrative or the narrative will control you, River reminded herself, but it was starting to feel like that laptop held way more control than she ever could.

"Everybody lies," River said. The doctor returned and tilted her head forward to start on the stitches. "Noelle's so desperate to be loved that I can see her saying, or doing, just about anything.

And Quintin . . ." She paused, swallowing the hesitation. But she couldn't stop, not even for her crush. "Quintin's drunk so often that I don't even know if he's lying on purpose or just forgetting what happens. But either way, his stories aren't adding up."

"What makes you think Dwayne's being dishonest?" Detective Franco asked.

"He's in love with Sydney. He'll do anything she asks him to. He's a politician's kid, just like her. They've been taught how to lie since they could talk."

"And you?" the detective asked, stroking his stubble. "What have you been lying about?"

River closed her eyes. Took a deep breath. If there was one narrative she'd control, it would be her own.

"I guess I'm more of my mother's daughter than I thought I was."

THE WEEK BEFORE:

FRIDAY

CHAPTER TWENTY

QUATRO

6:42 a.m.

HE HATED HIMSELF a little bit for it, sure, but what Quatro wanted more than anything was a drink. Just to . . . take the edge off. Dull his senses a little bit. The curtains were open, and it was finally sunny out—but the light was too damn bright, and the way it randomly bounced off the (creepily calm) water like camera flashes was making his stomach swim. There were too many colliding fragrances in the room—Dwayne swore by some cologne shit his dad put him onto, Sydney wore some super-flowery stuff, and the gently spicy scent on River that he typically couldn't get enough of was making his eyes water.

He felt like there were spiders crawling all over his skin, the birds outside were too damn loud—as were his friends' terse "whispering" voices—and he could swear he *tasted* death on the air. He kinda wanted to scream.

"I just . . . I don't know what to *do*," Dwayne was saying. "Like, I know what—or really *who*—my priorities are, but with Noelle knowing I'm planning to jet . . ." He shook his head. "If she makes a fuss and goes to the media and makes it seem like my dad doesn't care about anyone other than me—"

"Don't think like that, Dwayne," Sydney cut in. Quatro noticed the sweat beading at her hairline (because of course he did: the damp shine practically beamed at him) but tried not to think too much about it. "The most important thing here is getting off this island and away from this mess."

"I couldn't agree more," River said. "The narrative can be managed later. The narrative can *always* be managed . . ." (Spoken with unwavering conviction, but Quatro could tell she was trying to convince herself. He could *always* tell with River.)

Dwayne stared at the ceiling as if the answer would magically fall from it.

"Yeah, I hear that, River, but it doesn't take much to sway public opinion—"

"Dwayne." Sydney took Dwayne's face in her hands, and Quatro's eyes immediately went to River, who was standing across the room, looking right back at him. He felt like his chest was gonna crack open and spill all his organs out onto the floor.

"We gotta hold it together, okay?" Sydney said. "Things will be infinitely worse for your dad *and* my mom if we wind up dying in this place. We need to leave tonight. We can't wait until tomorrow. Prescott and Johnson have the SUV keys. We'll leave while the staff is in their nightly meeting."

It sobered the whole room.

River was still staring at him. His gut churned.

Sydney was right. They needed to get the hell out of there. No matter what.

"So what do we do about Noelle, then?" Dwayne asked, pulling Sydney's arms around his waist and wrapping her tight in his.

Quatro wished he could focus on the matter at hand. He really did. But everything was aggravating him. Like Sydney and Dwayne's political-ass PDA. (Because, let's be honest: the only people they were fooling with that shit was themselves. The children of governmental rivals couldn't be together. Their parents would never allow it.)

That's who was truly at fault in all this mess: everyone's parents. Quatro's included. If Dad didn't put so much damn pressure on Quatro—when he was *five,* the man put his size-fourteen shoes in front of Quatro and said, "Take a good look, son. These are what you will be required to fill." *Who* could manage under those sorts of expectations without some sort of . . . assistance?

"Quintin?" Now River was standing in front of him. "Are you okay? You . . ." She peeked over her shoulder and lowered her voice. "You look like you're about to 'detonate,' as you put it."

His gaze locked onto hers, and the memory crystallized: ninth grade, post-homecoming football game, some asshat from the rival school—which lost—had pushed up on River while their school was celebrating on the field. Quatro watched her tell him to back off multiple times, but he wouldn't. Then Quatro detonated.

They never played that school again.

The fear in her eyes knocked the concrete out of his muscles.

He grabbed her chin and grinned. (The girl was fine. There was no denying it.)

"I don't think we do anything about Noelle," he said aloud.

"But there's not enough room on the SUV for everyone," Dwayne said. "And I *know* she'll make a fuss. Especially when she sees I'm taking you three."

"Okay, well, leave me behind then, and take her instead," Quatro said. "As long as you two and Riv—"

"Umm, no," River replied, giving him a slight shove. "I'm *not* leaving you."

"Bro, don't be difficult, please—"

"No, Quintin! There's zero reason for stupid *Noelle* to go in your place!" She slapped him with the puppy dog face (which was mad unfair *and* uncalled for). "I need to be with you. It's the only place I feel safe right now—"

There was pounding on the door. The room went silent.

"Shit, security guards must be here," River said. "One of the staff probably heard us."

"You think it's the police?" Sydney asked.

Dwayne approached the door. "Can't think of anyone else who would beat on the door like that—"

It wasn't the security guards. Or the police from Islamorada.

It was Noelle.

River squeezed Quatro's forearm, and the air seemed to crackle.

"So you're all planning to just *leave* me here?" she said, hurt more than evident.

Dwayne sighed. "It's not like that, Noelle—"

"Sure seems to be . . ." She made a move to step into the room, but Dwayne blocked her path. "Those guards of yours know you're planning to leave?" she continued loud enough for the pair of them to hear her from where they were posted in the hallway. "If there's no room for me in that SUV, there surely isn't room for them either, right? You gonna leave the three of us here to die?"

"Oh my God," River piped. "Can you *please* cut the drama?"

"Couldn't have said it better myself," Sydney agreed. "We literally have no reason to prioritize you."

For a moment, Noelle looked stunned (Quatro couldn't seem to take his eyes off her). But she quickly recovered. "I mean, it's not like any of this is surprising . . ." The sound of her voice was so aggravating, Quatro had to fight to keep his mouth shut. Even though he *knew* she was about to say something she'd wind up regretting. You know, as was her habit these days. She zeroed in on Sydney. "I'm sure Sydney's the one *actually* calling the shots here. It's clear she's got Dwayne wrapped around her crooked little finger—"

"It's fascinating how bad you are at everything, including insults," Sydney shot back, unbothered.

"You're *just like Key*, Sydney," Noelle spat. "Only person you care about is *you*."

And there was Noelle's error. Quatro could literally *see* Future First Daughter Sydney Davis switch off as *Syd* came online. There would be no stopping the flames that were about to pour forth from down in her chest.

So he took a step back.

"I know your little no-friend-having ass isn't talking," Sydney began. "*You*, who spent the bulk of our childhood with your little lips glued to Keisha's butt cheeks, did whatever the hell she told you to like her little pet. Including talk shit about the rest of us. *And* you were clearly *so* obsessed with her, you chose her over us even though she's dead. Who exactly do *you* care about other than *yourself*, Noelle? The only reason you're even *here* is because of your little boyfrie—"

"Yeah, and now he's dead, so let's maybe not throw that in my face?" Noelle clenched her jaw.

Quatro had had enough. "All right, let's break this shit up—"

The moment he got close, Noelle threw her shoulder into the door, trying to barge her way in, but smacking Quatro with the heavy wood instead. Quatro heard the *thunk* before he felt it, but he dropped to the floor regardless.

"Oh my God, Quintin! Are you okay?" River appeared beside him. Wet warmth trickled down over his eyelid, but it wasn't until he saw blood on the back of his hand after wiping it away that the cut exploded with pain.

"What the hell is wrong with y'all, man?" Quatro barked as he let River help him to his feet. "Y'all are acting like you did the night Key died! Turning on each other and shit. Do you not remember? Everything worked out fine when we stuck together—"

"Yeah, until blabbermouth over there went and spilled her guts to that reporter," Sydney said.

"Look, I was tired of holding things *in*, okay? My best friend *died*: we were all *there* when it happened! And now it's happening again!" Noelle screamed.

"Let's dispense with the theatrics," Dwayne said. "No, it's not great that he died—"

"You mean was *murdered*?" Noelle corrected with tears streaming down her cheeks.

"Whatever. Point is, no one liked him any more than we liked Key—"

"Excuse you, speak for yourself!" Noelle shouted. "I happened to love them both!"

"Girl, please." Sydney threw her hands up. "You don't even love your *damn* self, the way you be acting. There's no way someone as narcissistic as you are could truly love another human being—"

"Come on." River tugged on Quatro's wrist and (thankfully) pulled him out of the verbal melee as Noelle sniped back and Dwayne jumped in. "Let's go get that cut cleaned up."

It *almost* felt like an escape . . .

But when Quatro realized that River had seen what was in the bathtub, he knew things were about to get infinitely worse.

"Umm . . . is that Ant's safe?" She pointed.

CHAPTER TWENTY-ONE

DWAYNE

7:02 a.m.

WHEN DWAYNE SAW River and Quatro disappear into the bathroom, he knew he was in trouble.

"Um, Sydney?" River called, and when her friend appeared at the bathroom door, River simply pointed.

"Is that the safe you said you found?" Sydney asked.

"Sure looks like it."

"What the hell is it doing in—?" Sydney looked at Dwayne, but he couldn't read her expression. "What's in it?" she asked River, turning away from him.

"Well, there was some cash, but it's gone. The weed and pills are still here, and so are—"

"A phone?"

Sydney's voice was barely a whisper, but the way she said it made Dwayne glance at her, just in time to catch it—the slight shift in Sydney's expression. It was barely anything—so subtle it would've gone unnoticed by anyone else. But Dwayne had known Sydney as long as he'd known the word *girl.*

Sydney was hiding something. Something that had to do with one (both?) of Ant's phones if he had to guess.

But why?

Dwayne wasn't about to put Sydney on blast, though—not now, with the tension in the room already so thick. But his mind raced, and one question rose above the rest: How soon would someone ask what the hell the safe was doing in the boys' bathtub?

"Everybody to the living room." River abandoned concern for Quatro and his bleeding cut and dragged him back into the suite's common area. Sydney and Dwayne followed without hesitation.

The quartet parted on its own: boys on one side of the room, girls on the other. A fucked-up school-dance scenario.

And River crossed her arms. "Why the hell do you two have that safe?" she said, her eyes volleying between the guys.

Dwayne barely blinked, as if she'd merely asked him what he wanted for breakfast. "I should be asking why you had it in the first place."

Quatro looked agog. Which made Dwayne feel bad for maybe a hair of a second.

Dwayne really should've taken the drugs out instead of the money.

River didn't take her eyes off Dwayne.

"Answer *my* question," she demanded. "Why the hell do you two have this safe?"

Something flickered in Dwayne's mind as the essence of Dana Reynolds seemed to rise out of River's very being. It had him squirming with the same unease Dana imposed on senators, congresspeople, CEOs. The ones who barely respected a powerful Black woman but feared her, nonetheless.

He cleared his throat and shrugged. "I saw you Wednesday morning. You snuck down to the yacht wreckage and came back with the safe."

The room tensed. All eyes turned to River.

"What was that about, River?" Dwayne continued.

But River wouldn't budge.

"So you broke into our room?" she asked, tilting her head slightly.

Dwayne's expression faltered. "Hold on—"

"You. Broke. Into. Our. Room," River repeated, razor sharp. "And stole the safe."

"The safe you stole in the first place!" he shot back.

"Wait, wait," Quatro cut in, stopping his second battle of the day. "Can we chill? We need to focus on getting the hell out of here. We can deal with this later—"

"No, we can't, Quatro." If River wasn't going to budge, Dwayne wasn't either. "Why was River out there? Why did she take Ant's safe? Do we all not deserve answers?"

River exhaled, annoyed. "I was trying to find Ant's laptop, all right?" she admitted. "I was curious about what might be on it. Whether there were some clues as to who might have killed him. Nasty text exchanges with resort staff, threatening emails . . . something. The last time I saw it was on the yacht ride from Key West, so that's where I decided to look."

She scanned the room.

"So why *did* you break into our room and take it, Dwayne?" Sydney said.

"Oh, so you knew she had it?" Dwayne replied.

"You should stop deflecting, Dwayne," River said. "It's a little disrespectful to the girl you've been all over for the past few days. I'm sure you've been whispering sweet nothings into her ear and shit. Might be good to just tell her the truth?"

Which . . . she had a point. Sydney did look stung, and the secret was eating him alive. Might as well spill it. What was the worst that could happen?

He lifted his chin. There would be no cowering. "I wanted the money from my and Ant's business arrangement. Figured it was in the safe. That's it."

"What sort of business arrangement, man?" Quatro asked. "Didn't you—"

"Irrelevant now. Why do you have his suitcase?"

"Really, dawg?" Quatro replied.

It was a low blow, and Dwayne knew it. But he needed to get the attention off himself before someone realized he was only telling a partial truth.

"I'm just saying: I can't be the only one with secrets Ant was keeping," Dwayne said.

No one replied.

"Well? Anybody else got something to confess?"

More silence.

"All right, then," Dwayne said. "Guess some of y'all are getting left behind."

Sydney drew back. "What?"

"The hell does that mean?" Quatro demanded.

Dwayne folded his arms. "New plan because I can't trust any of you right now. If any of you wanna be in that SUV and on *my* boat, you better come clean. Otherwise, you can take your chances at becoming the next dead body they find in this place."

He honestly couldn't believe he'd said the words aloud.

"What's gotten into you, Dwayne?" Sydney took a step away from him. Made his chest ache, but it was too late. He had to stay the course.

Another heavy silence filled the room.

Dwayne cleared his throat. "Last chance. If you got something to say, say it now. Otherwise? You're not coming. You can stay here and hope help is on the way."

Sydney looked at her feet and Quatro rolled his shoulders. River crossed her arms as though she was in the clear, but Dwayne knew her too well. He knew them *all* too damn well. "That goes for you too, River. There's no way you went looking for that laptop on some kid detective shit. What'd he have on you?"

River's mouth dropped . . . and then shut tight.

Dwayne raised a brow. "Nobody?"

Finally, Quatro sighed. "All right. Ant helped me get some . . . stuff. Performance enhancers. Not proud of it, but it is what it is."

River did a double take. "Wait, seriously?"

"Ant . . . tweaked some grades for me," Sydney said. "In calc."

Dwayne could tell that wasn't the full story, but he didn't press. It wasn't the time.

"River?" he said. "You wanna tell us what's *actually* on that laptop you went looking for?"

"Not until you *and* Syd spill the rest," River said. "What exactly was this 'business,' Dwayne?"

He kissed his teeth.

"Come on, man," Quatro added. "Just tell us. The only person who would use it against you isn't here cuz you closed the door in her face."

River snorted.

"Well, Dwayne?" Sydney pressed.

It was her eyes that made him crack. "Mostly green," he said.

"Huh?" Quatro threw his hands up.

"Green, man. Weed. Cannabis. Marijuana. Flower. Take your pick."

"*You* were selling *drugs*?" River looked like he'd told her he was the tooth fairy. "I'm . . . impressed? How the hell did you keep that a secret?"

"Man, whatever. Y'all don't know everything about me. Plus, most of my clients were from other schools, and I worked with a few people to make my deliveries. Kept my hands directly out of it, okay?" Dwayne said. "You got next. What was on the laptop, River?"

She hung her head. "Some stuff from one of my mom's cleanups," she said.

Definitely still lying.

"Sydney?" Quatro cut in. "What's the rest? Some changed test scores really ain't that big a deal. Go on 'head and air it all out."

Sydney glanced around the room and then let out a deep breath. The silence in the room boiled and Dwayne's stomach turned sour.

"My mother . . . she wanted me to get intel," Sydney said, quietly. "On you, Dwayne."

Dwayne's jaw flexed but he stayed quiet.

"I asked Ant to dig up some dirt to make her happy," she continued. "The day before we got here, he claimed he'd found something good—but he wanted a favor in return. We got into a fight over texts, and—"

"And you killed him?" Quatro said, aghast.

"Oh my God, Quintin! Of course she didn't kill him!" River snapped.

Dwayne stared at Sydney, absentmindedly rubbing the center of his chest. It was aching in a way it never had before. "So all this time . . . you were just spying on me for your mom?" he asked.

"No!" Sydney's response was immediate. "Dwayne, it wasn't like that! You and I— What we—"

"What we what, Sydney?" he asked. The aches spread into his arms and tingled in his fingertips. "Whatever it was, was it even real?"

And he could see the way Sydney's throat bobbed. How her lips pressed together. She was going to break. But he had no desire to stop it from happening.

"Dwayne." River stepped in front of Sydney. "I get it; you're upset, but we've got bigger problems right now. We need to get off this island, remember?"

Dwayne stared at Sydney for a minute and then sighed. "Let's just . . . meet behind the Meridian wing at eleven thirty tonight. The SUV will be ready."

"Meridian wing. Eleven thirty p.m.," River reiterated.

"Eleven thirty p.m. sharp. Johnson said that's when that asshole general manager has his nightly staff meeting in his office. They'll be distracted. Don't be late. You will be left—"

A sharp knock erased the rest of his sentence. Dwayne strode to the door. He peeked out the peephole, then yanked it open.

His heart jumped. The security guards looked a little too anxious for his liking. "Yes? What's going on?"

Johnson adjusted his stance, an air of no-nonsense rolling off him. "I need everyone to return to their rooms immediately."

"What? Why?" Quatro stood.

"This is not up for debate. Return to your rooms and stay there. I'll send word when I have it."

"Not without an explanation," Sydney said, fishing for eye contact from Prescott.

"Another dead body has been found," Prescott said.

The room went tomb silent.

No one moved.

No one breathed.

"Who?" River asked.

"I am not at liberty to say. This is a direct order. You are not to leave your rooms until it's time to leave. If you attempt to leave, you will be detained. Are we clear?"

The room blurred out of focus. Before he could overthink it (and even though he was gutted by what she'd done), Dwayne grabbed Sydney's hand. His fingers curled around hers; he needed her for stability just as much as she needed him.

Another dead body.

One by one, someone was picking them off.

And he had no idea who might be next.

CHAPTER TWENTY-TWO

SYDNEY

10:18 pm

HER GRANDMOTHER USED to say that if you shivered for no reason, it meant someone was walking on your grave. Sydney was sure that the "someone" was actually dancing on it because she could not stop shivering. They'd holed up in their rooms all day after Prescott had told them about the latest dead body. Every noise, every raindrop, every movement set Sydney and River on edge.

"You need to finish up," River said, voice panicked and urgent. "We need to be behind the Meridian wing in ten minutes."

"I'm going as fast as I can," Sydney snapped. Immediately, she regretted it. "I'm sorry. I'm just—" She didn't know what word to use to describe how she felt. Haunted, maybe? Some things you don't forget. Like the devastation on Dwayne's face after she confessed that she'd been spying on him for her mother. Or the way he'd rubbed at his chest—at his heart—over and over again, like she'd taken a sledgehammer to it. Like he was trying to soothe what she'd broken. But then, he'd still held her hand after the security guards brought up the newest dead body. So what did it all mean?

River sighed. "I get it, Sydney, but we have to go. Now."

Sydney stuffed her few remaining items into her suitcase and slammed it shut. "Let's go."

Outside, the weather deteriorated. Prescott was already waiting, her hair damp with sweat. "Aren't we missing Ms. Clarke?" she asked. And Sydney lied so quickly she surprised herself. "She'll be right along."

A sky full of gray clouds blocked the sun. The warm, gentle breeze from earlier in the day was now cool, gusting wind. Sydney zipped up her jacket and flipped her hoodie up. When would they catch a break? They were about to get in a car, and then on a boat. Now was not the time for yet another storm.

Quatro lurked behind one of the construction tarps draped across the Meridian wing's balconies. Buckets of indigo and blush paint spilled their guts across the cement floors of the shell of a building, the aesthetic promise of a setting sun theme all around them. Sydney wanted the sun to set on this nightmare spring break right now. She was beyond done.

Sydney looked past him, searching for Dwayne. "Where is he?"

Quatro ignored her, his eyes on River. "You good?"

River's shoulders sagged, like seeing Quatro had released all the tension from her body. She all but ran into his arms.

Sydney swallowed down the envy rising inside her. Would

Dwayne ever hold her like that again? Would he even talk to her after what she'd revealed earlier? Was the moment they'd shared earlier just because he was scared?

She gave their hug another few seconds before asking again. "Where is he?"

Quatro side-eyed her. "Said he'll be at the resort's mangrove entrance gate instead."

Sydney frowned. "That wasn't our plan."

"Plan changed without you," he said with a sneer. "What? You mad you don't have him all up in knots anymore? That he feels some type of way about your little setup? Your lies?"

River bumped his shoulder gently. "Lay off her," she said. "Now's not the time."

His sneer only deepened. "Now we all know the truth. She doesn't have to pretend to care about him."

"I do care about him!" Sydney said hotly. She was too angry to cry. Too devastated not to.

Part of her wanted to tell Quatro off. Who was he to judge her? He drank too much. Without his steroids or whatever, he wouldn't be any kind of anybody. He was just as big a fake, just as big a liar as she was. But another part of her, the part that understood she'd probably lost Dwayne forever, didn't have any fight left in her. They walked in silence toward the resort's other entrance in the Dusk wing.

Her heart lifted as she spotted the SUV ahead, shining like a yellow beacon. Their first step to a rescue.

The air grew heavier by the second. The clouds, darker. How long before the light drizzle became a downpour? Behind her, River and Quatro talked only to each other. As Sydney slid into the back seat, their heads were bent together. A small hope crept into her heart. If River and Quatro could forgive each other's lies and omissions, maybe Dwayne could forgive hers. It wasn't like he was blameless in all this. He'd broken into River's room. He'd sold literal drugs with Ant. Not that she gave a damn about that. She *did* care that he hadn't confided in her. Then again, she should've confessed, too. And the truth was, her crimes were bigger than his when it came to what mattered.

Dwayne wasn't at the resort's other entrance either. Sydney wrapped her arms around her waist tight and tried not to panic. What if he'd already left? Found another way to Vista Village? Did he hate her enough to leave them all behind? Would he punish her in this way?

Overhead, the clouds had darkened to near black. Wind whipped a stinging mix of water and sand into her eyes and hair. Sydney felt scrubbed raw, like someone had taken sandpaper to her skin. The open-air SUV would expose them to these elements. It would be a rough ride like this, but maybe they all deserved it.

Twenty minutes later, Dwayne still hadn't shown up. They stood in the shadows behind the SUV, engine off, ready to go, and trying not to draw attention in case one of the security guards was doing a round before their nightly staff meeting.

Quatro crossed his arms. "I don't like this," he muttered for the fourth time.

"Maybe we should go," River said.

"But it was *his* plan. He set this all up. We can't just leave him," Quatro added.

Instead of worrying that Dwayne had gone without them, Sydney was now worrying something bad had happened to him. What if he was lying hurt, or worse? What if he became another one of the dead bodies piling up? They still hadn't been told who'd been killed earlier.

"Maybe I should go check—" she began, but then there he was, jogging toward them, his executive protection security guard in tow.

Relief swamped her. He was alive. He was here.

Quatro didn't bother greeting him. "The hell you been?" he demanded.

More than anything, Sydney wanted to walk into Dwayne's arms, into the quiet safety he always made her feel. But he didn't say hello to her. Didn't even bother to look at her. She'd gotten used to the warmth of his eyes on her. How was she supposed to go back to being cold?

Dwayne shoved his hands into his pockets. "Man, lay off," he said to Quatro. "You don't think I had a good reason?" He palmed the back of his neck. "Something is up with the staff. I overheard them in their meeting."

"Why is that suspicious?" River asked.

"Their whole attitude was off. They didn't seem stressed or mad or anything. Seemed like they were having a grand old time. I couldn't get close enough to hear—"

"I knew it!" came Noelle's shrill voice from behind them. "I knew you would try to leave without me!" She was dragging suitcases and running toward them.

"Shit," Dwayne muttered. "Shit."

Instinctively, Sydney moved closer to him. Just as instinctively, Dwayne shifted away from her. He folded his arms across his chest and straightened himself up. Her greatest fear confirmed. That moment between them had been just that, a moment, and he might never forgive her.

Noelle descended on them. Her quiet seething reminded Sydney of Key. She was always the most dangerous, the most vicious, when she was silent. She looked pissed and smug at the same time. Sydney had a sudden urge to shove her to the ground. After this whole thing was over and done, she'd make it her mission to expose Noelle for the lying opportunist she was. She'd make sure that . . .

No. Sydney wouldn't be doing any of that. She was done with revenge and manipulation and pretense and lies. Done with being a part of the Six. Except for River and Dwayne, she didn't want anything to do with these people. Even now, she could barely stand to look at them. Disgusted, she turned away.

"So what are you gonna do?" Noelle challenged, arms crossed. "Because you're not leaving without me."

Prescott and Johnson tried to calm the situation, but Sydney could barely focus.

Dwayne paced. "We're out of time. We gotta go before we get caught out here."

Johnson's white cheeks shone with sweat. "Okay, we'll have to balance the weight. No suitcases."

"What?" Noelle said.

Everyone glared and she swallowed hard.

"So we're going to double up," Prescott directed. "Quatro and Dwayne in the back because your shoulders are broad. Then two girls will have to sit on your laps as we make our way through the forest. One will have to get in the trunk." She opened it and removed the luggage.

The boys hustled into the back of the SUV.

Noelle's eyes bounced between Sydney and River. "I'm not getting in there," she said.

"Yeah, well, suit yourself," Sydney said.

"I'm sitting on Quatro's lap." River turned on her heel and climbed up. Dwayne wouldn't look at Sydney, but he didn't block his lap.

Noelle burst into tears.

"Do you want to stay here or go?" Sydney said, and at this point, she didn't care. She just wanted to get out of there.

Prescott led a sulking Noelle to the trunk. Sydney heard Noelle's breath coming in sharp, short bursts, but she was too anxious herself to worry about Noelle. She pushed down anything that would soften her heart toward her former friend because this was survival and they had to move. She wanted to cover her ears as she climbed onto Dwayne's lap, but she heard Noelle begin to sob as the trunk slammed shut.

Sydney's pulse drummed and her hands went clammy as the engine started. Dwayne's upset radiated from him like steam in a kettle that was about to scream. But he held on to her, tentatively, as the SUV began making its way slowly over the bumpy, still partially flooded forest roads. She held her breath as the resort became smaller and smaller in the rearview mirror. Her heartbeat slowed as the SUV snaked along the road through the mangrove forest, the trees resembling twisted skeletons in the dark.

No one said a word until the small village came into view.

"Finally," Quatro mumbled.

A scattering of twinkling candlelight shone in various shops, and flashlights flickered in the distance.

This nightmare was almost over. Johnson parked the SUV near the storm-battered pier. They piled out, and Sydney saw that Noelle's cheeks were tear-streaked Prescott helped her out of the back. "You're okay, Miss Clarke," she heard her security guard whisper.

"Let's get out of here!" Dwayne led the way forward.

"What kind of decrepit-ass boat is that?" Quatro said as it got in close. Much as Sydney hated to agree with him about anything right now, he was right. *Decrepit* was too good a word for it. The thing was a cobbled-together assortment of bleached scrap wood. She saw cracks of moonlight between planks. The motor looked like a rusty leaf blower mounted on a pipe. No way could it take on the sheer power of a storm surge.

The boat wasn't the worst of it. The "captain," a grizzled and wrinkled husk of man who reeked of beer and rotten fish, didn't bother to greet them.

"Boat's only rated for five people," he said, and burped something foul.

"But there's seven of us," Sydney heard herself say, panic rising. "There's seven of us!"

"Well, three of you will have to hang back. I can make two trips if you can pay for two trips," the man said, with a gruff laugh.

Quatro wasn't having it. He grabbed River's hand and pushed forward. "All I know is me and Riv are getting on." He kept his voice low and his stance loose, like he was ready for a fight.

Johnson stepped forward, ready to negotiate, maybe to let Quatro or River or even Noelle go in his place, but Dwayne stopped him. He blew out a resigned breath and looked over at the captain. "How about I make it worth your while to take us all?"

The captain cackled. "Can't rightly spend it if I'm at the bottom of the ocean, now, can I?" But Sydney could spot greed on anyone. He was more than willing to take Dwayne's bribe.

He took a minute to size them up and then nodded. "Okay. Step lightly."

Dwayne got on first. He still hadn't looked at her once. Sydney tore her eyes away from him and stared out at the water. A crack of lightning ripped the sky open. For a moment during the flash, the world was a still photograph. Black waters under a black sky. All at once, Sydney knew: if she got on that boat, those waters were going to be her grave. She knew it the way she knew she loved Dwayne. Would always love him.

She backed away from the water's edge.

It didn't take long for River to notice. She grabbed Sydney's hand, tugged on it. "Let's go," she said, in her firmest no-nonsense voice.

Sydney shook her head. She remembered the way she hadn't been able to control her shivering earlier. Maybe her grandmother had been sending her a warning. "I'm not getting on that thing."

River pulled at her again. "Better than staying back here with some psycho picking us off."

Sydney gestured to Prescott standing behind them. "I promise I won't leave her side."

River opened her mouth to protest again, but Sydney stopped her. "You can't convince me." They'd been best friends for so long that Sydney knew the exact moment River understood she needed to give up.

Sydney pulled River in for a hug. "I'm so sorry about what I said before. I didn't mean it. I was just—"

"I know," River said, voice wavering. "I'm sorry too. I wanted to tell you my stuff, but I got in so deep."

Sydney squeezed her one last time. "I'll see you on the other side."

After that, it didn't take long for everyone to board the boat. Another ten minutes and they were off. Her security guard urged her to get out of the rain and get back inside the SUV. But something heavy and watchful inside her said not to leave.

Not yet.

She watched the boat approach the breakers. The waves were impossibly big, like dark mountains rising and collapsing. She watched as the boat climbed the face of a wave, becoming almost vertical, before sliding out of view down beyond its crest. The boat appeared again, climbing once more, then dipped. It did this four times until, to Sydney's horror, it capsized and vanished under a wave.

Sydney screamed her throat raw. "No!" Behind her, Prescott was saying something, but Sydney couldn't understand her. And then Prescott darted forward and dove into the water.

What had just happened?

This couldn't be real.

Had all her friends just died?

No.

Then she saw something white: an oar. Then something that could've been the motor. Then a plank. The boat had been pounded apart into junk pieces.

The bellhop, Cruz, was suddenly there. But how? He ran past her wearing a life vest, arms full of life preservers. He tossed them into the water, keeping hold of their ropes, and started swimming hard in their direction. This man was risking his own life. He was a better person than all of them combined.

The next few minutes were the longest of Sydney's life. For long stretches of time, there was nothing to see but the dark, churning ocean. It was as if the sea had swallowed everything she loved, and she held the cross around her neck so tightly her fingers ached as she silently begged God for her friends to be okay. Then, finally, a flash of orange. River's jacket? A few seconds later, she caught a glimpse of arms arcing in and out of water. Someone was swimming back to shore. The bellhop saw it too. He swam toward both figures with the life preservers in tow. River reached hers first. The second person—Quatro maybe—grabbed his next.

Standing there and doing nothing was agony. Maybe she should dive in and try to help too? But then she'd just be another person who needed rescuing. She watched, terrified, as her friends' heads vanished and reappeared in between waves. Each time they bobbed back into view, she allowed herself a shallow, panicked breath of relief.

River and Johnson were the first ones to make it back. With Johnson's help, Sydney pulled River out of the water. She collapsed on the dock and sputtered big wet messy breaths in and out.

Quatro was next back to shore. Then Noelle. Then the captain. All of them clutched at the surface of the undulating dock. They pressed their faces to it. All of them knew how close to death they'd come.

Sydney moved nearer to the edge. Where was Dwayne? And where was Prescott? A sole life preserver had drifted far away, tiny and white and still unclaimed. Had Dwayne been knocked out by debris? Was he gasping for his last breaths even now?

Behind her, she felt the others shuffling to their feet. She heard Noelle say, "Dwayne." Sydney wanted to scream at her, to tell her to keep his name out of her mouth.

River was suddenly right next to her, squeezing her hand. "Dwayne's gonna make it," she said. "Any second now, he'll be here with us."

Seconds became minutes. Three or four times, Sydney was sure she saw something out there that looked like a person, but it was never him.

Rain fell even harder. Noelle said something about being cold and needing to go inside because the wind had picked up. And then

River collapsed, like she hadn't been standing a moment earlier. Sydney crouched beside her and touched her face, but she could tell her friend was still breathing. Was Dwayne? Was her security guard?

Then she heard the bellhop say something about them all getting on the bus. A bus? Sydney turned to see a cheerful-looking resort shuttle with *Kuzimu Horizons Resort and Beach* emblazoned on the side, and it felt all wrong to climb aboard a vehicle that looked so clean and new. Where had the staff been hiding it? Johnson lifted River like she weighed nothing, and they all walked toward the shuttle, leaving Sydney behind for a moment, still staring at the waves.

"We can't leave Dwayne," she called out as everyone hustled to the bus to avoid the downpour. She couldn't leave him. She couldn't leave Prescott. Cruz tried to get her to join, but she begged him to help as the wind drowned out her voice. He promised he'd call for help if she got on the bus and out of the storm.

Months later, what Sydney would remember of the time she stood alone in that storm waiting for Dwayne to resurface was the bargain she made with God. Let him be alive, and she would do better. Be better. Let him be alive, and she would—finally—become something other than her mother's daughter.

THE WEEK BEFORE:

SATURDAY

CHAPTER TWENTY-THREE

RIVER

1:33 a.m.

RIVER KNEW SHE shouldn't have gotten on that boat.

The waves were like static, whooshing in a way that made them sound much more distant than they were. Her ears must have been clogged with seawater. She could feel sand gritty against her skin. It was under her nails, under her clothes, in her hair, in her bra, in her underwear. River coughed and looked around. They were all trembling, panting, and soaked, but that wasn't the worst part.

The worst part was the fact that they weren't all there.

Dwayne was still somewhere in the water. Washed away. Gone. And Sydney was wailing.

River must've lost consciousness after they'd all made it back to the beach, because when she came to, she was lying on the floor in the restaurant. She felt achy and confused, and it still sounded a bit like she was hearing everything from underwater. She had no idea how long she'd been out, but Sydney was calmer now, handing out bandages and antiseptic cream while tears ran silently down her face.

River's throat ached. Her nose stung with salt, and when she reached up to rub it, she realized it was bleeding. Something was off with her ankle too—when she tried to move, it hurt to straighten it. She wasn't the only one in awful shape.

Out on the beach she remembered seeing Quintin puking up what looked like foamy water in the sand and Noelle in the fetal position, rocking back and forth like every part of her was hurting.

River was almost certain she'd swallowed water. She tried to open her eyes but felt a wave of nausea, so she closed them again. She turned toward the sound of someone talking, waited a few seconds, and then opened her eyes again. But her sight was still bleary and unfocused. How did they get from the village back to Kuzimu? Her head felt too dizzy to piece it all together.

It was Quintin's voice she heard above the ringing in her ears, and she could see the shape of him, pacing.

"How the hell are we supposed to get out of here now?" he was shouting.

She tried to sit up. When Quintin saw her, he ran over to help. "You passed out on the beach. I was worried you were dry drowning."

River frowned. "Dry drowning?"

"It's a thing!" Quintin said.

"I believe you." River leaned into his side. "I'm okay," she told him.

"I don't know why you all jumped on the boat in the first place,"

Sydney said. "It was clearly unsafe, and still no one was being reasonable."

"I wasn't gonna be left behind here to die!" Noelle yelled.

"Great, and now Dwayne's dead," Sydney shouted back miserably. "And Prescott's . . ."

"What?" River asked.

"She jumped in after us," Quintin said quietly. He nodded at something covered in a wet sheet.

"Oh my God," River said, covering her mouth. She rubbed her eyes. "How did we even get back here?"

"The general manager had a shuttle all along," Sydney replied, swallowing a sob.

"And it was just our luck that we didn't know about that," Quintin added.

"Everything about the whole situation is a lose-lose," Noelle said. "I don't know what we're arguing about. We're stuck. We're in danger. And now most of us are hurt on top of everything else." Noelle reached up to touch the cut on her forehead and winced.

River saw the general manager pacing by the windows. It was so dark out that she couldn't tell where the sky ended and the ocean began. The chef was with him, and they were whispering. River thought she heard Chef Starlie say, "Where the hell is my son?" But the general manager told her to keep her voice down. Starlie looked anxious and angry, but she glanced around, nodded quickly and headed into the kitchens.

"I'm just going to get some ice for . . ." The chef gestured at all the kids, in their various states of distress.

"Why does it feel like she's lying?" River whispered to Quintin.

The double doors to the restaurant opened, and in walked the bartender, the groundskeeper, and the two security guards who had interrogated them. River expected them to rush over to make sure she and her friends were okay, but they lingered around the edges of the room.

"What are we going to do?" Noelle whined.

"Wait to be rescued, I guess," Sydney replied. She seemed more defeated than River had ever seen her.

"We can't just sit here," Quintin said.

None of the others had noticed the hotel staff edging around them, but River squeezed Quintin's hand to get his attention.

"What the hell are they all doing?" she whispered, but Quintin wasn't paying attention to her.

"We're on a goddamned island, Quatro! There's nowhere to run. Nothing can fly when the weather is so unpredictable. That crappy boat was our one ticket out of here. Now we just have to hope our parents figure out that we didn't make it to Islamorada, that we're on a murderous spring break, and somehow find a new way to get here before we're all dead!" Noelle shouted.

The door opened once again and in walked the bellhop. He rubbed his hands together, and River saw that his nails were painted a sickly shade of green. They looked like vomit.

"Okay, okay, settle down," he called out. "That was all very dramatic. But not to worry. Help is on the way."

River's eyes went wide, and Sydney turned around so quickly her locs flew over one of her shoulders.

"Really?" Noelle asked. "We're really going to be okay?"

That was when the laughter started. River thought she'd imagined it for a moment, but then it got louder and louder. The din bouncing off the walls. It was coming from the hotel staff, who had by now completely surrounded them. They were all laughing.

"What in the hell?" Quintin looked around as River grabbed his hand.

River hobbled to her feet. Her ankle was most certainly sprained or fractured. Quintin stood in front her, like his body would protect her from the crazed sound of their laughter. Sydney's hands began to tremble. River felt like shaking herself. It was all creepy as hell.

"I was kidding," the bellhop said.

The chef reentered the restaurant holding a tray of ice and a few kitchen towels. She looked around and slowly set the tray down.

"No one is coming," the bellhop continued. "I thought you'd have it all figured out by now. Rich, smart kids like you? But if you haven't, let me be clear: you've been our hostages this whole time."

The chef looked really confused now. She inched toward the door, but when the general manager saw her, he said, "Oh good. Now that everyone's here we can begin."

"Simply put," the general manager began, "we wanted to get paid. So when the opportunity to host the children of some of the nation's capital's elite presented itself, it was a no-brainer." He looked down at the draped body. "But then things got . . . messy."

River looked at Quintin, who looked at Noelle. River grabbed Sydney's arm and Noelle just stared at the general manager with her mouth hanging open.

"I'm sorry, Starlie. When you told me you weren't interested in joining in on our plan and then showed up with your son, I needed to make sure you'd keep your mouth shut. And when you didn't and I found out he knew. . . He became the perfect . . . body . . . we needed for this whole arrangement."

"What the fuck?" Quintin asked.

The general manager shrugged as the chef started crying. River watched as the woman folded in on herself and seemed to be having a hard time breathing. A classic panic attack. No one attempted to help her as she hit the floor, sobbing out a name that sounded like *Orion*.

"We had to blow up the boat after it docked because we couldn't have you all setting sail in the middle of the week. I thought the captain would just drop you off. I had no idea he planned to stay the whole time! And when we planned the explosion, I didn't count on him still being on board. Whoops."

"Oh my god," Noelle whispered. River slowly backed away from them, as if distance could make everything Mr. Chandler was saying less real.

"And then, well, P.J. let his so-called *God* determine how far he was willing to go. And I couldn't have that. Religious guilt can make people do dangerous, crazy things. Like talk a little too much."

Now River froze. She felt pinned in place, a butterfly pressed beneath glass with its wings on display and ready for inspection.

None of this felt real.

"Just like Orion, the writer wasn't even supposed to be here this week. And Gloria—well, all I wanted was to talk to her, and when I saw what she was up to, the old broad just killed over from shock at being caught, I guess."

"Jesus," River heard Quintin whisper.

"All these people were ruining my carefully laid out plans. It was supposed to be us and you six. That's it. And we were supposed to tell your parents if they didn't pay up, you wouldn't come home. But none of it worked!"

The general manager was screaming now. And River couldn't believe her ears. This man was deranged.

"We didn't count on this damn storm. We couldn't even reach anyone to ask for the goddamn money! So now I don't really know what to do. I think we have to kill you all now? Because no one can know. No one can find out what happened here."

The doors swung open again. Johnson stumbled in, dripping wet, supporting someone with his head down.

"Dwayne?" Sydney called out, and at the sound of her voice, he looked up. "Dwayne!" She ran to him, arms outstretched.

River watched as they embraced, and then Johnson began moving toward the bellhop, gun drawn. The bartender and groundskeeper grabbed him and shoved him to the ground. Then Dwayne stumbled toward the general manager. Quatro followed, jumping in to help, but the bartender and the groundskeeper were suddenly there, too, pulling the boys away from the general manager. Everyone was yelling and fighting, and River was still so confused.

Hostages? Getting paid? Did someone who worked for the hotel kill Ant? Were they all really about to die?

She should have known not to get on that boat.

It was all becoming too much, and River knew she couldn't take much more. She eased toward the back of the room, and it was so chaotic, so full of people screaming and bleeding, girls sobbing and guys fighting, that no one noticed. She would find her own way out of here, her own way off this godforsaken island.

She'd known for days that something was off. That someone, or maybe everyone, was lying. She should have trusted her gut and tried to figure out a way out of here instead of trying to find the truth. She'd never make that mistake again.

River remembered Dwayne saying something about a satellite phone. She wondered if she could find it and use it if it was still in his room. It was the only hope she had left, and so she turned and hobbled toward the exit, her injuries making the long hallway seem even longer. Her nose was still bleeding and something was definitely wrong with her ankle, but she pushed through the pain. Just before she reached the door, someone else opened it. It was dark outside, but she saw flashing red and white lights, and her legs almost gave out with relief. Help, at last. She could just make out that the person who opened the door had a tall silhouette and broad shoulders—a cop, she thought, until he stepped into the light.

River stopped dead.

"Ant?" she said.

FLORENCE BENNETT

Housekeeper

12:00 p.m.

FLORENCE BENNETT KNEW mess when she saw it.

And this was a mess unlike any other.

For thirty of her sixty years on this earth, Florence had worked at the Kuzimu Horizons Resort and Beach. She'd seen it all—new ownership, flashy renovations, guests from countries she couldn't point to on a map, managers who thought their suits and ties gave them the right to talk to her any old kind of way.

But in all her years, she'd never seen a dead body.

This week, she'd seen too many.

Florence sighed as she stood by the floor-to-ceiling windows of the Sunset wing's presidential suite, rubbing the small of her lower back. The way some people swore their aching joints could predict rain, Florence's back always knew when trouble was brewing. A trashed room. An unruly guest. A scandal waiting to happen.

This week, the trouble had come wrapped up in designer clothes and teenage recklessness.

Beyond the window out on the dock, the Islamorada police ferry pulled away from the island into the night, carrying away those spoiled, entitled, troublesome kids. She'd used the extra satellite phone in the housekeeping office to call. She'd had enough of this game.

Good riddance. Hopefully they took their chaos and bad luck with them.

Florence had always thought it was foolish to let teenagers run wild at the resort. They should've banned guests under eighteen. But ownership didn't take advice from the housekeepers. They never had to clean up the broken glass, mop up the vomit and the blood, deliver towels to underage girls who were nursing their first hangover. No, ownership just collected the money while Florence scrubbed away the evidence.

She should've been used to it by now, but this bunch was different. For one, Mr. Brooks's son, Anthony, had been part of their little clique. In fact, he was the one who'd brought them here. And now . . .

Florence shook her head, turning back to the mess of the room. The storm and power outage alone had seemed like signs from God almighty Himself. Then the yacht exploded, and the dead bodies started piling up. It was like evil itself had checked into the resort.

But Florence had kept her hands as spotless as the luxury sheets she was now pulling from her cart. Good thing, too, because she still had a pension to look forward to. But her coworkers?

She yanked the comforter off the bed, her lips pressed tight. They'd gone too far. She never liked those kids from the moment they arrived, but playing God was a fool's errand—she wasn't about to torment them. Her coworkers had tried to drag her into their little games, whispering about justice and teaching lessons, but she was too old for all that foolishness. Florence called it what it was—stupid. She'd scrub every toilet at the resort with a toothbrush before she got roped into that.

And now? While she was still earning her paycheck, was still *free*, her coworkers were about to trade their uniforms for orange jumpsuits.

Lord, have mercy.

Florence tucked the corners of the new sheets tight and smoothed her palm over the fresh linen. The suite was clean again—new sheets, new towels, a restocked minibar, waiting for a new guest. One who would hopefully bring new energy. No blood, no bodies, no schemes.

God willing.

Florence took one last glance at the ferry, then grabbed her cart and rolled it out of the suite, making her way down to the lobby.

The air was thick and heavy. But that damn storm was gone now. The hum of police radios filled the space as officers moved around. Florence kept her head down, like she always did, but then she saw them.

The bodies being wheeled out. The black bags now tagged with the names.

Orion Parsons.

Ade Diallo.

Gloria Platt.

Patrick James Morgan.

Sabine Richardson.

She inhaled sharply and made the sign of the cross. But not for the dead.

For herself.

By the grace of God, she wasn't being loaded into the coroner's van.

Because Florence Bennett knew mess when she saw it.

But more importantly, she knew how to keep her hands clean.

PRESENT DAY

DWAYNE HARRIS

April 6

8:56 p.m.

"HELLO, DWAYNE. I'M Detective Franco. And I just have a few questions. What exactly happened?"

Dwayne Harris couldn't believe this detective was talking to him when the general manager of the Kuzimu was basically a certified sociopath.

"I was told that there was a boat? Who exactly was on it?"

Dwayne couldn't understand why *he* was being questioned when the bellhop, groundskeeper, and bartender had helped hold them hostage.

"What exactly was the plan? Where were you all headed?"

And he definitely couldn't wrap his head around why this man and his badge were in here in *his* face when there were full-grown adults he should be questioning. Murderous ones. Not to mention that Anthony Brooks, the resort owner's son and the kid they'd all presumed was dead, was completely unharmed in the room next door.

"I'm sorry," Dwayne said, shaking his pounding head. He wondered if he had a concussion. "But I just got tossed around underwater, nearly drowned, and I'm still hooked up to"—he gestured to the machines beeping and whirring around him, monitoring his vitals—"all this shit."

He leaned forward and shifted his shoulders in a way that he knew from experience made him look bigger.

"Why the hell are you talking to me?"

ANTHONY BROOKS

April 6
9:11 p.m.

ANTHONY COULDN'T HELP himself: he smiled. Nah, things hadn't gone precisely as planned—he definitely hadn't counted on people *actually* dying (big *oops!* there). But all in all, he'd accomplished his mission.

Shit felt good. Even with this goofy-ass "detective" glaring at him.

"You sure look happy for a kid who was supposedly murdered," the guy said.

Ant shrugged. "I'm sure you'd be happy, too, if you'd come back from the dead."

The guy's eyes narrowed. He wanted to say some shit he knew he shouldn't. Ant could see it all over him. And could also see his Adam's apple bob as he swallowed it down.

"So, who are you exactly?" Dude leaned back in his chair and crossed his arms.

"What do you mean?"

It was fun watching the red creep up his neck and fill his face from the bottom. Like a human thermometer.

"Everybody else here—all your 'friends'—has told me a completely different story about what happened on that island. But there's one thing they all seem to agree on . . ."

A chill shot down Ant's arms. Yeah, he'd done his due diligence with regard to entrenching himself as an invaluable resource in each of their lives, while also collecting dirt on them in the process. But it hadn't occurred to him that, while each of them had a *little* dirt on him as well, collectively . . . they had a whole lot. It had been the gamble he'd taken to gain their trust.

He gulped and lifted his chin. Plausible deniability would work in his favor. It *always* did.

Didn't it?

"And what was that?" Ant asked, cool as a cucumber.

The detective sat forward and put his elbow on his knees. "Not a single one of them seemed to know a whole lot about you, their benevolent trip planner."

The tension went out of Ant's shoulders. So, none of them narc'd. Getting himself off the hook here would (should) be a piece of cake.

"So, I'll ask you again: Who are you?"

It was all over now. Might as well tell the truth. Might as well revel in what he'd accomplished. It was a feat, after all.

Ant adjusted his chain and settled into his seat. "My name is Anthony Brooks," he began. "I'm sure you already know–slash–have heard, but around this same time last year, a girl died. She was good friends with all the other kids who came on this trip. You familiar?"

The guy consulted his notes. "Keisha White, I presume?"

Ant nodded. "Yeah. That's her. She was my cousin." His head dropped. "My favorite cousin, in fact. Not that any of *them* know that."

When he forced his chin back up to lock eyes with the detective, they were damp. It hit Ant hard: he hadn't actually grieved. From the moment his mama had told him Keisha was dead, that she'd supposedly "drowned," he'd been in private-eye mode.

Because Key had been an even stronger swimmer than Ant was.

They'd spent most summers together on their grandfather's ten acres in South Carolina, and he remembered how when high school started, she used to call him all the time and tell him how out of place she'd felt around her friends. She would talk about how everyone seemed to be "chasing adulthood" and "morphing into their pushy parents" except her. She just wanted to have a regular high school life and do "dumb teenage shit" she wouldn't be able to get away with once she got older.

"I'll tell you everything . . ." Ant leaned back against the hospital bed, ready to tell the story of a lifetime.

River's videos had been a bright spot for a minute—Key loved the thrill of anonymously spilling tea through River's little blog thing—but Key eventually recognized that River wasn't ever being real with her. She could tell by the way River would look at Key's boyfriend, Quatro, when she thought Key wasn't watching.

And as Ant came to discover through his master plan—which took *months* of effort and late nights and collecting information and strategizing—River's little crush on Quatro was what had started the firestorm that burned his cousin to the ground.

It had come to him piecemeal, but once he'd gotten that pivotal part, it wasn't too hard to put the rest together. Had he felt a little guilty about bugging everyone's rooms on the island? Ehh . . . maybe. But if not for River slipping back out to the pool that first night after everyone had gone to bed—delaying Ant's plan by an hour (which was stressful as hell at the time)—he wouldn't have known how to put together the snippets and bits he'd gathered from their private conversations.

River had scared the shit out of Ant at first. He was still swimming laps, waiting for his cue from the groundskeeper he'd recruited to be the lookout in case any of them came out of their rooms in the middle of the night. Not that the dude had wound up being necessary: they'd all had more to drink than they'd realized, as Ant had been deliberately heavy-handed with his pours.

So heavy, apparently, that River wandered back down to the pool an hour or so after everyone had left, drunk as shit. The sight of her suddenly sitting at the end of a lounger, red-eyed and looking off into the distance like her soul had been sucked from her body made Ant lose his butterfly stroke and come down so hard, water shot up his nose.

The drizzle hadn't turned to a downpour quite yet, though the sky threatened to open any minute.

He swam over to the edge where she sat under a pool cabana. "Uhh, River? You good?"

"This is the anniversary," she said to the sky, a brief pause in the rain letting her catch a glimpse of a few stars. When she looked at Ant, he could see she was crying. "It was tonight. Did you know that?"

Ant hadn't responded.

"It was all my fault. I just . . ." She shut her eyes and shook her head. "The way she *came* at me was . . . and I *reacted* . . . I didn't know . . ." Her face dropped into her hands.

Ant got out of the pool then. Draped a towel over *her* shoulders—which, despite being in pajamas, she wrapped tightly around her like a blanket—and pulled up a lounger beside her. The moment his butt hit the thick, cream-colored linen of the seat, ol' girl cracked and spilled like a busted piñata.

"It was *the worst night* of my life," she blubbered, almost incoherently. "And I didn't mean for . . . UGH!"

Ant looked around and sent up a silent prayer that no one had heard her exclamation. He needed her to go away, not for more people to come . . . but first, he needed to know what the hell she was talking about. "Go on ahead and get your shit off, River. I won't judge."

She sniffled, then took a deep breath. "Keisha and I weren't . . . getting along, I guess you could say. We were hanging out more because of MANIfest the Mess, and she'd tell me things, you know? Stuff she didn't tell anyone. Even Noelle. The more we talked, the more I realized how sad she was deep down and how alone she felt. I could also tell our *friends* were getting sick of her." She shook her head. "And the more I hung out with *them*, the less I wanted to be around *her* . . . even though I totally knew her meanness came from sadness, and she needed a real friend." More tears fell.

Ant didn't say a word.

"I didn't, like . . . *mean* to zoom in on Quatro. I really, really didn't. He's obviously hot and was—is—so, so great or whatever, but I wasn't *trying* to get with him or anything. Well . . . not at first, really. We just *got* each other? There was this one night we'd all gone to this off-the-grid party in Rock Creek Park. When Key got there, she was already messy. She'd eaten too much of a canna cookie some 'friend of a friend' had given her and was acting all paranoid. She exploded on everyone, saying she knew everyone had turned on her and was talking about her behind her back and judging her because she didn't know what she wanted to do with her life or something? She wasn't making a ton of sense."

Ant had heard about this night, though Keisha hadn't been able to remember exactly what she'd said during her midnight rant. Only that she was "pretty sure" she'd "further isolated" herself from the people she cared about most, and that she "didn't know what the hell was *wrong*" with her. She'd cried on that call.

"Anyway," River continued, "there was this moment at the park when Dwayne said, 'Ey, get your girl,' to Quatro at the exact same time Sydney said, 'Noelle, *please* get your friend.' Quatro and I locked eyes and I just, like . . . I felt so *bad* for him, you know? Keisha used to really put him through it."

Her face morphed. "I was *not* 'trying to steal him,' though," she said (in a tone that made it clear to Ant that "stealing him" was precisely what River was trying to do, even if the motivation itself was subconscious). "She was awful to him sometimes, so I made it a point to be the opposite. Give the guy a break, you know? Looking back, it probably did seem strange that I was calling to check up on him and stuff, to make sure he didn't need anything—she sure as hell wasn't giving him the sort of support a girlfriend was supposed to. But that night at the gala . . ."

She put her face in her hands again as if she could hide away from all that she'd said, and Ant's irritation spiked. So he came right out with it: "What happened that night, River?"

"I blacked out, but lately every time I drink it comes back to me. She just . . . *came* at me! We were at the gala in our gowns or whatever, and she got us to sneak to the hotel's indoor pool . . . she had this *way* about her, you know? There's a reason everyone was sort of at her beck and call. She was really hard to say no to. I should've known some shit was up. There was *always* something up with Key at that point." She shut her eyes and shook her head, then barreled on: "So we all sneak through the hotel and get into the pool area, and we walk to the edge of it to look around. We were partying and she, like, *flipped* on me. Said she was sick of watching me make 'sex eyes'—whatever the hell that meant—at her boyfriend or whatever. 'You think I don't see that you *want* him, Riv? You think I don't know about how often you text him, offering him shit like *I*, his literal *girl*, don't even exist?' And she was, like . . . unhinged. Her eyes were all bloodshot and there were veins bulging in her neck."

She turned to Ant then and put a hand over her heart. "I was literally afraid for my *life*, Ant. *Literally.*"

It was the most bullshit thing he'd ever heard. But he bit his tongue. Because he knew there was more to come.

"So, of course, I'm all like, 'Key, no! I would NEVER disrespect you like that! In fact, I'm a little worried about you . . . Are you all right?' You know, actually being a good friend?"

(Ant could see that she'd worked hard to convince herself that was true.)

"And the next thing I knew, she'd gotten right up in my face with her weird eyes, looking like she wanted blood. 'Oh, a good friend? Is that why you recorded those videos about me? Because you're such a *good friend*?'"

Ant's ears perked up.

"Mind you, I hadn't actually posted them yet. Yes, I'd *recorded* a few MANIfest videos about stuff Key told me in confidence. Like *just in case* I wound up needing them or whatever, because *she* was the one pushing me to make the really awful ones about people at Marshall. But I hadn't *posted* the ones about her. I don't even know how she *knew* about them."

Ant did. Keisha knew about the videos . . . because he'd told her.

It had taken everything in him to swallow his rage at that point. Which was coming from multiple directions: first, he realized his cousin hadn't been totally honest with him. Key had called Ant one night, (seemingly) distraught about some gossip blog that "someone" was posting online that was leaking secrets about people at her school. "I'm really nervous I'm going to be targeted," she'd told him.

And there was nothing Anthony wouldn't do for his favorite cousin. So when she asked him to hack the account and screen-record everything in the drafts folder and send it to her, he'd done it without asking any questions. There were four of them, three about Keisha. And he was livid when he watched them.

After Ant moved to Thurgood Marshall, he did his best to figure out who was behind the blog, but everyone he managed to ask about it claimed it had been *Keisha's* blog—which was easy to assume as the posts stopped once Keisha was gone. He even started sending threatening messages from Key's account to try to flush the person out. But there was never a response.

To find out River was the one behind it—and that Key not only knew that, but was telling her what to post? Well, Ant didn't have the slightest idea what to do with that.

"I pushed her in," River said, yanking Ant back to the pool lounger and cabana. The biggest lightning bolt Ant had ever seen lit the sky just before a terrifying roll of thunder cracked it open, but the silence that followed was so dense, it almost seemed as if the cosmos had fallen.

"Say that again?"

"I pushed her, okay? She was . . . UGH! I just hated her so *fucking* much, and I hated everything she stood for, and I hated that she could seemingly make the world kneel at her feet by sheer force of will and that *she'd* managed to land a guy like Quintin.

And I hated that she'd found out about the videos. She was always somehow a step ahead of everybody! So, I just . . . reacted." She put her hand over her eyes. "She said what she said about the videos, and the next thing I knew, my arms were extended in front of me as her arms were spiraling, and she was falling backward into the pool with this look of panic on her face."

Ant could hardly breathe. "And then what happened?"

River sighed and let her head drop back. "I don't know—"

"Huh? Whatchu mean?"

"I ran." She shook her head as fresh tears began to fall. "I shoved her, and then I turned around and ran. I didn't even see her hit the water. And then I posted one of the videos about her. Because *fuck* her."

Ant was speechless.

"When I heard she'd drowned, I didn't know what to do. I didn't delete the video because I thought that would make me look more guilty than leaving it up. Honestly, I've been waiting a year now for cops to show up and tell me someone came forward and told them Keisha had sneaked into the pool area before winding up dead. And like I said: I don't know precisely how she drowned because I wasn't there. I left her. But I'm also the one who pushed her in, so—ugh, this is why I don't drink. Haven't drank since that night . . . It makes me lose control and I *hate* losing control."

There was another jagged crack of lightning and roll of thunder. Ant looked at his watch. Another round of rain was about to pour down on them. "You need to go back in now; okay, River? This storm is coming in strong, and as a good host, I need you to be safe."

To his relief, she nodded, got up, and went inside without another word.

And there, poolside, Ant allowed himself to do the one thing he'd been resisting for a year: cry. The rain trickled across his forehead, taking his tears with it.

"If I learned nothing else from this whole adventure," he said to the detective, "it's that nobody really *knows* anybody else because we are too busy trying to manage what other people *think*."

The detective's eyebrows lifted as he considered that. "Go on."

"Nobody knew my cousin for real. Not even me. The things I heard about her from the others shocked me, but I also knew they were true. And there were things about each of them that I knew, but the others didn't."

"And I'm guessing none of them knew you were the type to invite them to some remote island to fake your death?"

Ant smiled. "Touché."

"And if I understand correctly, you're saying they also didn't know you were this girl's cousin."

Ant felt his smile shift to a scowl, but he nodded.

"So run me through what all you learned from this little fake-death adventure."

Again: might as well tell the truth. Though Ant doubted there would be any real consequences for anyone: Key's death was ruled an accident, and even with everything he'd gathered, there was no way to prove otherwise. He knew from conversations he'd overheard that there was no security footage from the pool that night because the Six had somehow pulled strings to have the cameras turned off (it was Noelle's family's hotel, after all) so they could party in the pool area—but putting it all out there was its own type of justice, was it not?

He leaned forward in his seat and put his fingertips together. "Nobody ever wanted to talk about the night my cousin died because every single person who was there did something they didn't want anyone to know. River is the person who pushed Keisha in the pool and ran, but Dwayne was the person who'd given her the drugs she'd taken that'd had her acting out of sorts for months. Sydney and Noelle were the ones who came in and found Key floating in the water. They pulled her out, and Noelle tried to do CPR while Sydney ran to allegedly go and find help, but instead of coming back with, you know, an *adult*, she brought the others.

"When they all realized Keisha was gone, everyone freaked out, Sydney most of all. So she convinced them *not* to call the cops. Couldn't have anyone who would've been useful learning that the daughter of a senator trying to land 'the Dem nom for POTUS,' as she put it, was underage and wasted at a party *and* had discovered the dead body of a childhood friend who was drunk *and* on drugs. Dwayne went with it as the person who'd given her the drugs, and was in the same position as Sydney and didn't want the smoke clouding *his* dad's campaign, River certainly didn't want *her* Little Miss Perfect reputation thrown in a blender by being wrapped up in the bad press fallout that even her powerful mother couldn't fix, and Quatro's simp ass will do anything River wants despite him supposedly being in love with my cousin for years."

"Okay, so the girl gets pushed in the pool by one of the other kids here, two other girls pulled her out and realized she was dead in the water. One of them went and got the others, and they all agreed to . . . what?"

This was the part that really ate Ant up. It had fueled his whole plan and kept him going when there were bumps in the execution. Because what they had collectively decided to do was so diabolical to Ant, he wanted them all to spend the rest of their lives afraid they'd been found out and real repercussions were imminent. "They decided to act like they had no idea about any of it."

On night three, Ant overheard Dwayne and Quintin discussing "what the hell we're gonna do now that Noelle is runnin' her damn mouth to reporters," which was how he learned that Dwayne was the one who'd put Keisha's body back in the water, and Quintin and River had cleaned up the pool area.

He remembered reading the news articles where they were all acting surprised and pretending to be distraught at the loss of their "good friend" Keisha. He'd seen right through that shit.

"So, you faked your death on the anniversary of your cousin's death to—"

"Get them talking about what actually happened to her," Ant said. "I needed to know, man. I needed to see just how far they'd go to hide the truth."

The detective nodded, then smiled, showing a row of crooked teeth. And Ant could swear his stomach jumped up and swallowed his heart. "That's a fascinating story, kid," he began. "Truly. I was on the edge of my seat. But you're still in deep shit. 'Cause we got a slew of *actual* dead bodies to deal with—"

"Nah, but that don't have nothin' to do with me."

The detective spread his hands. "That's not what the staff is saying."

Ant shook his head. "Don't trust a word they say, man. That was *my* biggest error in all this: thinking they were trustworthy. Greed will make a person do wild things—"

"Yeah, well, *they're* saying luring all your rich friends to your dad's island so they could be ransomed back to their rich parents was *your* idea."

"What? That's not true! I shot that shit down and told them that if they didn't stick to the plan, they wouldn't get paid at all—"

"And yet, as I mentioned, there are five *actual* dead bodies that have to be accounted for. And while we do have a couple of confessions on record—Cruz Ramirez and Glenn Chandler were very cooperative—both men are saying they were acting on your instructions."

Ant had to fight to keep from jumping to his feet; he didn't want the detective to say he'd felt "threatened." "But that's not true!" He thought about telling him more, but the man was turning on him.

The detective raised his hands in an exaggerated shrug before *he* stood. "Case is being handed over to the FBI."

"The *FBI*? Are you *serious*?"

"As a heart attack, kid. You've made quite a mess."

Ant didn't respond to that. What could he even say? He kept his eyes glued to the detective's empty chair as the man made his way to the door.

"Oh, and Mr. Brooks?"

Ant didn't reply. And didn't need to.

"A piece of unsolicited advice in case you ever decide to play this friends-close-enemies-closer game again: when you're pretending to be a friend to someone—or I guess a *boyfriend*, in this case—for the sake of gaining an advantage, stay mindful of the fact that they could very well be doing the same to you." He put his hat on. "And be sure to get a lawyer."

And then he was gone.

EPILOGUE

NOELLE CLARKE

THAT NIGHT AIR tasted like a secret. Bitter as a lie told to keep someone safe, metallic as blood. Noelle waited for her parents' black town car to pull around. She steeled herself, willing her legs not to let her turn and look back at the hospital behind her. She didn't want to see a single glimpse of her ex-friends.

She wanted to be done with spring break.

Done with the Florida Keys.

Done with it all.

She wanted to never think of what happened last week . . . or them . . . ever again. As she waited with her suitcase, a hospital janitor drew closer and closer, dragging a rattling wheeled trash can along the sidewalk, cleaning up some sort of mess from a person heading toward the emergency room.

"Good evening," Noelle said, trying her best to return to her old self: a good girl, the girl her mother raised. Polite. Polished. Perfect. But as the humidity coated her skin and the sharp scent of whatever was in the garbage bag found her nose, she fought with more secrets she needed to remain buried.

The car pulled up. Both her mother and father jumped out and hugged her close. Not saying a word for a long moment. Just holding her there. The three peas in a pod.

Another car slowed as it passed. Noelle's gaze followed it as she rested her chin on her mother's shoulder. The car window cracked open. She spotted Anthony Brooks. Their eyes burned into each other's and they both nodded. The car window shut, and the car continued out of the parking lot.

"I'm fine." Noelle peeled herself from her parents' arms and made sure to erase any expression on her face.

"You sure?" Noelle felt her mother's sharp eyes comb over every dirty inch of her, and then she fell back into her father's arms, the scent of his cologne mixed with the signature smell of Red Bone's kitchens filling her nose and slowing her heart.

She was safe.

This was over.

Her mother peppered her with questions and commentary:

"What actually happened? They didn't give us much information over the phone."

"Are you sure they've examined you thoroughly? That cut looks bad."

"I can't believe you all went through this. Where are the other parents?"

"Those twin hurricanes were both category four. The worst of the decade so far, and back-to-back. Surprise for the whole country. I can't believe you all had to suffer through that."

"I need to make a million phone calls. I need to make sure our Marshall students are all right. Did you see them before you came outside?"

Luckily, her father rushed them both into the car and they started to make their way out of the hospital parking lot. Noelle wanted as much space as possible between her and the Six, her and what happened last week, her and all these memories.

She plugged her phone into the back-seat port with eager fingers and waited for it to gain enough power to turn on. They'd had no charging cables at the hospital. It had been a week without service, and she worried her phone had gotten waterlogged when they'd tried to escape the island and capsized in the ocean. But the device illuminated. She nibbled her bottom lip, breaking the fragile scab once more as notifications flooded the screen. Mostly social media tags, school emails, new recipe alerts from the cooking apps she used.

But one notification caused her heart to backflip in her chest. The *Washington Post* headline hit her like a splatter of hot grease: **IN MEMORIAM—A YEAR LATER BELOVED TEEN'S DEATH STILL HAUNTS A LOCAL COMMUNITY.**

The article. The one she'd provided an interview for, angering everyone around her. Noelle tucked her knees to her chest and clicked it open to read. The sophomore-class photo of Key filled her screen, her intense eyes almost finding her there in the dark. Noelle couldn't resist reading.

A year later, Keisha White's death still remains a mystery, leaving a tight-knit Washington, DC, Black community riddled with questions. The daughter of Octavius and Dr. Roslyn White, and an accomplished high school sophomore at Thurgood Marshall Academy, she had the world at her feet until her untimely drowning after the annual fundraiser for her prestigious school. I met with her best friend, Noelle Clarke, the daughter of the principal of Thurgood Marshall Academy and a Michelin-star restaurant owner, to remember the teen. We grabbed root beer floats at Lulu's on U Street, one of their favorite spots, a few weeks before the anniversary of White's death.

"What do you miss most about her?" I asked.

"Everything," Noelle answered, gazing into the dark puddle of her glass.

Noelle closed her eyes, willing away the images she'd fought so hard to keep at bay. The scent of chlorine and blood rushing back. She remembered how bright Key's eyes looked after she'd fished her out of the pool that night: the blue eye as clear as the pool water itself and the green eye like a marble, the broken capillaries stitched around Key's pupils like crimson lightning bolts.

She'd coughed up water and struggled to speak as Noelle gazed down at her.

"I need some air." Her father's words and the warm blast from the window snatched her back into the car.

Noelle gulped. She knew she should stop reading and answer some of her mother's incessant questions, but she couldn't. Her biggest secret wanted out as if it was clawing itself from beneath her stomach, where she'd tucked it away for so long. It made its way through her veins, forcing her to contend with it.

She continued to read:

"Not many who were close to Keisha would speak to me, I must admit. Especially those from Thurgood Marshall. Maybe because she was so talented and beautiful and popular. From what I've gathered, she had quite the effect on people. Would you agree?"

I watched as Noelle squirmed and bit her lips until they bloomed with pinkness. It took her a few moments to respond as if she was carefully measuring her words.

"She was the sun of our group—the Six. She was . . . like the force of gravity. Resisting her was impossible." A tear skated down her brown cheek and gave me a glimpse of the little girl inside her, the one yearning for a lost friend.

Noelle could feel those tears return in this moment, the tide of memory pointless to fight after all she'd been through the past week. Twin emotions of rage and passion surged in her chest as flashes of Key played on a loop. The same feelings the night Key died. She rubbed her knees as if the hard grit from the poolside still pressed against them as she'd hovered over Key's sputtering body. Tears coated her eyes, blurring the phone screen.

They'd been fighting for days leading up to the gala, arguing about Key's latest shady projects—the MANIfest videos with River—and even worse, she'd been more off the rails than usual since finding out her parents were splitting up. When Key was hurting, she wanted everyone else to hurt too. They'd fought about the fact that Noelle wanted her to be different, better. More like the old version of her that Noelle missed from when they were little kids.

But Key hadn't listened. If anything, she countered Noelle's softness with an unwillingness to bend—the more vulnerable Noelle was, the angrier Key seemed to get. She started to feel less and less like a friend and more like someone who hated her, someone Noelle was starting to hate back.

The fighting got worse. And while Noelle would cry and beg, Key would yell. One night when Key told her she wanted to slash her parents' divorce attorneys' tires, Noelle said she had to draw the line. And Key lost it. Key's insults blended with Chef Donaldson's belittling barks, morphing into a cacophony of Noelle's failures:

"You spend so much time being afraid. Why don't you stand up for yourself and stop being such a whiny little bitch?"

"You'll regret spending high school trying to be mommy's perfect little angel and daddy's perfect little chef! You're screwing everything up anyway!"

"You said you loved me and that we'd make this year count! That we'd do things together, but I knew you'd never do anything that meant taking a risk. I knew you were a coward. You never show up for me—not when it really matters."

As Noelle stared down at her best friend gasping for breath, she saw an enemy instead, that blue eye as cold as Chef Donaldson's gaze, that pale skin sallow now like his always was. She looked left and right, then behind her. They were alone poolside. Noelle reached for one of the nearby towels, soggy and soaked with pool water, then placed it over Key's mouth. She pressed down. Hard.

She thought back to how Chef Donaldson used to lock her in the pantry or the walk-in, only allowing her out if she promised to obey. She thought back to how Keisha used to force her to harm people with secrets. She thought back to how she'd scalded herself so many nights trying to get clean of it all.

She watched as Key writhed and wriggled, unable to cough up the rest of the water in her lungs, sucking down more as the sodden fibers of the towel filled her mouth. Her arms eventually went limp. The coughing stopped. Noelle put two fingers to Key's neck, waiting for a pulse, part of her not believing what she'd just done. Nothing about the moment felt real.

But the heartbeat she'd spent so much time memorizing as they'd tangled up with each other in bed during sleepovers . . . was gone.

Key was dead.

Weeks later, the coroner's report would say *accidental drowning.*

The phone screen darkened. The absence of light forced Noelle to sit with her secret on the tip of her tongue.

Her father leaned over to kiss her forehead. Noelle flinched. "I see you're reading the article. Just wanted to tell you how proud I am of you, sweetheart. I read those beautiful words you said about Key. They'll give her family comfort. After all of the pain, you're still so eloquent. My good girl."

"Yes, yes," her mother chimed in, while digging in her purse. "I put the newspaper clipping in here somewhere." She unearthed it, then unfolded it and slipped on her reading glasses. "This line especially: 'She was my best friend and I loved her.' We should start sessions back up with Dr. Monroe after all of this. It's just all too much, and you have senior year to contend with. The college-application season will be brutal on your mental health. I need you ready. I need you okay, sweet pea."

Noelle stared out the window. The headlights and highway lamps left halos along the road. The green of the spring trees and the blue of the sky lightening with the dawn made her think of Key again. Those unforgettable eyes.

And she really did believe what she'd told the reporter.

Noelle really did love her.